PAST REFLECTIONS

Wings Press, Inc.

Sandra Bonaldi

Past Reflections

Their eyes collided and Julie's heart began to race wildly. "Do you?" She breathed, her heart shining within her eyes.

"Yeah." He was going to kiss her. Even through the haze she knew it. And this time she was going to be ready. As his lips touched hers lightly she wound her arms around his neck pulling him closer. Before she realized anything else Kevin was easing her back down onto a soft bed of moss kissing her all the time. She would not fight the feelings this time she vowed. She wanted this. She wanted him as much as he wanted her. Why fight what was inevitable? The time was right and she was ready.

As Kevin's body covered her lightly his lips trailed sweet kisses all over her face. Over and over he kissed her until she was breathless and quivering beneath him. The kisses began gently but soon turned to an urgency and Julie arched her back as passion assailed her in waves. Their hearts beat as one as she clung to him. At that moment nothing existed but what she felt for Kevin. She wanted him, needed him, as she had never needed anyone before.

Other Works From The Pen Of

Sandra Bonaldi

<u>Midnight Magic 03-2010</u>
Nick Roland never had a problem playing the white knight. The problem was that Victoria's form of protection was not of the ordinary variety.

PAST REFLECTIONS

Sandra Bonaldi

A Wings ePress, Inc.
Contemporary Romance Novel

Wings ePress, Inc.

Edited by: Leslie Hodges
Copy Edited by: Joan Powell
Senior Editor: Anita York
Executive Editor: Marilyn Kapp
Cover Artist: Richard Stroud

Wings ePress Books
http://www.books-by-wings-epress.com/

Published In the United States Of America

Wings ePress Inc.
3000 N. Rock Road
Newton, KS 67114

Dedication

The Lord above always. My husband Tom – for his immeasurable amount of support. Joey, Jackie and Mark Vin and Nic Chase & Chelsea – Two pups with attitude.

In Memory of: Jesus (Jay) V. Alvarez – Forever Purple Flowers

One

Camp Wiskle was everything Julie had imagined and so much more. It was absolutely breathtaking with nothing but greenery as far as the eye could see. The trees were green and full. The bushes lush but well maintained. After pulling into the parking area off of the main road Julie knew that this was not going to be a walk in the park. This was the country, a whole other world than that of which she was accustomed. She was a city girl pure and simple.

Looking around there was also a wide variety of sports offered at Camp Wiskle. Basketball, tennis and softball were just to name a few. But there were many more. There was also a wide range of water sports, some of which were swimming and canoeing.

This would be a summer to remember. Julie certainly wouldn't have any extra time to spend thinking about her past. There would be too much to do. After all, this was going to be a big responsibility. Even more so, considering that this was Julie's first job. She wanted to do her absolute best. And she certainly did not want to disappoint Tracey.

Although a few years older, Tracey Collins was Julie's best friend, and had been for the past three years. From the day they had first met they became inseparable. This job had been one of Tracey's brilliant ideas. The only drawback had been that Julie would have to expand her age, just a little, to obtain the last counselor position available. Although she had never made it a habit to lie she felt that getting the position was too important not to. So she upped her age a few years and cinched the position. It had also helped that Tracey's parents had known the Wiskles for years. That was how Tracey had first obtained her position two years ago, and that was also what had gotten Julie the job as well.

Julie had always led a sheltered life. Until recently. She had only barely graduated from high school when her Mom had signed herself into a rehabilitation center. It hadn't come as a big surprise as her Mom had done it before and had gone back to drinking. But it seemed this time she was more serious. Then again, a lot more was riding on this than before.

Up until a few weeks ago Julie had attended a catholic high school for girls. Saint Anne's School for Girls, to be exact. All of her life she had gone to an all-girls school. She had never really known what it felt like to have a boyfriend as the only dates that she'd ever had were for the regular school dances. And those had always been limited. Limited, to the point of being almost nonexistent as the boys who had escorted her were usually sons of her parents friends. She usually suffered through the dances with no interest one way or the other. That could not be considered much of a social life.

After some very brief introductions with just a few of the counselors in the parking lot, Julie and Tracey started in the direction of the girls' cabins, their home away from home for the next hectic eight weeks. "Cheer up." Tracey laughed, her bright blue eyes shining. "You'll like it." She lowered her voice to a faint whisper. "No one but you or I know the truth. Stop worrying, all right."

"I know but…"

"But what?" She was totally serious. "If you don't tell I won't tell. We're gonna have a fabulous time." That was Tracey, one minute she was joking, the next, serious as all get out. She was always bubbling and so full of life. She lived life to the fullest while Julie usually hung back, uncertain and unsure. Tracey had the nerve to try anything at least once. She claimed it was something in her blood.

This, her senior year in high school, had been a rough year for Julie. She needed this job as well as the diversion. She needed to become somewhat independent. Camp Wiskle, according to Tracey, would be that diversion. Then there would be college in the fall. But that was not something that she was ready to think about. Not yet anyway. "This is what we call the lighted path," Tracey was saying. "It will be lit up every night. See how the lights are strung." She pointed to the trees overhead which now shaded the path because of their large sprawling branches. It was as though they were walking beneath a lush green canopy. "They need every light they can get because it really gets dark out here. You'll see what I mean tonight."

Julie's arm was beginning to ache under the weight of the suitcase. "The lake is off that path." She pointed towards the left. "There are about six or seven docks. Some are restricted from the camp's use. I am not sure why." She paused for a breath, which was just as well, as she was beginning to sound like a tour guide with every word. "Jake is usually our lifeguard but who knows if he's making it this year. He's also a counselor. And someone to stay away from, if you know what I mean."

"Are we almost there?"

"Almost." She stopped and put down her case. "I took the long way to show you around." She met Julie's eyes evenly.

It was the look that she gave her, the look that Julie had come to know so well. With a sigh she dropped her case and began rummaging through her handbag. "You don't really need it." Tracey said with a small smile.

"Sure." Julie shot her a look. "We both know better than that." She studied her complexion critically in the compact mirror. The jagged scar on her left cheek brought back a bitter taste of reality. Not only had it crushed her dreams but it had crushed her self-esteem as well. It certainly had not been an easy year. So much had happened to change Julie's almost normal life.

Even before the car accident Julie Finch could hardly consider herself pretty. She considered herself to be about average. Her best feature was her big brown eyes. Other than that she had an okay nose, almost clear complexion and dimples when she smiled. She was a mere five feet one weighing in at a whopping one hundred and five pounds. Her mousey brown hair was well past her shoulders and was a little on the wild side. She used to tie it back to restrain her curls. But that was before the accident. Now she kept it long hoping to hide her scar, if only a little bit. She had been reassured often enough that none of her scars mattered. That she was still such a pretty girl. All nonsense as far as she was concerned. Hadn't Scott Rourke proved that?

She remembered looking into the mirror for the first time after the accident. It had been awful. She was now deformed. She was ugly. All Doctor Paulson could say was how lucky she was to be alive. But she wasn't thinking along those lines. No way. Couldn't he see that her face was now imperfect? Not that it had ever been perfect from the beginning. Only a few little scars. Little! What the hell did he know? What did any of them know about how she really felt? True. It could have been worse. She could have died in that car crash. She realized that but what did that matter after she lost Scott. She may as well have died because it felt as though her heart had. But she had survived and now had to live with the telltale scar that marred her left cheek. It was approximately four inches long and jagged. It was amazing how a windshield could shatter into a million pieces right before your eyes. There were many other scars as well. Especially the one high up on her left thigh as it had somehow gotten caught and twisted under the dashboard upon impact. She could not remember how that had happened.

After the accident she had withdrawn from almost everyone. She refused to wear any of the clothes she had once loved so much. It would be a cold day in hell before she'd wear another pair of shorts or one of her miniskirts.

That day was permanently burned into her mind. Almost as clear as the day it had actually happened. Why couldn't her Mom ever just admit when she'd had one drink too many? And It usually wasn't one drink too many. It always went well beyond that. It had been obvious from the very beginning that Marie Finch had been in no condition what-so-ever to operate a car on that particular blustery cold day.

~ * ~

"I can drive, Mom," Julie's voice caught. She knew Marie had been drinking since early that afternoon. Although it was almost four and she had stopped drinking close to an hour ago she somehow thought that she was okay. But Julie knew better and Marie was definitely drunk. In another hour Dad would come home from work and all hell would break loose. Especially if he saw her in this condition. "It isn't that far."

Marie shot her a disgusted look. "You don't even have a license." Her words slurred slightly. "Sit back and relax." She revved the motor as though they were entering some kind of a race.

"Please, Mom." Her voice was now bordering on panic. "We can call Dad." Just then the light turned green and Marie accelerated.

"I don't know who's more of a worry wart, you or your father."

"Please watch the road..."

"Please watch the road," she mimicked in a mocking tone. "You sure give me a lot of credit." She was now becoming quickly annoyed. "My daughter is now telling me what to do."

A car horn blared and Julie cringed. "I wish you'd pull over."

"I'm sure you would." Her voice was dripping with sarcasm. But the more Julie pleaded with her mother to slow down the more Marie did just the opposite and hit the gas pedal. "We're almost home."

Thank goodness they were wearing their seatbelts. Just another few blocks. It couldn't pass quickly enough. Julie squeezed her eyes closed as they turned onto Evergreen. Two more blocks. The screech of the tires and Marie's quick intake of breath had Julie opening her eyes. To her horror they were heading straight for a utility pole. At that moment she gripped the arm rest as the pole was closing in with amazing speed. She froze with fear as the tires screeched in protest once again. As the brakes locked and the airbags deployed there was a shrill scream; she wasn't sure whose, as the impact was tremendous and the windshield shattered into a million pieces. Then all Julie could remember was a thick blanket of blackness reaching out to meet her.

~ * ~

"Are you going to stare into that mirror all day?" Tracey demanded causing Julie to return to the present with a start. "You look fine."

Julie applied just the right amount of powder with a careful hand. She was accustomed to fast touch-ups as her compact was never far out of her reach. Call it a measure of security considering that was exactly what it was. It made her feel better about the way she looked not to see that marring scar stare back at her untouched. Just the right amount of powder and she could temporarily erase it. She could deal with that.

Since it was quite humid, probably in the nineties and still rising, Julie could feel beads of perspiration breaking out on her forehead. "Here's my cabin." Tracey said simply. "Yours is the next around the bend. I'll be sure to come by before dinner time."

"Sounds good." She watched Tracey climb the rickety stairs and with a small wave she continued on her way. It looked to be a good three city blocks just to reach the bend, never mind how much further beyond that point that she had to walk to reach her cabin. The path was very well shaded and every once in a while a bird would chirp and the leaves on the trees would bristle as a bird took flight. There were also the buzzing sounds of flying insects. The path was narrow but wide enough for two or three people to walk side by side. There were trees all around and Julie could see where the lights were strung. She could only imagine how dark it got out here at night.

Without missing a step she switched the heavy suitcase to her other hand. By the time she reached the next bend in the path she was out of breath. Just a little bit further. She could now see the cabin from where she stood.

"Can I help you with that?" A thoroughly masculine voice seemed to come out of nowhere. Rather, from just beyond the trees. Automatically her hand went to her scarred cheek. Just another annoying habit she had acquired after the accident. And even more so when she met an attractive guy. And from where she stood he was gorgeous. Tall and built. His bright hazel eyes looked like they could go from blue to green at a moment's notice. They were totally breathtaking. His light sandy hair hung over his forehead innocently. But Julie could guess that he knew nothing about innocence. His features were rugged yet handsome. Strong nose, pouting mouth and square jaw completed the picture. He was definitely all male. Dangerously so. To her complete surprise all he wore were a pair of denim cut-off shorts and no shirt. He had a deep golden tan which emphasized his muscular biceps and strong chest. "Where you headed?" He rocked back on his heels smiling. It was obvious that she had been caught in the act of sizing him up.

"Cabin Three," she returned lightly while at the same time trying not to blush.

"Well Darlin'." He smirked. "That's a little ways ahead."

Julie knew exactly where it was but said nothing. "I'll take that." He picked up her case with ease. "First time at camp." It was not a question but rather a statement. "My name's Kevin, in case you were wondering."

She had to smile at that. "Julie Finch."

"It's nice to meet you Julie Finch." They started on their way. Which was another few city blocks. *Just around the bend, my foot*, she thought. "Who's the counselor at Cabin Three?"

"I am," she returned lightly and he laughed.

"You're kidding, right?" He arched an eyebrow and she almost panicked. What if no one believed she was twenty as she had stated on her application?

"No. I'm not."

Kevin still snickered. It was not going to be as easy as Tracey had first led her to believe. No one was going to believe she was a day over seventeen never mind twenty. "I'm sorry." He suddenly became serious. "I didn't mean to offend you. If you say so then I believe it. We're here." He stopped in front of the small wooden cabin. "Not exactly all the comforts of home." He went up the rickety stairs and placed her suitcase at the top. "I'll be seeing you soon, Julie." With a mock salute and a small smile he walked away, leaving her too speechless to say anything.

The cabin was in pretty good condition considering. But Kevin had been right. It certainly did not have any of the comforts of home. Not by any stretch of the imagination. But it would have to do. The first thing Julie noticed was the five huge screened in windows. Although not in the best condition they looked like they would pass the mosquito test. The room itself was very plain. After all, it was a regular wooden cabin. There were a total of eight cots lined side by side. None of which looked at all comfortable. Along the far-side wall there was a larger cot, a makeshift closet, and a small end table with a working clock on top which she supposed was for her.

It was quite obvious that most, if not all, of the campers had arrived. There were suitcases on some of the cots, including hers. Shoes, makeup, and clothes were also scattered about. Julie found an available cot before going to investigate the bathroom. The bathroom, on the other hand, shocked her, though it shouldn't have. What had she expected? There were four showers but none with stalls which meant no privacy. Thank goodness the toilet area was private or she'd really have a problem. At least everything was clean. She'd have to live with it. After all, she was going to have to tolerate it for the next eight weeks. It made her appreciate home all the more.

As she was coming out of the bathroom she met up with two young girls. Actually they were probably her age. One was a tall stunning blonde. The other was Julie's height with a large thick braid hanging halfway down her back. Both girls had brown eyes and pencil thin eyebrows. How the hell was she going to pull this off without screwing up?

"Hello." The blonde said coolly. "I'm Nancy. Junior Counselor." She had an air about her and instantly Julie's heart sank. This girl was going to rival her at any given opportunity. She knew the type.

"Hi." She smiled warmly. "I'm the new counselor."

Nancy just looked at her as though she had just been dropped from another planet. That of course she had to be kidding. "I'm Lorna." The other girl spoke up but it did little to break the mounting tension. "Sort of a Junior Counselor in training." She giggled softly.

"A Junior Counselor in training?" Julie questioned.

"You have to be one before you're a junior," Nancy returned as though everyone knew that. Everyone with half a brain. "But you got the Counselor position." Her gaze narrowed. "Usually the Wiskles' like their counselors to be juniors first, you must rate."

Julie knew that she was walking on thin ice with Nancy. She had to be handled with kid gloves there was no doubt about it. "Is everyone here? She asked just to break the tension.

"They're around." It was Lorna who answered while Nancy tried to stare Julie down. She had to be careful where Nancy was concerned. She could see that much already.

"You don't look like you're old enough to be a counselor." Nancy snorted waving a hand aside. "You look younger than we are." She met her eyes evenly. "How old are you anyway?"

Julie took a deep breath as her nerves were already jumping. She'd have to try another tactic. "Listen, Nancy," she began sweetly since they had gotten off on the wrong foot. She had to make this better now before it all blew up before she even got out of the starting gate. "Since I'm new around here I could really use some help. I'm going to need it."

Nancy looked as though she could care less. "So what."

"I figured you would know the grounds..."

"Like the back of my hand."

"Good." Julie paused then went on. "Because I need more of an assistant, not a junior counselor."

At that moment Nancy's eyes widened in surprise. "You're kidding me, right?"

"Not at all. This is new to me." She looked around at the cabin. "This camp is huge. Nothing like what I'm used to. I don't know the grounds at all and since you have done this already you have to know what I'm up against. And whenever I feel like I might need a break you can help me out unless you'd rather not..."

"Just like that?" She was skeptical and Julie didn't blame her. After her, she hadn't made such a good impression. Hopefully this would make up for it and help save her job at the same time.

"Just like that," Julie returned simply. "Are you up to all that responsibility?"

At that moment it seemed that the shudders had come down. "Of course." Her brown eyes seemed to soften.

"Thank you. Now, which cot is mine?"

Nancy went and started moving her belongings from the larger cot. "Right here." It was as Julie had thought. The cot right beside the closet. Things would go on as planned. All she had to do was keep Nancy in her corner and it would be downhill from here on in. At least she hoped so.

After placing her suitcase beside the small closet Julie plopped on the cot. "Okay, Nance." She began. "You can start by getting the girls together for our first meeting of the minds."

At first the girls were quiet as they gathered in a circle in the middle of the cabin. They were young, probably about fourteen or so. How she remembered that awkward age. But it was Nancy who got the ball rolling. It seemed that she had been coming to the same camp for the last three years and knew practically everyone. This was her second year as a junior and she had been hoping to shoot for a counselor this year but she had been told that she was still too young.

Nancy had that tone of authority and the girls looked at her with awe. Julie didn't have a problem with it because she had to keep Nancy on her side. And she was beginning to enjoy watching the way she drew the girls out. In fact, Julie was actually beginning to have fun. There were five girls in her charge. They were between the ages of fourteen and fifteen. They were practically in her age group. She needed to pull this off without a hitch.

The hour went fast but soon Julie learned their names, their hobbies and some of their interests. Julie had hardly spoken as they went on about high school, the courses that they were going to take and the upcoming junior prom. All things that interested a normal teen aged girl. All things that Julie could in some way identify with. As the meeting was slowly winding down, Ellen, a red head with freckles, turned to her and questioned. "So Julie. What do you like to do?"

She thought about that. "Anything you care to tell." Ellen prompted.

"Let's see." Julie paused. "I like chocolate cake. And I like hanging out with my friends." She smiled. "And I like you guys." She paused for a breath and continued. "I think we're off to a great start."

But they weren't interested in hearing that. They wanted to hear the real stuff. They wanted to hear the juicy stuff. "Do you have a boyfriend?" Carol and Maria asked at the same time and laughed.

"No." She didn't want to think about that.

"We'll have to change that." Lorna said with a big smile.

"Really?" Julie had to laugh at that one. "I think I'm much too busy to have a boyfriend right now."

"No one's ever that busy," Nancy said, matter-of-fact. "Don't you trust us?" She waved a well-manicured hand aside. "We'll find you a nice respectable guy and this way on your nights off he can take you out to dinner in town. I'll take care of everything."

"Well thank you, Nance." She snickered. "I guess we covered everything, including my love life."

"Okay, Girls." She took on that tone of authority which seemed to come naturally. "We should all get unpacked before dinner."

"Good idea." Julie seconded it and to her complete amazement they gained their feet and went about getting their things in order. All suitcases and footlockers were to be kept at the bottom of each bunk and they were to remain closed at all times. No one wanted any surprises jumping out when they opened their suitcases.

Within the hour Julie was pretty much settled in. Her suitcase was unpacked and all of her tops were hanging in her small closet. Her jeans she placed neatly on the bottom shelf. She had even brought a few dressy outfits as Tracey had suggested, minus any short sets. On that issue she had been most adamant.

"It's time for dinner." Nancy came over to her. "I doubt they're going to ring the bell tonight." She had changed from jeans into a pretty light blue short set. She was a very pretty girl. So sure of herself. So outgoing. If only Julie could be more like that. "I can show you where the dining hall is and where we usually sit. Unless you're not ready."

"I'm ready." She turned her attention to Lorna who was trying to stuff a silky red dress in the top flap of her suitcase. "Lorna, hang that up in the closet."

"You wouldn't mind?" She came over, dress in hand.

"Of course not. You can't stuff that in a suitcase. It will get wrinkled."

"I brought an iron." She protested but Julie wasn't hearing any of it.

"Hang it up. And while you're at it, see if anyone else needs to hang anything. There is plenty of room." She turned back to Nancy. "I'm ready," she said again. "Is there anything I need to know or do before we go?"

Nancy shook her head in wonder. "You really surprise me."

"Why?"

"Well for one, you act just like one of us."

"I am one of you," she said in all honesty.

"No, it's different. Most of the counselors here like to flaunt their authority. You know. They wouldn't dream of letting a lowly camper use their closet. Or anything else."

"Really?" Julie's eyes widened. "That's silly. By the way," she began on a very serious note. "You can use the closet too."

Nancy laughed. Soon after that everyone in the cabin was laughing as well. It was great. She was glad she had decided to come. "I'm happy to see that everyone is in such a good mood." Tracey came inside the door smiling. "Because wait until you see what we're having for dinner." She paused trying to keep them from guessing. "It's pot luck."

"Using last summer's leftovers." Nancy supplied and everyone in the cabin was laughing all over again.

"So," Tracey began on a more serious note. "What do you Girls think of Julie?"

"I think she's..." Nancy paused. "She's okay." She finally got out and Tracey looked as though she might faint away.

"I'm glad to hear that." Tracey looked at her watch. "Time for dinner." She waited until the girls filed outside and were halfway down the path before saying. "I knew you'd be a hit. Like I said before, this is going to be a summer to remember. Wait and see." She paused. "You worried all for nothing. Now all we have to do is find you a man..."

"Tracey." She put up a hand. "You know how I feel about blind dates."

"Oh please." Tracey sighed. "You need to loosen up. One day you're going to find this guy who is going to knock you off your feet."

"I thought the term was sweep you off your feet," she said as they started for the cafeteria trailing after the girls.

"Not in your case." She met her eyes evenly. "First of all," her voice was hardly a whisper. "You know I have an excellent knack for these things. And second," she put her hand up as Julie was about to interrupt. "I have the perfect guy in mind."

Julie rolled her eyes as Tracey continued. "Just meet him." Her eyes were pleading. "He's a good friend of Keith's. I would never steer you wrong, Julie. There's a meeting tonight at ten, after lights out. All I'm asking is that you meet him and then you can take it from there."

Julie thought about it. "You can't keep living in the past, Julie. I know how you felt about Scott." She paused. "But that's over now."

Scott. Why did she have to bring Scott up at all? Especially now. Tracey was the only one who knew about that episode in her life. The only person Julie had trusted enough with the truth. The only one who had somewhat understood her feelings concerning Scott. Would the pain ever go away? In her mind she knew it was over, and had been for a long time. It was her heart that refused to accept that. It all went back to that fateful car accident and her scars. After that he no longer felt anything for her. That realization in itself had hurt like hell.

"Just keep an open mind, Julie." Tracey went on as they filed into the cafeteria. "I only want for you to be happy."

Tracey just didn't get it. There was no way she was going to be happy if Scott wasn't a part of her life. Sometimes Julie could hate him almost as much as she loved him. "I know." Was all that she could reply.

After they retrieved their trays they stood on line to get their dinner. To Julie's delight the dining hall did actually resemble a small functional cafeteria. When Tracey had first explained it to her she hadn't believed it to be true. As everyone passed their trays on the metal rail there were food choices all the way down the line. There were healthy foods such as salads and fruits. There were choices of breads, rolls and pitas. There were beverage choices of bottled water, milk and apple juice. Tonight there were two choices of entrées. "Take the roast beef." Tracey mumbled. "The pot luck is horrible."

Julie did as she was told without even a single glance at the pot luck. Why tempt fate. As she followed Tracey further down the line she grabbed an apple instead of the rice pudding for dessert. Napkins, salt, pepper and silverware followed. By now her tray was almost full. Next, they found their way to a long table up in the front. It was where all the juniors and counselors were seated. The campers usually sat in groups rather than by cabin numbers. Basically everyone sat wherever there was room.

At least they weren't the last to arrive. Quickly Tracey made the introductions, if you could even call them that. Nothing fancy but definitely to the point. "Hi everyone." She began while standing at the head of the table. "This is Julie. She's the new counselor in Cabin Three." Then she went around the table quickly. "Christine, John, and you already know Nancy." She took a breath. "Kevin and Anna." She finished while looking around. "I thought Mike was here already," she said simply. And Julie knew almost immediately why she had asked that question. It was obvious that Mike had to be the one that Tracey wanted her to meet. Tracey had never minced words and it looked like she wasn't about to start now. But it was seeing Kevin again which had caused her heart to skip a beat.

"He'll be here." It was Kevin who answered.

"I guess not everyone's here yet." Tracey said, more to herself than anyone at the table.

After taking their seats Julie met Kevin's eyes over her water glass. He gave her a small flirty smile which had her flushing. It had been a long time since she had felt a flush of anything for anyone. When she and Scott had parted ways he had taken her heart with him. Now it seemed that she was feeling something and she had to admit that it wasn't a bad thing. In fact she liked the fact that he would even find her attractive enough to flirt with her. It made her feel like a woman.

The buzz going around the tables at the moment were how the teams were going to be assigned. "Rob wants everyone involved in the morning jog. He wants calisthenics around the flag pole. This is Wiskle history that we're talking about." John smiled warmly. "Whatever happens, happens. But we do know he's always been big on the morning run."

Tracey elbowed her. "The morning run can be a mile run."

From the moment that Julie had looked at Kevin it seemed so had Nancy. They were sitting close and whispering which caused Julie to think that maybe they could be considered a couple. Julie shook herself into the present as John was still going on about early morning exercise around the flagpole. After that Julie's focus was to be the absolute best counselor that she could be. And if everyone was required to do that mile run, then she would have to do it as well. She wasn't here to meet a boyfriend. She didn't need a boyfriend. With that thought in mind she was so wrapped up in pushing her mashed potatoes around her plate that she hadn't realized that Tracey had been speaking until she got a nudge. "I'm sorry." She put her fork down on her tray and looked up. "I didn't hear you."

Tracey gave her that all too knowing look. "Nancy was just telling us how you've appointed her assistant." Her blue eyes were wide, almost accusing.

"I think it's a good idea," Nancy put in quickly. "Of course Julie is still in charge..." It seemed as though Nancy was floundering and was sorry she had opened her mouth in the first place.

"Whose idea was it?" Tracey asked bluntly.

"It was mine," Julie stated. "And I think it's a good idea too. I don't know the grounds at all. I have a map, but what good will that do?" Suddenly she felt out of her element. Tracey was acting as though she had done something wrong. "I feel that Nancy will be a big help." With that said she went back to picking at her dinner but she did not miss the look of admiration that Kevin had given her. Not at all.

Two

It was exactly nine forty when Julie collapsed on her bunk. Only twenty minutes until lights out. At least she had a little time to relax. It had been a long day and she was exhausted. Rob Wiskle was holding a meeting promptly at ten thirty and it was mandatory that all counselors attend, so she had to be there.

As Julie leaned against the pillows wearily she could hear the girls chatting in the distance. They were all seated in the center of the room sitting on blankets Indian style. It seemed their main topic of conversation centered on the different dances that were held weekly. Who was going, what they would wear, and who did they want to go with.

Julie hadn't really been listening until a familiar name was mentioned. And to Julie's surprise it hadn't been Nancy who had brought it up. "Kevin's looking mighty fine this year." It had been Lorna who had broached the subject. "Mighty fine."

"Any ideas, Lorna?" Nancy queried, eyes wide.

"Of course not," she said quickly. "I do know the score, Nancy," she said before changing the subject immediately.

Julie wondered what that was all about but thought better of asking. It seemed that Nancy and Kevin could be considered a couple. And that was that. Why should she care anyway? She was there to do her job and that was all. Of course, she had promised Tracey that she would meet Mike. But that's where it ended. There would be no more match making. She didn't need any other complications in her life. Things were complicated enough.

If only she had been a little more like Nancy about a year ago. That had been before the accident had shattered her dreams. That had been when she had been hopelessly in love with Scott. There hadn't been any problems back then, only secrets.

As the girls went on about clothing, Julie let her mind drift. It didn't take long before the memories came flooding back.

~ * ~

Scott stood before her scowling. "Matt would blow a fuse." He shook his head adamantly. "I can't do that, Julie. It would destroy our friendship." His blue eyes were intense. "Not to mention what it will do to our relationship."

"Oh, is that what it's called?" She was angry. But more than that, she was hurt.

"We'll tell him when you turn seventeen."

"That's more than a year away." She was shocked. "And until then?" She demanded.

"Until then it will be our secret." He swept her into his arms ever so gently and she could feel herself softening. "A year isn't a long time. Then we'll tell Matt everything."

"Promise?" Her heart was in her soft brown eyes.

"I promise." He kissed her. "Until then, this will be our little secret."

~ * ~

"It's almost ten." Suddenly Nancy was standing beside her bunk.

She shook her head to clear away the fog and came back to the present. "I think you can handle it from here." She gained her feet just as Tracey entered the cabin.

"I wasn't going to let you walk alone on your first night here." Tracey said. "But tomorrow you're on your own."

Julie laughed. "Thanks."

"You're not ready yet, are you?" She pulled a careful hand through her short blonde curls. My, she looked exceptionally pretty tonight. She was wearing a modest pair of pink cotton shorts with a matching short cropped shirt, just enough to show a little skin. Tonight she looked like she was having a good time. Even her bright blue eyes were shining.

"I'm ready."

"Don't you want to change into something a little more... You know..." She wrinkled her nose. "Comfortable?" She asked but then went on before Julie could answer. "You weren't serious when you said you weren't bringing shorts, were you?"

"Did you think I was kidding?"

"Julie." She groaned. "What are you going to do, play basketball in jeans?"

"Why not?"

Instead of replying Tracey went to her closet and opened it. "Are you sure you brought enough?"

"It's not all mine." Carefully she was studying her scar in the compact. "I let the girls hang a few things of their own."

"You can borrow something of mine." Lorna offered while rooting through her suitcase. "We look about the same size."

"No thanks," Julie returned gently but firmly. "I'm wearing what I have on." She shot Tracey a look not to argue with.

"Let's get out of here then. We're running late enough as it is."

"You're really angry." Julie stated the minute they were on their way and out of ear-shot.

Tracey sighed. "You know better than anyone that you can't play basketball or tennis in jeans. Your father's a coach for Pete's sake."

"Was a coach," Julie corrected.

"Whatever." She shot Julie a look. "He was a good one too. And you have that same knack. It must run in the family."

Jackson Finch had been the best basketball coach in the county. Everyone knew it and everyone respected him for it. Some of the top colleges sought him out as they had wanted him to coach their teams to victory. It was something he was still considering for the future. But as for the present, he was still on a leave of absence.

"Basketball isn't my game." Julie said at last.

"You know how to play."

"Just the basics." Julie said evenly. "Anybody can throw a ball into a net."

"You'd be surprised."

At that moment Julie turned her attention to her surroundings. They were now on the lighted path, which could hardly be considered as lit by any stretch of the imagination. It was very dark as it was just as frightening. The trees cast eerie shadows all around them making them moving shadows that loomed in the dimmest of light. "It's not that bad." It was as though Tracey could read her mind. Which, in fact she had.

"You call this lit?" Julie giggled nervously. "I'm definitely a city girl."

"If you think this is bad," Tracey snickered. "Wait until you see the turn-off. Now that's an experience."

They were silent for a few minutes. All that could be heard were some lonely crickets tuning into the night. "Did Nancy bully you into anything?"

Julie looked at her friend in surprise. "No. I just felt it would be better to have her on my side rather than against me."

"You worry too much. Who in their right mind is going to challenge your age? Who would even care for that matter?"

"So, I really look twenty?"

"Do I look twenty-two?"

"No." Julie sighed. "But she's older than I am."

Tracey snorted. "By a week. Don't worry about it."

"Besides, I don't know the grounds yet. She would be a help." She paused. "I know it will help."

"It doesn't matter one way or the other to me." Tracey shrugged. "As long as it was your idea." Then they were there, the turn-off. Julie blinked rapidly so her eyes would adjust to the darkness. Dark wasn't the word for this place. It was pitch black. Downright scary was more like it. "This is the turn-off." She announced as though Julie needed an introduction.

"I can see what you mean." She took a deep breath in hopes it would still the wild pounding of her heart. In the distance, far distance, she could see the main house. There was a small lamp burning on the porch. But other than that there was nothing but utter darkness.

"It's now or never." Tracey breathed and Julie knew that she was just as frightened by the darkness. "Let's go." They walked close together in complete silence their eyes trained on that light in the distance. Julie's ears were straining for the slightest sound. Although she didn't know how she would possibly hear anything above the beating of her heart. This was the fastest pace Julie had ever walked in her whole life. When finally they reached the house and were at the foot of the stairs a man stepped out of the shadows. Julie's heart jumped wildly when Tracey exclaimed. "Keith! Are you trying to scare me senseless?" By now she was laughing, probably more out of relief rather than anything else. But Keith was laughing too. Only Julie stood there still trying to calm her beating heart.

"Did you really think I could desert you?" He opened his arms and Tracey fell inside. It was a happy reunion. "Never." He kissed her lips hungrily.

"I thought you said that last year was it." She didn't meet his eyes. "The end."

Julie felt silly just standing there. Especially considering that she remembered when Tracey had come home last year, how upset she had been because she and Keith had said goodbye. All the nights she had cried because she thought she'd never see him again. Now she looked so jubilant. Julie was happy for her friend.

Tracey turned towards her then, as though just remembering she was there. "This is my best friend in the whole world, Julie. Julie, my best guy, Keith."

"It's nice to meet you."

"The one and only Julie, huh." He extended his free hand which she took shyly. "The pleasure is all mine."

She flushed pink. "Well, here we are again. The big meeting." He lowered his voice then. "I've heard that the Wiskles' aren't here yet." He paused as Tracey took all this in. "Rob is taking charge, for now anyway."

"That's interesting." Tracey whispered as all three started up the stairs.

"So, here we are again. One year later. Remember what we were doing at this time last year?" He had a gleam in his bright blue eyes.

As they went back in time so did Julie. She could recall last year as though it were yesterday. Last year around this very time Julie had been lying in a hospital bed her face scarred for life. To her complete surprise and dismay Scott had come to see her. He'd brought a lovely bouquet of daisies. It had been a few days after the accident when she had been looking her worse. Black and blue, battered and bruised. In he came, like a breath of fresh spring air.

~ * ~

"Hello Beautiful." Scott handed her the flowers. His blond hair was slightly mussed but his blue eyes seemed distant somehow. "How do you feel?" He kissed her forehead absently. "Better, I hope." He sat beside her on the bed.

"I missed you." Then before she knew it, she was in his arms the tears flowing down her cheeks. "I didn't think you would come." Julie clutched the front of his shirt as though she'd never let go.

"It's okay." He held her close his hands sifting through her long hair. "I'm here, sweetie."

"I can't wait to get out of here." She shuddered but smiled through her tears as she nestled into his crisp cotton white tee shirt. Everything was all right now that Scott was here. "Next week is my birthday, Scott." Her heart was in her eyes. "I know you wanted to wait but I thought..." She trailed off as he swiftly gained his feet. Then suddenly she knew what she had been denying all along. He had never had any intention of telling Matt or anyone else for that matter. He'd just used her age as an excuse to keep her where he wanted her, at arm's length. But now... Now she was angry. "I know you wanted to wait until next year." She began while trying desperately not to cry. She refused to cry. Not after this latest realization. "You said that we would tell him..."

"I know what I said, damnit!" He shouted then quickly lowered his voice as though remembering where he was. "But now is not the time..."

"When is the right time?" Her voice broke and tears threatened her eyes once again. "It's because of the accident, right?" she said knowingly. "It's the scars... My face..." She broke off but the list went on and on.

"Julie..."

"That's it, isn't it?" She demanded. "Just say it, damnit. For once, be honest with me."

"Julie..."

"Get out!" Suddenly she didn't want to know the reason. It hurt too much already and without another thought she thrust the flowers back at him. "Get the hell out!"

"If you'd just let me..."

"I'll make it easy for you. I never want to see you again." She turned her back and waited for him to leave. Never before had she felt as terrible as she had at that moment.

~ * ~

"I think the meeting has already started." Keith said interrupting her train of thought. "After you, Ladies."

As they climbed the cement stairs leading into the main house Julie realized what a lovely house it truly was. In awe she took in the main foyer. It was gorgeous in beige stripes amidst thinner brown and pink pin stripes. Next, they stepped into a large room which looked to be a lounge where the meeting was already underway. "Come in, Counselors." A man in his early to mid-thirties motioned for them to be seated. "We have just started." All three took their seats on a large rose colored sofa. Julie tried not to appear curious. "As you may have guessed, I am Mr. Wiskle."

This did not look like the Mr. Wiskle Tracey had described. Not in the least. Julie had almost expected an old man complete with white hair and cane in hand. This man was young, vibrant, and handsome. "There's a list of rules on the table in the foyer." He began again. "I expect that they will be followed just as I expect the very best from all of you."

"The Wiskles' aren't here yet." Tracey whispered close to her ear. "That is Robert Wiskle, one of their sons."

Julie nodded absently. She was trying to listen to whatever else was being said but with Tracey talking away, that was next to impossible. "I'm here to help out in any way I can." He poured himself a glass of water and took a few sips before continuing. "From what I've been hearing, the juniors are restless this year. Let's try to remember that they are future counselors. Don't be afraid to put them to work." He laughed mildly. "That's about all I can think of for now besides the basic rules of the camp, but I won't get into that. You can read them at your leisure." He held up his copy, which looked to be the size of a small book. "Are there any questions?" He looked around the room once before finishing his monologue. "Okay. Then I guess we're finished here for now. Good luck."

The moment everyone got to their feet instant chatter filled the room. As all of the counselors began to mingle about there were some that were rebuilding old friendships or creating new ones.

"Hello there, Brown Eyes." A tall, rather handsome young man came to stand before her smiling warmly. The first thing Julie could not help but notice was his dazzling blue eyes. Eyes that were as blue as a summer sky. He had just a hint of stubble on his chin which gave him a dangerous air. "Jake White." He extended a hand still smiling. "First year at camp." It was a statement. "Welcome."

She took his hand and to her complete surprise he raised it to his lips kissing it lightly. "Julie." She mumbled as he finally released her hand.

"It's nice to meet you. We need some new faces around here." This man reeked of masculinity. In fact, he was a knock-out. He had light brown hair, almost a dirty blond, which although it was short on top it reached his collar in the back. He was tall, about six feet tall, and built. Talk about muscles.

"Come on, Julie." Tracey came to stand beside her. "Jake." She acknowledged with a tight smile.

"Hi, Trace." His blue eyes widened in surprise. "The scene: Camp Wiskle. Two years in a row. Or has it been three?"

"I see that you've already met Julie."

"It was a pleasure." His eyes met Julie's evenly. Then before walking away he shot her an incredible sexy smile.

"What did you do that for?" Julie turned towards her friend scowling. "He was only being friendly."

"Friendly." She snorted. "Jake is anything but friendly, unless you consider a rattlesnake friendly." Then rather abruptly she proceeded to change the subject. "Are you ready to head out? We've all decided to go swimming."

"Now?"

"Why not?" She smiled. "It's definitely hot enough."

"Well... I'm..."

"Julie Catherine Finch." Someone was calling out her name. It seemed for the moment she might be saved. From the way Mr. Wiskle was scanning the room it looked as though he was the one who had called her. "Miss Finch." He called out again.

"You go. Maybe I'll meet up with you later." Julie then excused herself and went to see what Mr. Wiskle wanted. "I'm Julie Finch." She gave him a small smile as she stood before him a little ill at ease.

"Hi." He was holding her application in one hand and a rule book in the other. "You're short enough to pass for a camper." He laughed out loud and she knew he was only joking. "Everything checks out here."

Julie breathed a sigh of relief. "Since you're new around here, I figured maybe you would like a grand tour of the grounds." He went on with a smile. "I'd be happy to assist you in any way that I can." He left the invitation open.

"Thank you, Mr. Wiskle but I'm sure I can manage."

He shrugged. "It's up to you." He lowered his voice then. "I was wondering if you could do something for me."

She met his eyes carefully. She was almost afraid to ask what that something was. But she did ask none-the-less. "Yes?"

"For starters you can call me Rob." He grinned. "There's no need to be so formal around here. We're like one big happy family." He pushed out a short laugh. "If you have any questions at all I am always available."

"Thank you." For now she seemed safe.

"In the rule book you'll find a map of the grounds. I believe it's on the back cover. It pretty much explains where everything is." He paused. "And now I will let you get back to your campers."

"Thank you, Rob. Good night."

"Good night." He left the room and took the stairs in the hall leading upstairs and as she looked around she had discovered that everyone else had already left the house. Well, she was on her own. What a wonderful way to end the evening.

~ * ~

The darkness seemed endless as she made her way back in the general direction of the cabins. As Julie kept up a steady pace she strained her ears for the slightest sound. The silence was almost deafening. Suddenly, in the distance, a howl sounded that had Julie off and running blindly in the dark. It seemed an eternity before she reached the lighted path when that dreaded howl sounded again, only this time it sounded as though this animal was getting closer. She broke out in a cold sweat just thinking about what kind of animal she might be up against but still she pressed on. There was the bend, a little ways ahead. A large tree marked the path. Funny, she couldn't remember seeing a tree there before. But she kept on running, not even slowing down to round the bend. That was when she collided head-on into something. The impact had her reeling backwards and falling into the trunk of that enormous tree. It had winded her and she lay motionless at the foot of the tree. "What the hell!"

She had run into someone. "Are you crazy?!" It sounded like Kevin. She was too shaken to move when finally he stepped out of the shadows and into the dimmest of light. "Julie, my gosh." He went to her and bent down. "Are you hurt?"

"It's you." She breathed a great sigh of relief and placed a hand to her pounding heart. "I'm sorry. I didn't see you."

"Are you all right?"

No! She was embarrassed. "I'm okay." She giggled nervously. "I just didn't expect anyone to be there."

"Here, let me help you up." He took her hand gently and pulled her to her feet. She swayed slightly and leaned against him. "You're not okay, are you?"

"I'm just a little shaken. But I'm fine, really." She looked up at him and smiled. They stood awfully close. Too close. And Julie found herself backing away. "I really have to go." For that one heart stopping moment she had thought that he was going to kiss her. Just the thought frightened her.

"I'll walk you back to your cabin."

As much as she had wanted to walk away unscathed she could not as she had no idea as to where she was as she had somehow gotten off the beaten path. "That would be nice, thank you."

At first they walked in silence. As they walked on the awkwardness quickly faded. And soon after that they were talking and laughing quite easily. Julie discovered that they lived only miles away from each other. It certainly was a small world. "What made you decide to become a counselor?" Kevin asked.

"I don't really know. It was Tracey's suggestion and she had helped me get the job." She paused. "I guess what I really needed at the time was to get away for a while."

"A vacation, huh?"

"I guess you can say that."

"I don't want to disappoint you but after this you're going to need a vacation."

They both laughed at that. "You're probably right." She agreed. "But it's been fun so far."

"So, you're twenty?"

"Yes." She answered simply while at the same time trying to take notice of where she was. And she was really off the beaten path, so to speak. She looked to have been going in the opposite direction of the cabins altogether. She'd have to study that map. Maybe even carry it around for a few days.

"What were you running from?"

She looked at him and he laughed. "When you ran into me. Not that I minded." He added quickly. "But next time give me fair warning."

"I will." She promised. "I let my imagination run wild. I was hearing all these weird noises. Howling. Or maybe it was growling. I'm not even sure."

"It was a barn owl hooting. You'll get used to it," he returned, matter-of-fact. "Give it a good week."

"Think I'll survive that long?"

"You look like a natural to me."

"Thanks for walking me back," she said when they finally reached her cabin. "I couldn't have done it without you."

"I should be thanking you." Kevin met her eyes.

"For what?" Her eyes didn't leave his. It was as though they were a magnet, drawing her closer and closer with each passing moment.

"For running into me," he said simply. There was that look again. Her heart turned over. But once again, she backed away.

"I'd better go in." Somehow she knew he wanted to kiss her. And she wasn't quite sure how she felt about that. "Good night, Kevin." She gave him a quick smile before going inside.

Three

The very next morning Julie awoke to a loud clanging bell. It was off key, which made it sound terrible. Nancy rolled over and muttered aloud. "Shut that stupid thing off, will ya."

"Rise and shine Girls." Julie forced a cheerfulness she did not feel. Last night had been positively awful. Every little noise had her eyes straining against the darkness. When all was said and done she'd had a few short hours of sleep and felt completely drained, physically as well as mentally. She would have liked nothing more but to roll over and go back to sleep. It was a tempting thought but she knew better.

As she gathered her clothes together she protectively pulled a letter from the pocket of her suitcase. It was a letter she had written to Scott right before coming to camp. It was a therapy she had given herself but she hadn't the nerve to mail it. She had figured that maybe if she had put some of her feelings down on paper that it would help, just another one of Tracey's brilliant ideas. But no such luck. The only thing she had discovered upon writing the letter was how deep her feelings for Scott actually ran. Not good for the heart.

Of course, seeing Scott the week before leaving for camp hadn't been much help either. In fact, that had been what had actually prompted her to write the letter in the first place. She knew that she wouldn't mail it. She didn't have the nerve. She didn't, and probably never would, understand what actually motivated a man like Scott? And what could possibly change all of their feelings, his feelings, in the space of a few short days? And all she really wanted to know was why he was still so hell-bent on hurting her?

~ * ~

When she went next door to borrow her brother's luggage she had never expected to see Scott. The last she had heard was that he was getting an apartment closer to the college, which was hours away from all of them. It was obvious to Julie that they wouldn't be running into each other any time soon. At first she didn't know if that were good or bad considering it still hurt either way.

Scott had certainly changed in the last year. He had lost some weight. But that was probably because he was too busy with his social life to find the time for something as simple as eating. His blond hair was really short, as short as a buzz cut. Gone was that thick curly hair she had once run her fingers through. But he was still as handsome as ever. With those deep blue eyes that could always look right through her and always had.

Although Matt wasn't at home Scott seemed to be in capable hands. He and Janet, Matt's wife, were seated at the kitchen table having coffee chatting and laughing, probably talking about the good old days. They gained their feet when she came in through the back door breathlessly. She stopped short upon meeting his intense blue eyes and her sister-in-law said sweetly. "You have to remember Matt's little sister."

Julie could have pinched her. But Janet didn't seem to notice anything out of the ordinary. And of course Julie looked a sight wearing her oldest pair of jeans and faded tee shirt. But worse than that was the fact that she wore no makeup. Her first reaction had her placing her hand to her cheek protectively. A gesture Scott didn't miss. "Of course I remember Julie." He smiled warmly. "How are you?"

She forced a quick smile that didn't quite reach her eyes. "Fine, and you?" She could have choked as the pretense was sickening.

"Great." He was actually beaming.

"You came for the suitcase," Janet said, matter-of-fact. "I think Matt left it out for you. I'll go and see." She excused herself then left them alone. Mistake number one.

"You're looking good," he said the minute Janet was out of ear-shot.

"Thank you." Her voice was crisp, tense.

"It's been a long time." His tone was light. "Almost a year is it."

"Should I be honored that you remembered." Her brown eyes flashed. At that moment she was sorry she had opened her mouth at all.

"Still mad at me, huh?" He was trying to get a rise out of her. Not that he had to try that hard. "I thought that the situation..."

"There was never any damned situation," she hissed cutting him off. "You wanted it all Scott. Why can't you just be honest enough to admit that?" She met his eyes evenly and was rather taken aback at what she found lurking there. It seemed to her that in the past year he had, in fact, changed. He looked older and tired. However, she would not soften. He had hurt her deeply and she wasn't ready to forgive and forget. Not yet.

"Maybe I wasn't completely honest with you." He started towards her with a purpose. "But you always knew how I felt..."

"Disgusted," she finished for him. "Everything changed after the accident." Upon first meeting his gaze she had promised

herself she would not get upset. And she wouldn't. It was over and had been for a long time.

"You're still hung up about those scars." He shook his head sadly. "It's amazing how some things never change."

"I don't want to discuss my scars with you." She found herself backing away. "You've already made your feelings clear."

"You never gave me a chance..." He broke off suddenly as Janet came back into the room suitcase in hand.

"I think this one is the biggest out of the three." She placed it on the floor right on the threshold. "I'm sure Scott wouldn't mind carrying it..."

"That's okay." She hedged backing towards the door. "I'll pick it up later." Then she got out of there as though the devil himself were chasing her.

~ * ~

Julie powdered her cheek with an expert hand while waiting for her turn in the bathroom. She would have loved a nice cool shower but there wasn't enough time. Maybe after breakfast she'd find a few spare minutes. She doubted it as everyone was to meet on the baseball diamond promptly at seven in time for the morning warm up. It was something Julie and her campers could have done without, and would have if it weren't one of the camp's requirements.

Almost immediately the temperature had begun to rise. An early weather broadcast had predicted high humidity and they weren't kidding. She looked down at her jeans and knew she had made a bad judgment call. Scars or no scars, she should have listened to Tracey. It didn't take long for her to find a solution. A little bit of Tracey had to be rubbing off she realized.

Carefully she laid out three pair of jeans across her cot. Don't think. Just do it, her mind reasoned. Next, she took out a pair of scissors from her emergency sewing kit and proceeded to cut off the legs of those jeans before she could talk herself out of it. The task wasn't an easy one but she pulled it off. In less than twenty minutes she had three pair of shorts. She held them up and searched for any flaws. Of course they weren't perfect as she wasn't a seamstress by any stretch of the imagination and they only came to the knee. But she could roll them up once to make a small cuff and they would still hide her scars. That in itself was a small miracle. Wouldn't Tracey be surprised!

"Are we playing tennis today?" It was Lorna who had presented that question.

"I'm not sure." Julie tossed the letter to Scott on the end table before picking up the weekly schedule. "No, we're playing tomorrow." She flipped the schedule on the bed and proceeded to pull on a pair of the cut-offs beneath her nightshirt as they were already running against the clock.

"That's a good idea." Lorna looked over the shorts with a smile.

"I hate to say this." Nancy stated simply from the bathroom doorway. "But we're already almost five minutes late."

Everyone picked up speed after hearing that as it was clearly understood that Mr. Robert Wiskle liked promptness. Everything was to run by the book and there were to be no exceptions.

All in all they were only five minutes late. Rob gave them a look as if to say, 'Don't let it happen again' which Julie understood perfectly. And it was her job to make sure that it wouldn't happen again.

"We'll start with our famous jumping jacks." Rob shouted so everyone could hear. "Four sets. And everyone does them."

To Julie's surprise he joined them in the exercising as well. "Get moving Girls. Julie." He gave her a smile which was warm. "Not quite Nancy." He shouted but his eyes were still trained on Julie, which was something that made her feel uncomfortable. Then again he probably thought her to be a woman of the world. Not so as she was only seventeen. With that thought in mind she kept her eyes straight ahead. She was letting her thoughts spin out of control. But Kevin? Now Kevin was definitely another story.

After another few sets of push-ups followed by some crunches they were finished and seemingly out of breath. Thank goodness. "Breakfast." Rob shouted which sent everyone running for the dining hall. But Julie remained where she had collapsed.

"Sleep okay last night?" Kevin asked.

"Not really." Julie sat up to find him sitting beside her. "I think it's going to take some getting used to."

"It always does." He got to his feet lazily. "Hungry?"

"A little."

"Well, let me escort you to breakfast."

She got to her feet smiling. Yes, Kevin was definitely another story.

The cafeteria was certainly buzzing. Julie got onto the line right behind Tracey who was waiting patiently for the next batch of scrambled eggs. "I'm not surprised that you did it." She sampled a piece of dry toast on her tray. "I told you that you would need shorts. And by the way, you look good." She took the next plate of eggs that was offered. "Now we have to go shopping."

"Shopping?"

"Yes. Shopping. Hi, Kev." She smiled at him just taking notice that he was standing behind Julie. "Thursday night we'll go. I know a great shop where all they sell are short sets and miniskirts. Wait until you see it."

Julie poured herself a cup of coffee listening to Tracey who was still talking about the local shop before jumping to the next topic. "You still have to meet Mike." She went on. "I really think you two will hit it off."

"I don't know, Trace." She placed a half grapefruit on her tray beside the coffee. "You know how I feel..." She stopped short as she didn't want Kevin to hear any more than he already had. "I just don't think it would be a good idea right now." They cleared the line with Kevin still right behind them.

"I'm only asking you to meet him. You don't have to go out with him or anything." Tracey threw over her shoulder as Julie followed her to the table. "You have to learn how to relax. You think way too much."

She was probably right about that. But Julie couldn't help it. Scott had been her first true love and that was just the way it was. And it would always be that way. But Tracey didn't want to hear any of that. In her opinion, Julie should have been over Scott a long time ago. And maybe she was right. But the truth still remained that she wasn't. And it was that simple. Now it was time to change the subject since they had finally reached the table. "Where's the list for clean-up posted?" Julie asked just to change the subject.

"Behind the kitchen door." Tracey took her seat and motioned for Julie to do the same. Right across from Kevin no less. "And don't change the subject." They sat side by side. "We were talking about..."

"Tracey." She shot her a look. "I'd rather not talk about it right now." She didn't miss the way Kevin was trying not to smile. Sometimes Tracey pushed too far.

"All right." She waved a hand aside. "I won't say another word. But if I were you I'd forget all about Scott..."

"Tracey." Julie shot her a look which said more than any words could.

"Okay. Okay." Tracey made a small face before attacking her breakfast with gusto. For the moment Julie was relieved.

The cafeteria was certainly noisy this morning. Not all of the counselors had arrived yet as there was only a handful seated. Tracey, Nancy, Jake, Kevin, and she all told. Where was everyone else? That was when she noticed another table, just like theirs, situated on the other side of the room. So, there were two tables. That was a nice fact to know.

"Keith is on mail call today." Tracey said to no one in particular. "A real pain in the neck if you ask me."

"We're slated for basketball this morning." Jake gave her a small smile. "Are you up for the challenge?" His blue eyes twinkled mischievously. "You do know how to play?"

"Of course." She quipped.

"Good. Get your campers together and we'll meet you down on the court in half an hour." He paused. "It's down by the lake, off the lighted path. I can wait for you..."

"No, you go on. I'm sure I can find it."

"Let's go, Kev." Both he and Kevin gained their feet, trays in hand. "We'll have a chance to warm up."

"I'm going too." Nancy followed suit. "I'll get the campers together Julie."

"Thank you, Nance."

When they were alone at the table Tracey said. "I can't believe how nice Nancy is being."

"Why?" Julie finished off her coffee.

"She's never that nice to anyone." She shrugged. "Maybe she likes you." Tracey pushed her tray off to the side. "Now, about Mike..."

Julie rolled her eyes upwards. "I told you I will meet him. But that's all."

"Good." That seemed to make her happy for the moment. "I know you'll like him."

"What cabin is Kevin in?" Julie changed the subject completely as she popped a spoonful of grapefruit into her mouth.

"Seven." Her gaze narrowed. "Why?" She kept her eyes carefully trained on Julie's expression. "He's a junior you know."

No, she hadn't known. "You're kidding?" Now, why wasn't she surprised?

"I think that he likes you."

Julie didn't say anything. She knew the rules just as well as Tracey knew the rules. Counselors and Junior Counselors did not go out. It was a rule plain and simple. And she most certainly was not going to get into a habit of breaking any of the rules. "We don't need any problems right now, Julie."

"There won't be any problems," she returned lightly while gaining her feet. "I have to look at the clean-up list before I go. Do you think I have enough time to run back to the cabin?" She picked up her tray while Tracey got up and did the same.

"We'll check out the list later. I'll walk back to your cabin with you." She paused taking in a deep breath. "I think we need to talk."

Four

They made it back to the cabin in record time. Tracey started in immediately regarding the different rules and regulations governing Camp Wiskle. Julie remained silent as she had other things on her mind. She also had every intention of honoring all of the rules that pertained to Camp Wiskle. As though she could afford any slip ups, especially since she had lied from day one regarding the age requirements. "I have Dance in ten minutes." Tracey's conversation took another turn. "And I can't be late, so get what you need and let's get out of here."

Julie went directly to the night stand which was where she had left her compact. "That's what we came back for?"

"Yes," came Julie's crisp reply. "Don't you start." She was tired of hearing the same old story. After pocketing the compact she picked up the schedule off of her cot before placing it neatly on the table. That was when she noticed that something was amiss.

The letter! Her heart jumped into her throat as she discovered that the letter she had written to Scott was missing!

Without another thought she was down on the floor on hands and knees searching for the letter while her heart was hammering wildly. Don't panic, her head screamed. "It has to be here somewhere." Her voice broke as sweat beaded her brow and she thought she might be ill at any given moment.

"What is it?" Tracey got down on the floor right beside her.

"It's a letter. I have to find it."

"A letter! A letter for whom?" It was apparent Tracey was confused.

"To Scott." Frantically she was looking under all of the cots now. "Remember, after the accident, when you told me to put my feelings down on paper, when I was angry about my scars. After I threw the flowers at him." She elaborated further as she met Tracey's blue eyes evenly. "Well, I did it. I wrote the letter."

"For once you listened to me." Tracey actually cracked up. "I don't believe it."

"I'm glad you find it funny." She got to her feet in despair. The letter was nowhere in sight. That had to mean, according to Julie, that someone must have taken it. But why?

"It has to be here somewhere. Don't worry, we'll find it." Tracey glanced at her watch. "We're late enough as it is. We have to go. But I'll help you look for it later."

Reluctantly Julie followed Tracey out of the cabin and into the bright sunshine. "We'll look again after lunch." She patted Julie's arm for reassurance. "The only thing I can think of is that maybe someone threw it away accidentally."

Julie didn't even want to think of the many possibilities, the worse of those being that someone had come across it and mailed it. Hopefully she was worrying over nothing. "Keith is on mail duty all this week. Being he's a guy he wouldn't have come into the cabin. It's against the rules. Unless someone let him in." She waved a hand aside as though dismissing that idea altogether. "But I doubt that's the case. I'll ask him..."

"Would you?" Julie breathed a small sigh of relief.

"I should see him before lunch. Don't look so down we'll find it." She gave Julie a wave as she left her at the edge of the lighted path, now basked in nothing but glorious sunlight. It was hard to believe that it had been so dark the night before.

Julie made it down to the basketball court only to find the game already in progress. She took a seat on the bench beside Jake who already looked as though he were ready to throw in the towel. "Don't you look like the happy camper? You look like you lost your last friend," he returned his attention back to the game. "Kevin." He called. "You can consider yourself benched." He snorted. "We have our work cut out for us this year." He blew the whistle that was hanging around his neck and everyone came to a standstill on the court. "One more personal foul and I'm calling this game off." He sauntered onto the court. "And don't get any smart ideas. Because if you do, instead of playing basketball we'll all write a nice composition about how the game should be played."

Everyone groaned but Jake wasn't hearing any of it. "You either play the game right or you don't play at all." He blew the whistle again which set the game in motion. "So," He turned his attention back to her. "What's up?"

"Sorry I was late."

"I'll let it slide this time." He gave her a sly smile. "Besides, you showed up just in time. I'm on guard duty in about fifteen minutes. I'm leaving Kevin in charge here, so don't worry."

She was only worried about one thing. And it certainly had nothing to do with the basketball game. "Usually Mike fills in for me but he hasn't reported in at the office yet. I don't even know that he will show up this year. But Kevin knows the drill."

As Kevin made his way over to them Jake gained his feet. "I'm leaving you in very capable hands." He handed the whistle to Kevin. "I'll see you both later."

Kevin sat beside her as Jake made his way down to the lake. At least he would get a swim in before lunch. With this heat it sounded very appealing, even to Julie. "We meet again."

Julie didn't meet his eyes. She was afraid of what might be lurking in their blue-green depths. "Yes. I'm a Junior Counselor."

"I don't remember asking," she returned lightly while twisting a white string round her finger from her cutoffs.

"Ah, but you were thinking of asking me." He jested.

"Was I?" She tried not to smile.

"Lucky guess." He stretched out his long honey tanned legs in front of him sighing lazily. It was going to be hard to concentrate on this game. Especially with him sitting so close. The silence seemed to drag on. Julie wasn't fond of making small talk. It was polite when you had nothing to say she supposed. But her mind was on other things, the letter being foremost. She had to find it and fast.

The game seemed to drag on endlessly. Basketball, although an active sport, was not an interesting sport, from Julie's perspective, to watch. Kevin stretched again and this time she watched him carefully out of the corner of her eye. It was completely beyond her how he could be a junior counselor when he looked so much older. "Is the game almost over?" She asked just for something to break the silence.

"Another few minutes. I really wasn't paying much attention."

Julie carefully kept her gaze averted. "What's next on your schedule?" he asked.

"Arts and crafts." She wrinkled her nose prettily. "I think that we're making key chains."

"Sounds like fun."

"What are you doing after this?"

"Swimming."

"That sounds better than making a keychain." They were making small talk and they both knew it.

"Are you looking forward to the campfire tonight?"

Julie looked at him. She hadn't heard about a campfire. Maybe he had some inside information. "We usually have one once a week." He continued. "It's a way for everyone to mingle. Meet new people. That's not always easy to do in the cafeteria or in chapel. The campfires are fun and relaxing."

The basketball game was now officially over. Many of the campers came off of the court heading in the direction of the nearby water fountain. "I think that the campfires are listed on the back of the schedule." Kevin gained his feet. "Maybe I'll see you there." His eyebrows rose a fraction. "See you later, Julie."

She watched him walk away. He was a strange guy. Yet she found that whenever he was around that she enjoyed his company. There was something about him. A positive force that emanated from him and Julie felt drawn to him by that force. Her heart would flutter when he looked at her with that soul searching gaze. It was a feeling that she had felt before almost in another place in time. It was scary yet exciting. But then reality came crashing through because there was Scott. He was the man that she loved with all of her heart. Could it be possible to love someone and yet be attracted to someone else?

There wasn't time to think about that now as the girls were waiting for her. Jake's campers had already moved on with Kevin leading the way. She had to get her emotions in check. "Is everyone ready?" She forced a faint smile that didn't quite reach her eyes.

"Where do we go from here?" Ellen asked. But it was Nancy who answered.

"Arts and crafts." She solemnly waited for Julie as the girls started up the hill in the direction of the cafeteria. "You and Kevin seem to have a lot in common." It came as a cool remark.

"We were just making small talk." Why did Julie feel as though she had to defend herself? It wasn't as though Nancy had accused her of anything, not yet anyway.

"We were sort of seeing each other last year." So, that was where this conversation had been leading. Nancy was marking her territory. Little did she know but she had nothing to worry about. Julie knew where her priorities stood. And she was also in love with Scott, very much so. "We went to most of the dances together." She went on. "We were even crowned King and Queen."

"That's nice." Julie mumbled absently as they reached the cafeteria where arts and crafts were held daily. She honestly didn't know what else to say. If she defended herself as she felt the need then Nancy would pick up on it like a dog with a bone. She could not afford to run the risk of getting on Nancy's bad side. It was too early for that.

"Kevin could never resist a challenge." Nancy met her eyes evenly. "But since you're the counselor..." She pushed out a small strained laugh as she walked away. "I'm sure I don't have to tell you the rules."

As Julie entered the building she had noticed that Tracey and her campers were already inside waiting. All of the necessary materials were laid out on one large table. The girls were just beginning to form a line while waiting for instructions as well. Tracey walked up to her as soon as she came inside. "How's it going so far?"

Julie pushed out a short laugh. There were so many different ways to answer that loaded question. "Well," she began hesitantly. "I'm nervous about the letter. I believe that Nancy just laid it on the line where she stands with Kevin and is under some false impression that I am after her boyfriend." She shrugged carelessly. "Aside from that, I would have to say that everything else is fine."

"I told you that he was interested and you didn't believe me." Tracey's voice was hardly a whisper. "But it's obvious."

"Well, it's not happening." Julie said simply, as though anything were that simple. But in her opinion it was cut and dry.

"Listen, Julie." Her friend faced her. "Sooner or later you're going to have to accept the fact that you and Scott are history."

Julie didn't think that she could ever accept that. In her heart she believed that Scott had loved her. She had to keep believing that. Someday he would realize it as well and they would be together.

"It's been over a year." Tracey continued softly. "It's time to forget him. You have to move on with your life."

That was easy for her to say. "It was a year for you and Keith too." She pointed out. "Or did you forget that?"

Tracey sighed. "You know how it was. You told me yourself. We went over it a million times. Scott wanted it all. You gave him your all, and what did he give you?" She demanded. "Absolutely nothing. Nothing at all."

Julie didn't want to hear it. Tracey didn't know everything. "I don't want to see you get hurt. He's already hurt you in so many ways. It's time to pick up the pieces."

Julie looked away. "You don't want to hear it." Tracey continued none-the-less. "But it's reality. You're going to have to face it now."

"I have faced it."

"I suppose that's why you haven't gone out with anyone in the past year." She had the last word again as she went to the front of the room to begin the class. It wasn't at all unusual that Tracey got in the last word. In fact, Julie would have been more surprised if she hadn't.

As it turned out the girls didn't have enough time to complete their key chains so Tracey collected them, placing them in a small box to be put aside for their next class. Their next class would be held the following week. They had one half hour before lunch to get the cafeteria clean as the staff was already in the kitchen preparing the midday meal. Julie kept pretty much to herself as they went about the cleanup which included gathering together the stray strands of twine and small leather pieces.

Sometimes she was sorry she had told Tracey anything at all. Tracey would never understand and Julie was tired of repeating herself. Sure, it had been great that she could tell her parents that she was over at Tracey's, when in fact, she had been with Scott. Tracey had been good at covering up. But now it was different. It seemed that everything had changed. She surely hadn't changed. Her feelings were still the same. It was everyone else around her that had changed. It had to be.

Julie was still wiping up the tables as the kitchen staff began to bring out the food. Some of the campers had arrived and were already waiting in line. It was a good thing that they hadn't come in all at once but instead came in at a steady pace. Slowly the cafeteria was filling up. "I haven't forgotten." Tracey said as Julie got in line behind her. "We'll go and look right after lunch."

"Thanks."

The line was finally beginning to move. Lunch consisted of a ham and cheese sandwich, juice, coffee, and an apple for dessert. "Not bad." Tracey commented. "I've seen worse."

They were the first to be seated at their table. "I'll ask Keith as soon as he gets here." Tracey fixed her coffee. "I haven't seen him all day."

Nancy, followed by Jake and Kevin, joined them a few minutes later. This time Kevin sat beside her while Nancy opted to sit on the other side. Tracey gave her a knowing glance but said nothing.

Although the cafeteria was already quite full, Keith still had not arrived. Nancy was busy trying to engage Kevin in some type of conversation while Julie ate her lunch silently. "Mike should be here later on tonight." Jake said. "Better late than never, I guess."

"You can meet him at the campfire." Tracey whispered close to her ear. "This is working out perfectly."

Julie didn't say a word. However, she could not help but notice the side glances she had been receiving from Kevin throughout their meal. Although she was a little uncomfortable she tried not to let it show and obviously it had been working as everyone was busy with their own conversations. "Has anyone seen Keith this morning?" Although Tracey had voiced that question casually it seemed that everyone around the table became quiet.

"I have." Nancy said while munching on her apple. "He was getting the mail this morning."

"Where?" Tracey questioned blue eyes wide.

"Around."

"One of Julie's letters is missing." Tracey went on simply. "She left it on her night stand and when she came back this morning it was gone."

There was a slight pause. "I gave it to Keith."

Julie actually choked on her apple juice. "What?" She came up sputtering her eyes tearing. This was not happening. All the blood must have drained from her face. It seemed although there was chatter in the background she could actually hear her heart beat. It seemed unreal.

"Who gave you permission to touch anything in that cabin?" She demanded angrily. Never before had Julie seen her friend so angry. "Never mind something that was not yours to begin with…"

"Do you think it made it to the post office yet?" Julie queried softly.

"I would think so." Nancy continued to eat her apple right down to the core. "It was addressed to go out so I thought…"

"That's the problem." Tracey cut in bitterly. "You didn't think at all."

"I'm sorry." Nancy kept her eyes lowered while Julie forced a smile, which on the inside was just ripping her to shreds. Her mind was racing wildly in every direction. Nancy had forced a hand that she had been holding for a long time. It wasn't the end of the world but maybe it was the beginning. She still couldn't believe this was happening. The letter had been addressed and stamped. Who would have thought otherwise? It had been a mistake.

"You're awfully calm." Tracey acknowledged a few minutes later when Julie had remained quiet.

"I think I'm in shock." She shook her head in amazement. But something else was going on inside her. Somewhere deep inside there was a flicker of hope. Something that she had thought died a long time ago. But it was there, slow and steady as though it still had a chance.

"Why don't you let the rest of us in on your little secret?" Jake wanted to know.

"It's not important." Julie returned, while her heart was hammering wildly.

"The one and only time you listen to me." Now Tracey was snickering. "Look at it this way." She tried to keep a straight face. "You're almost four hundred miles away. It's not like he could jump in his jeep to come all the way out here just to confront you."

"You don't know Scott very well, do you?"

Her blue eyes widened. "Would he?"

Julie took a careful sip of apple juice while trying not to think of how Scott was going to react to that letter. After all, it was full of some deep thoughts. "So, what was in this letter exactly?" She whispered her blue eyes twinkling with delight.

"I can't say." She pushed her tray away. Suddenly she didn't have any appetite left. "You were right about one thing, Trace." She paused. "This is going to be a summer to remember."

~ * ~

Julie went through the rest of the day in some kind of daze. Every nerve seemed to be on edge. She was almost afraid to think of how Scott was going to react when she finally did come home. Then what? She'd have to face him then. What would he say? Would he be angry? Or would he just laugh it off as being unimportant? Laugh her off as being unimportant.

If Julie hadn't have known better she would have guessed that the girls were going to a party. They had to look their absolute best before leaving the cabin and were fighting over bathroom rights. From the bits and pieces of the flowing conversation Julie assumed everyone had a date. Although Nancy didn't come out and say that she was going with Kevin, she may as well have. In the faint distance she could hear Tracey's crew, before they even reached the bend. Why was everyone so delighted over a campfire? If it weren't a requirement Julie wouldn't be going at all.

Julie opted for a pair of black leggings instead of shorts, which almost everyone was wearing. As she draped a pink sweater about her shoulders Tracey came inside. "You can start down the path." She told the girls. Julie's campers included. "But wait at the turn-off."

"What about our dates?" It was Nancy who questioned.

"They will just have to meet you there." Nancy stormed outside muttering something about fairness under her breath. Tracey just waved that aside with a smile. "A firm answer." She turned towards Julie then. "You've been quiet all day?" she said when they were finally left alone. "Are you all right?"

When Julie didn't reply she went on. "You haven't changed your mind about meeting Mike, have you?"

Julie wavered. "I'm beginning to think this was a big mistake. Coming here. But especially lying about my age." She shrugged. "Maybe it's me. Maybe I just want to be seventeen again."

"You're thinking again, Julie Finch." She smiled. "If you convinced Rob and Nancy, you're home free. Believe me; no one else is smart enough to figure it out." She paused. "Give it some time. It's only the first day."

Tracey was probably right. It was only the first day. It might take well over a week before she adjusted to camp life. She wasn't sure. Then again, she wasn't sure of much of anything anymore. "Come on. We'll have a good time. You'll see."

The campfire was well underway by the time they had arrived. Julie was surprised to find any sort of clearing off the lighted path. The forest had seemed so dense before, almost formidable. But there was a clearing, nestled in the midst of some large oak and pine trees, only a few feet off of the path itself.

There were a few fallen oak trees, now just logs, which were situated all around the large fire. Most of the campers seemed content with sitting on the ground. There were some counselors sitting together on a large flannel blanket while some of the campers were talking and others playing a game of hide and seek.

Julie peered nervously over her shoulder as they entered the clearing. She couldn't shake the feeling that she and Tracey had been followed or watched as they had walked the path. The reason she hadn't mentioned it was because Tracey had been so engrossed in talking about Keith and their small age difference. Besides, Tracey wouldn't have believed it anyway. She would have thought Julie paranoid as this was her first camping experience. Now that they were surrounded by people Julie felt a little better and was glad she hadn't said anything. "There's Mike." Tracey whispered close to her ear. "Do you see him?" She didn't point as he would see them if she had. "He's sitting next to Jake." Quite frankly, she didn't know what all the fuss was about. Okay, so he was handsome, but so was every other guy there. "Come on, I'll introduce you." Tracey grabbed her arm and made a bee-line towards them, as though that weren't obvious. She may as well have pointed him out before, after that display. "Hi, Guys." She turned on the charm full force. "We didn't think you were going to make it this year." She directed at Mike. "I was just telling Julie this morning... Oh, how rude." She turned to Julie and gave her a wink. "This is my very best friend Julie. Julie, this is Mike."

Julie didn't know how she managed to keep a straight face. But she did. "It's nice to meet you." He held out his hand in a friendly gesture and Julie shook it with a smile. Okay, so maybe he was drop dead handsome. What she wouldn't have given up for a prom date like that. Then again, on the other hand, he really wasn't Julie's type. And Tracey should have known that. He had curly black hair and light brown eyes. He looked to be well over six feet tall and was built like a truck. He looked to be in his late twenties and at this stage of the game that would be playing with fire and she wasn't ready for that.

"You're new this year." It was a statement.

"Yes." She could feel her palms getting clammy. She could feel the air sizzle and with the smile he had given her she wanted to run. "Well, it was nice meeting you." This time she took Tracey's arm firmly. "If you'll excuse us. We're waiting for Keith." Her tongue actually stuck to the roof of her mouth. "There he is." With a quick tug she steered Tracey back towards the campfire.

Tracey looked angry but suddenly she didn't care. Never before had she felt so out of place. He was practically undressing her with his eyes. Besides, she had only promised Tracey an introduction not that she would go out with him. "Why did you say we had to meet Keith?" She demanded the moment they were out of earshot. "You didn't even give him a fair chance. How are you ever going to meet anyone with that kind of attitude?"

"Maybe I don't want to meet anyone." She took a deep breath. "He seemed nice, Trace, just not my type."

"I give up." She threw her hands up in disgust. "There's more to life than Scott Rourke." She spat then walked away.

Julie helped herself to a glass of soda before wandering around as Ann, one of the counselor's in Cabin One was playing folk songs on a guitar. After placing her sweater on the ground Julie took a seat and leaned back against the giant oak tree. The music was soft and soothing. Very soon she was being lulled away as she let the soft melody sweep her far, far away, back into another place in time.

~ * ~

"You know how I feel, Brown Eyes." Scott looked down at her with a smile. He looked so carefree at that moment. Like maybe their secret didn't matter anymore. Then again, she should have known better.

"So, I can tell Matt all about us?"

"Are you crazy?!" Suddenly his eyes turned to ice. "You're the only one who has to know how I feel."

"How do you feel, Scott?"

He turned away thrusting his hands into the pockets of his blue jeans. "You're very special to me, Julie. You know that."

She snorted. "Your dog's special to you too, Scott. Can't you just come out and say it?"

"I shouldn't have to." He kept his back to her. "You know I have trouble putting how I feel into words."

She'd heard it all before. Rather, she had never heard it which was part of the problem, if not the whole problem. "I love you too, Scott." She whispered. But he didn't hear her. Or maybe, he just wasn't listening.

~ * ~

"No date tonight?" Rob came and sat down beside her. "Somehow I find that hard to believe."

Julie shook herself free of the memories. Although deep down inside she knew she'd never be free. She was only torturing herself, and all for what? The past was over. She had other things to concern herself with now. "How was your first day?"

"Exhausting," she admitted. "But it was fun. A real experience."

"I'm glad to hear that." He too leaned against the tree trunk lazily. "This is what I consider to be the best part of the day, a time to kick back and forget everything."

If only she could forget everything. "What's on your agenda for tomorrow?" He was trying to draw her out.

"I'm not sure." Wrong thing to say to the camp director. "I haven't had a chance to look at the schedule but I'm almost sure that it includes swimming," she returned on a light note.

"Probably." He was scanning the crowd obviously making the necessary rounds. "If you need anything you know where to find me."

She let her breath out slowly while he walked away. Wearily she leaned back against the tree again carefully tucking her legs beneath her. Everyone seemed to be having a good time. And of course almost everyone was paired off. Everyone except her, or so it seemed.

Julie hadn't realized she'd been dozing until Kevin plopped down next to her. And to her surprise, as well as relief, Nancy was not with him. "You're not falling asleep on us, are you?" He teased but then became quite serious. "Why are you sitting here all alone?"

"I like sitting alone," she said simply.

"Where's Tracey?"

"I don't know." She stifled a yawn. "Probably with Keith somewhere."

"We should have come together tonight." He lowered his voice. But no one could hear them from where they were sitting. "I wanted to." He met her eyes. "I think you did too."

She was too stunned to say anything. But for one heart stopping moment she thought that maybe he was right. It was an interesting thought. "Next week you'll come with me." It was not a question.

"I really don't think that's such a good idea."

Kevin stood to his feet his eyes not leaving hers. "I know the score, Julie Finch."

She didn't say anything. For starters she didn't know what he was talking about. "I know how you landed this job." He rocked back on his heels smirking. "Need I say anything more?"

"I don't know what you're talking about." She raised her chin defiantly.

"It's such a shame. Really it is." He shook his head sadly but smiled none-the-less. "I know your secret," he said simply while looking her over carefully. "I think that you're younger than I am." His eyes looked awfully blue tonight. It was probably because of the deep blue tee shirt he was wearing. "You may have gotten one over on Old Man Wiskle but you didn't get close enough to get anything over on me."

He knew! How was that possible? Her head was spinning. She was at a loss for words. It seemed that Kevin could see right through her. "Aren't you going to say anything?" Kevin asked. "Aren't you going to deny it?"

She cleared her throat nervously. He was daring her with his eyes. Daring her to lie. "What would you like for me to say?"

"You may as well tell me what I already know." He got down on one knee so he could be closer to her. "Basically all I want to hear is that I'm right."

"Why?" Her breath caught as he was so close.

"Because I don't want to believe that I'm out of my league by asking you out," he returned simply. "And I don't want to be shot down."

"You don't want to ask me out, Kevin." she returned evenly. "Besides, there's Nancy to consider..."

"My asking you out has absolutely nothing to do with Nancy." He cut in quickly. "I wanted to ask you tonight."

Julie gained her feet carefully. It was almost time to turn in for the night. And right now she'd do just about anything to get out of this present situation. She didn't like feeling trapped and it felt as though Kevin was boxing her in. Maybe she could try another tactic. "I'm flattered, Kevin." She began hesitantly but with a smile. "But I have to be honest with you and I do have a boyfriend back home." God forgive her but it was a half-truth.

"Scott," he said knowingly. "Yeah. I've heard you talk about him." He gained his feet his eyes never leaving hers. "And it sounded to me like that relationship died a long time ago."

She actually gasped as she couldn't believe he'd said that. Her eyes met his evenly. "That doesn't mean my feelings died with it." After that was said she walked away. She refused to discuss her personal life regarding Scott with anyone, including Kevin. Especially not with Kevin. Of that she was most certain.

Much later, after everyone had gone to bed, Julie thought again about what Kevin had said. How it sounded to her ears. How it had stung. She'd never looked at it in that light. Had their relationship really died? Did they ever have a relationship? Was she just grasping at memories? Some happy times shared with her brother's best friend. Whatever it had been, she was determined not to let go.

Five

Soon a whole week had passed. Dragged, was more like it. Finally it seemed that Julie was adjusting. It felt great to walk the lighted path and for once know exactly where she was going. Of course, she still wouldn't walk it alone at night if she could help it. Then again, she was not the only one that felt that way. There were some guys that wouldn't walk it alone either. They might not admit to it but that did not make it so.

It felt good to finally belong, or to fit in. The days were filled with activities galore. There was always something to do. Then there were chapel services on Sunday morning. It was refreshing to attend these services. She felt invigorated and motivated and it showed. There were some people who just sat there and stared off into the distance but Julie soaked it in. And although it was not something that she was accustomed to, she enjoyed it none-the-less. A minister came in from one of the surrounding towns and gave a message every Sunday. Everyone met in the dance hall.

There was music, which was then followed by the weekly message. It was not exactly a requirement that everyone attend but no one had a problem with attending. This was just fine with Julie.

By now she'd assumed that Scott had received her letter, and knew exactly how she felt. Maybe he'd even consider writing back. Now that was wishful thinking. To Julie's surprise as well as to her dismay Kevin had kept his distance. She wasn't really sure how she felt about that. But she did miss him. She had noticed, on several occasions, Kevin sneaking glances her way. He'd had that all too knowing look. The look that said if she crossed him in any way he would have no problem telling everyone her secret. He hadn't been teasing that night at the campfire. He really knew.

It was Wednesday night at dinner when finally he did approach her. She had been waiting for Tracey and was alone at the table, for once the first to arrive. "I'll see you at the campfire tonight." It was a statement. His bright blue eyes openly dared her to refuse. He was patiently awaiting her answer.

"Can we talk about this later, Kevin?" She had just spotted Tracey who was weaving her way across the cafeteria on her way to the table.

"I can always take a walk down to Wiskle's office..."

"I really had you figured all wrong." She hissed.

"You want to know something; you're beautiful when you get angry." He blew her a kiss, his blue-green eyes laughing. "I'd better go and sit with Nancy, looks like she's shooting daggers at both of us. But I will see you later at the campfire."

"Sure. Whatever." She turned her attention to Tracey who had reached the table with Keith just a few steps behind her.

"You're not sitting here, Kev?" Keith put his tray down before taking his seat beside Tracey. "What is it? Nobody wants to sit here anymore. We don't have cooties you know."

"I'm sitting here." Kevin said taking the seat across from Julie. "If nobody else minds." His eyes never left hers.

"Good." Keith said unaware of the new-found tension at the table. "I told Rob about these ridiculous seating arrangements. There should be one long table for the counselors and juniors." He started eating. "Why split everyone up."

"I really should ask Nancy to join us." Julie found her voice at last. She met Kevin's eyes with a smile, one of which he did not return. One point for her. Then again, after catching a glimpse of the dirty looks she was now receiving from Nancy she quickly dismissed that idea. She could just imagine what Nancy was thinking. Not that Julie blamed her. In fact, she'd be thinking the same thing had she been in Nancy's place. Kevin was putting her in an awkward position and she didn't like it one bit. He had her over a barrel and he knew it.

Absently Julie pushed her dinner around the plate. Lately she had been so tired. On top of that, the weather had been so hot and muggy. It seemed to drain the energy right out of her. Tonight was of no exception. The humidity was not letting up.

"After the campfire we're going swimming." Tracey suddenly announced. "I already got the okay from Rob."

"It's gonna be like an all-night party." Keith too seemed to get caught up in Tracey's excitement.

"I'm in." Kevin said his eyes intent on Julie.

"What about you, Julie?" Tracey looked at her. "Are you going to show up this time?"

Julie was almost afraid to answer. It would be an excuse for Kevin to blow the whistle. "I don't know." She tried biding her time while fixing her coffee. "If I'm not too tired I'll come."

"Good." Thank goodness Tracey didn't persist. As was her usual custom with everything. Especially if one did not agree with her. "Rob said we could use either docks three or four."

"Dock three," Kevin said simply. "It has a better ladder."

"Fine with me," Tracey agreed. "I can hardly wait." She went back to her dinner. "It's a new week starting tomorrow morning." She changed the subject. "Who's on clean-up?"

Julie had meant to look when she had come in but had forgotten. No one else seemed to have remembered to have looked either. "I'll take a peek when I'm finished." Keith offered and everyone went back to eating their dinner.

~ * ~

Although it was inevitable Julie almost dreaded the thought of seeing Nancy after dinner. All of the girls were present when she arrived at the cabin, all except for Nancy who was already in the shower preparing for the upcoming night. As she plopped down wearily on the bunk Lorna came over. "You look beat." She took a seat on the bunk opposite Julie's. "It's got to be the country air."

"Could be." Julie said with a sigh.

"Nancy is in a rotten mood tonight," she said, matter-of-fact. It was almost as though she were trying to warn Julie indirectly. "She's really mad. I think she got into a fight with Kevin."

Now, why wasn't Julie surprised? "Did she say that?" Julie decided to play it safe. Why offer any information. Not that she had any information to begin with.

"Not exactly. But she didn't have to. I know Nancy."

Julie nodded. She knew Nancy had been angry as well. But she also knew that Nancy wasn't angry with Kevin. She was angry with Julie. Which at this point, Julie was too tired to worry about. Lorna tugged at her long braid, pulling it loose. "It seems that things aren't the same as they were last year. He doesn't seem interested anymore. Not like he was last year," she said absently.

"A year is a long time." Julie said deep in thought. She had learned that lesson the hard way herself.

"I guess." She began to brush out her long hair. "I never thought they had much in common anyway."

Julie didn't say anything. What could she say about the situation? She wasn't all that fond of Kevin's tactics either. Yet there was something about him. It was like an unspoken power between them. She could feel it whenever he was around. But that still didn't make it right. The right thing to do would be to stay away from him. Far away. But since when had she ever done the right thing? Probably never. Well, it was high time she did.

From the very beginning she knew she should have stayed away from Scott. But that hadn't stopped Julie. No, she had to learn the hard way. And that, more often than not, led to getting hurt. Their relationship had been doomed from the very beginning. She knew damn well what would eventually happen, but had that stopped her? No! She had been hell-bent on making Scott fall in love with her. And now she was paying for that mistake ten times over.

The entire cabin fell silent as Nancy emerged from the bathroom. She was certainly dressed to the hilt in a black mini skirt and hot pink sleeveless tee shirt. Although her hair was wrapped in a towel, turban style, she still looked lovely. She went to her bunk without uttering a word. This was so unlike Nancy who always had something to say.

Although Julie felt Nancy was inappropriately dressed she said nothing. It wasn't the time or the place to lock horns. It would happen sooner or later. The tension since Nancy came into the room was unnerving. Even Lorna picked up on it. "What's wrong?" She whispered her brown eyes wide.

"Nothing." Julie gained her feet slowly. The silence in the cabin was almost deafening. Something had to give. She could feel the tension peaking. It was up to her to set the record straight. Especially considering Nancy was not about to budge. "I want everyone to take a walk over to Tracey's cabin. You can wait for me there." She'd expected some kind of resistance but surprisingly met none. "Not you, Nance," she said as Nancy was about to file out behind them. "I think we need to have a little talk, don't you?"

Nancy turned around then. And the look she gave Julie was remarkable. Her brown eyes were ice cold and shooting sparks at the same time. "I have nothing to say to you," she said through clenched teeth.

"I doubt that." Julie stood her ground.

"All right. I will say this," she began. "I don't know what's going on between you and Kevin." Her breath caught and held. "But there are rules…"

"Yes. There are rules." Julie said simply. "And I've followed every one of them."

"Have you?" She smiled like the cat that had finally cornered the mouse. "I suppose by going to the campfire with Kevin and seeing him as well…"

"I am not seeing Kevin. Or going to the campfire with Kevin, or anyone else for that matter." Julie was appalled at this latest piece of information.

"It's obvious to me…"

"Listen." Julie cut in quickly. "I don't care what is, or is not, obvious."

"Oh really?" Nancy stood hands on hips. "I guess we'll see tonight since Kevin is not taking you to the campfire."

Julie was at a loss for words. And Nancy picked up on that like a dog with a bone. She wasn't about to let Julie off the hook without an explanation. "You must think we're all stupid." She snorted. "It's the way he looks at you. And the way you look at him." Nancy shrugged her shoulders. "I'm not blind, you know."

How dare Kevin open his big mouth. How dare he let people believe they were seeing each other. Oh, she'd see him tonight. And he'd get what she should have given Scott a long time ago. Was she ever angry! He was going to regret everything that had passed his lips without a thought. "We'll talk about this later, Nance." She looked up to find Nancy watching her intently. "In fact, I'm putting you in charge tonight." She went to her closet and opened it with a vengeance. Tonight was going to be a night Kevin would never forget. "Do you have any questions?" She met Nancy's eyes evenly daring her to refute anything.

"No."

"Good." Julie wiggled out of her jean cut-offs and stood in her red skimpy panties. "What are you waiting for? Do your hair and go get the girls."

Nancy did as she was told. Although she gave Julie the oddest look as she combed her blonde hair. Never before had Julie showered and dressed so quickly. The first thing she pulled out of the closet was the outfit she chose for the evening. It didn't matter that the outfit belonged to Lorna, a pair of peach shorts with a matching short cropped shirt.

As she applied her makeup with a steady hand Nancy was out the door and on her way to get their campers. Now Julie was really racing against the clock.

She had come up with the perfect plan. At first it had seemed too perfect. But the way she figured it, she wouldn't have to seek Kevin out. Given enough time he would come looking for her. And then everything would come full circle. She'd give it to him, and she'd give it to him good.

Then just as she had planned, just as her compact clicked shut, there was a knock on the door. A little sooner than she had expected but it would do. "Come in." She remained completely calm. No need for hysterics. She was in complete control. Of course it was Kevin. "Hi, Kevin." She met those deep blue-green eyes. Mistake number one. He was certainly dressed up, for what she did not know. He wore a pair of black khakis with a green shirt. His eyes were the color of his shirt and the way his dirty blond hair fell over the collar looked so innocent. At that moment her breath caught and all of the previous felt anger melted instantly away.

"You look very pretty tonight." Those green eyes took in her appearance with appreciation. His intense gaze missed nothing and especially not the scars on her left thigh. Although he said nothing she knew he had seen them. Maybe that would work to her advantage. But could she stand another rejection due to that damned car accident? "Are you ready?" He asked finally bringing his eyes to meet hers once again.

"Kevin." The rest of the words stuck in her throat. Deep down she knew what she had to do, so why wasn't she doing it? "Kevin." She'd try it again. "It's not the proper thing to do." That really sounded good. "Being a counselor I have to follow the rules." That sounded a little better. "Please understand that."

He smiled. "The circumstances have just changed."

She didn't understand. Or perhaps she did. "Why?"

"Not all of us are in a position to lie about our ages," he said simply. "If we were, who knows." He shrugged. "I guess I'd be a counselor too."

"What do you want me to do, Kevin?" She crossed her arms to her chest. "Do you want me to go to Rob and tell him? Would that make you happy?"

"Yes."

She couldn't believe he'd said that. "Rob would demote you in a heartbeat."

"And you'd just love that, wouldn't you?" She raised her chin a notch. "All right." She agreed. "I'll tell him." She smiled. "But it won't matter at all, Kevin. Because in the end I'll just go home. It won't change anything. I still won't go out with you."

Kevin started towards her. For once Julie thought she had over-stepped her boundaries, yet she would not back down. "How can you stand there and tell me you won't go out with me." He stopped short in front of her. "Maybe you should try it before making any rash decisions."

Her breath caught. He was standing so close. Too close. "Why do you want to run away?" His voice was like a silky caress, his eyes held hers as though a magnet. "Why don't you try it first? You might just like it."

He was going to kiss her. And she was too shaken to move. Deep down she supposed she wanted him to kiss her. At this point she really wasn't sure. But she wasn't going to back away. That would mean that she was allowing her fears to take over. "Kev…" Her breath caught as his mouth descended lower until his lips were just barely touching hers. It felt perfect. "Kev…" As she sighed his name he kissed her thoroughly. The kiss was light and sweet. Then suddenly it deepened and she could feel herself melting. Of their own accord her arms wound around his neck as his hands rested at her waist. She could actually feel the heat emanating from the both of them.

"Step up." He still held her loosely about the waist.

Kevin ran his hands gently through her long hair as he deepened the kiss.

The kiss was light and sweet. As his arms went around her she was blasted by the memories. They were there and now they crashed upon her in waves. They consumed every part of her. The very way that Kevin was holding her it was almost as though it could have been Scott's touch. And that scared her. This wasn't right. It was too soon. The pain was still fresh, almost like rubbing salt into a wound. Her breath caught and she backed away as pain filled her big brown eyes. Instantly the mood was broken. "I can't." The rest of the words got lodged somewhere in her throat. "Please say you understand, Kevin."

"I don't understand," he said softly. "Why don't you explain it to me?"

Explain it! How could she explain it to him when she didn't understand it herself? What did he want to hear? What could she say that would change anything? "Is this just another excuse?" He questioned. "Will you come with me to the campfire tonight?"

She looked at him blinking back tears. This had been the closest she had ever come to feeling anything for anyone besides Scott.

"You don't have to consider it a date." He gave her one of his dazzling smiles. "We can go as friends." He paused. "We are friends, aren't we?"

"Yes, but…"

"Why is there always a but in there somewhere?" They were still standing close. "Just say yes, Julie. And I promise that I won't pressure you."

He sounded so sincere. But could she trust him? Could she trust herself? Could she believe him? "All right, Kevin." She began. "I'll go to the campfire with you." She met his eyes. "But I don't want to hear anything else about my age. So if you have any intention of going to Rob or to the Wiskles' you may as well tell me where I stand right now."

He snickered. "Tough little cookie." He rocked back on his heels grinning. "Just tell me one thing," he came a little bit closer which sent Julie's heart to beating wildly once again. "If I were a counselor…"

As though he really had to ask that question? The problem was could she admit it? "Don't answer that." He looked at his watch. "We'd better get out of here. Who knows what everyone would think." He laughed as he led her to the door and out into the breezy night air. It wasn't a laughing matter as she had thought along those very same lines herself. What would everyone think? So much for her brilliant plan!

Six

They walked to the campfire in total silence. The only sounds
that could be heard were those of the crickets tuning into the
night. It was a cool night tonight as the air was just a little crisp.
Not a good night for wearing shorts, Julie had soon discovered.
Aside from the lighted path, there was just a sliver of moon to
light their way. Something in which Julie had never considered lit
to begin with. "You're awfully quiet." Kevin remarked lightly.
"Julie," he stopped suddenly then. "I won't go to Wiskle. I guess I
went a little too far."

She faced him. "Thank you, Kevin." As he came closer she
backed away laughing. "Don't push your luck."

As they started on their way once again Julie felt much better.
Light hearted actually. Soon she and Kevin were talking and
joking as before, the strain of the past week now forgotten. It felt
good not to constantly be on guard. So, someone else knew her
secret. It had been bound to happen. At least she was safe enough,
for now anyway.

The fire was roaring when they arrived. Everyone seemed to be scattered about. No one seemed to notice that they had arrived together. Hopefully no one would. But if they did, Julie would be ready. "We can sit over here." Kevin took her arm gently. "Mike brought a blanket. He won't mind if we sit there." They walked over together and Mike looked up.

"Hey, Kev. What's up?" He gained his feet respectfully. "And you're Julie, right?"

She nodded. "Sit down. Kev, get your lady a drink."

Julie almost choked at that remark. "Unless you'd prefer a beer." Mike had lowered his voice significantly. "I have a few tucked away for safe-keeping."

"No thank you." She took a seat at the edge of the red heavy blanket while Kevin went to get their drinks.

"You're Tracey's friend," Mike said taking a pull of his beer. "Nice girl, that Tracey."

If Julie didn't know better she would have thought that Mike had one too many of those beers he had tucked away. She knew that whole scenario rather well. After all, she'd been through it enough times with her mother, to know. Marie Finch, at one point, had a major drinking problem. However, that was something that Julie didn't even want to think about now. She was far enough away that Marie's drinking couldn't touch her. Physically anyway.

"Is punch all right with you?" Kevin sat down beside her.

"Thanks." She took the cup with a smile. The punch was excellent, like nothing she had ever tasted before. Although it had an unfamiliar twang it had a nice mixed berry taste. It went down cool and was refreshing. She drank it all down rather quickly, actually within seconds as she had been quite thirsty. "Can you get me another?" She met Kevin's eyes.

"That good, huh?" He handed her his cup. "Drink this one nice and slow." He scrambled to his feet. "I'll be right back."

As Julie watched him walk away she took another sip. "Did that come from Jake's private stock?"

"Excuse me?"

At that moment Mike leaned over and peered into her cup. "He makes the best berry punch around."

"What's in this?"

"Probably a little bit of everything."

Julie looked into the cup. "You mean alcohol?" She whispered, brown eyes wide.

"Yeah." He gave her this odd look as if to say, 'haven't you ever had a drink before?' Well she hadn't and she had no intention of starting now. If Rob knew what was going on he'd have all of their hides. No Alcohol! Rule Number One. They were breaking the rules.

"Did you miss me?"

"There's alcohol in here." She whispered before he sat down. "That's against the rules."

"What Rob doesn't know won't hurt him."

"Oh really?" She wanted to be serious. In fact, it had started out that way. Only now she felt airy and light. So instead of telling him what she had at first intended, she sighed. She felt too good to argue with him. Why bother with it now. They were here. They were together. "Sit back and relax. Tracey is right about one thing," he placed an arm across her shoulders. "You worry too much."

She leaned into his embrace. He was so warm that she snuggled even closer. "This is nice." Kevin took a sip of his own drink. "Being here with you." His breath was warm on her neck. He was so close and for once in her life she felt completely at ease. "I like spending time with you, Julie."

"Yeah?" She met his eyes.

"I like you." He whispered. "And more than just a friend."

Julie was hypnotized by those blue-green eyes. "I like you too," she returned softly, meaning every word. If it weren't for their current predicament she might be able to fall in love with him. However, at this point in time that was definitely out of the question. Not under these circumstances. The time wasn't right. Then again, when love came knocking, would the time ever be right?

"Let's take a walk. Everyone's already doing their own thing. Nobody will even miss us." He got to his feet then held his hand out for her to take. When she did, he pulled her up and she practically fell into his arms. "Take it easy."

She laughed up at him. "Sorry." She mumbled. "That punch had some kick."

"I'll say." Their eyes met and held and Julie found it impossible to look away. "Let's get out of here. All I want to do is kiss you." He took her hand and they started for the lighted path. Once they were on the path and away from everyone's eyes he faced her. "I can't help myself, Julie." He placed a gentle hand to her cheek his eyes never leaving hers. "Can I kiss you?"

She didn't even hesitate. What the hell was she doing? "Yes." She breathed and he kissed her. It was a moment of pure bliss as their lips went on a mission of touching and tasting. It was heaven being in his arms. His hands were sifting through her hair as he pulled her even closer. Without a conscious thought she wound her arms around his neck as he kissed her over and over again. At that very moment she felt as though she could spread wings and fly.

"You're beautiful," he said against her lips.

No one had ever said that to her before and meant it. She knew that Kevin wasn't handing her a line. She could feel it in his kiss. "I want us to be together, Julie. I want you to be my girl."

Suddenly Julie's heart froze as her mind went on instant rewind, racing back to another place in time.

~ * ~

Scott gave her a big smile. "You know I'm not the type to commit. But Julie," He swept her into his arms. "I want you to be mine. And only mine."

~ * ~

"What do you say?" Kevin was looking down at her waiting for an answer.

"I have to get back." She moved away from him then. Thinking of Scott had actually thrown her for a loop and now the moment was gone.

"Damnit." He hissed through his teeth. "You're doing it again. Why are you running away from me?"

"I'm not running. It's getting late..."

"Okay." He threw his hands up in disgust. "You must like playing games with people's minds. Is that what it is?"

"I wasn't..."

"Like hell you weren't." His eyes flashed dangerously. "I'm practically telling you that I'm falling in love with you..." He stopped suddenly. "Why don't you just kick me in the teeth? Because that's exactly what you keep doing."

"You knew I had a boyfriend back home. Why did you have to push it?" Her voice quivered.

"Fine. You want me to back off, I'll back off." He took a few steps away from her as well. "Go back to Scott, if there even is a Scott, but don't you ever play head games with me again." He was definitely angry. And she really couldn't blame him at this point. "What are you waiting for? Go home little girl." With that said he stomped off into the darkness leaving Julie to stare after him.

At first she felt too numb to move. If it weren't for her emotions running rampant she would be angry. But above all, she was not going to cry. That would be the ultimate in defeat. And she would not let Scott or his memory overcome her.

For once since she had arrived at Camp Wiskle walking through the darkness did not seem to bother her. Maybe that was because she had absolutely no feelings left. If her heart weren't so numb it would be shredded into little pieces by now. Why couldn't she just admit that she did feel something for Kevin? Why was she still allowing Scott to control her heart?

Finally, after what seemed like hours, she made it back to the cabin. The girls, minus Nancy, were already in bed and fast asleep. The soft glow of the night light shone softly in the large room. Nancy had probably decided to go swimming with the others. No big deal. "You're back." Lorna propped herself up on an elbow. "We were starting to get worried."

Julie sat at the edge of her own bunk which was adjacent to Lorna's. "Nancy went swimming with the rest of the counselors." She sighed wearily. "Why didn't you go too?"

"I'm really bushed."

"It's only a little after eleven." She noticed that Julie was wearing one of her outfits. "That short set looks great on you." She snickered. "Better than it does on me."

"I'm sorry, Lorna I really should have asked…"

"That's okay." She pulled herself up to a sitting position. "Are you sure you're feeling all right, Julie?"

Julie forced a smile. "I'm just tired."

"I know the feeling. This country air knocks me out too." She stifled a yawn.

"Go back to sleep." Julie collected her nightshirt and towel before heading for the bathroom. All she needed was a nice cool shower before turning in.

All night Julie tossed and turned. Not only did she have plenty on her mind but the heat was horrendous. Although she had feigned sleep when Nancy came in she had noticed the time on the small travel alarm beside her bunk. To her dismay it had been half past three. Surely they hadn't been swimming for the past five hours. At that very moment her mind kicked into overdrive, had Nancy been with Kevin? She had to get a grip on the way her thoughts were turning. She took a deep breath and let it out slowly. She refused to think of Kevin in that light again. It served no purpose at all for her to get angry. In fact, she had no right to feel the way that she did. It would only create further complications. This situation was out of her hands. Being a good counselor had to remain her objective right now. And to be the best counselor she could be she had to follow the rules. It did not matter if she agreed with them or not. The rules had been established for a reason. It was that simple. It had to be. On that note she finally fell asleep.

~ * ~

The next morning dawned bright but cool. Finally, a much needed break from the heat wave of the previous week. After the bell sounded Rob's voice could be heard over the intercom. "Good morning, campers." There was only a brief pause. "This morning will be a little different."

Everyone in Cabin Three stopped what they were doing at the moment to listen. "All juniors and campers are to go to the baseball diamond as usual. All counselors are to report to the main house for a meeting." The intercom crackled. "Carry on."

"I wonder what that's all about." Nancy remarked before going into the bathroom for a shower. But something told Julie that she already knew what it was all about but Julie said nothing. The girls continued as usual with their morning rituals. No one else seemed to be put off by Rob calling a meeting but Julie's stomach was suddenly tied in knots. As if that weren't enough, she had a splitting headache.

Julie dressed quickly, opting for jeans, just as the girls were making their way out the door and into the bright sunshine. She was only a little surprised when Tracey came in a few minutes later. "Hi." She took a seat on Lorna's freshly made bunk, looking unusually pale with dark circles beneath her blue eyes.

"Late night last night?" Julie was putting on her sneakers.

"You never showed up." She wagged a finger and smiled. "But you didn't really miss anything anyway."

Julie met her friend's eyes evenly. "What do you think this meeting is all about?"

"Who knows?" Tracey waved a hand aside carelessly. "It could be anything. Rob is like that. He'll have a meeting about what is on the breakfast menu."

"It can't be about me, can it?"

"Not if you didn't open your mouth about our little sneaky maneuver." She looked at Julie then. "Who did you tell?"

"I didn't tell anyone." She began. "But Kevin knows."

Tracey groaned. "How the hell did he find out?"

"I don't know. But he knows. And for the first time, I didn't say a single word."

"All right. Let's think about this rationally." Tracey continued deep in thought. "First of all, this is a meeting for all of the counselors. If Rob had found out the deal, he would have only paged you."

"It sounds logical enough to me. We'd better get down there then. Why flirt with any more trouble."

All the way to the main house Julie's heart was racing. What if Kevin had opened his big mouth? If he had he would definitely be sorry. Hopefully it was something trivial. But she knew that she couldn't completely relax until she knew for sure exactly what this meeting was about.

They were the last to arrive, as usual. It seemed everyone had turned around when they came into the room and at that moment Julie wished she were somewhere else. "Close the door." Rob said from where he was standing at the front of the room. "And take your seats." He looked awfully grim. As soon as they took their seats he began. "I'm just a little bit disturbed about last night's behavior." He looked around the room. "We, being counselors, are here to set a good example. The rule book cannot state that fact any clearer than it does." He took a deep breath before continuing. "There will be absolutely no liquor allowed on these grounds."

Julie listened intently while her heart beat slowly returned to normal. She was so thankful that this meeting wasn't about her that she sighed aloud. "There will be a punishment." Rob went on. "There will be no night off allowed for anyone this week."

Almost everyone in the room groaned aloud. "Also, I want all remaining liquor to be turned in as soon as possible." He looked around at the quiet room. "That is all I have to say for now. But I can tell you this much, if it happens again, and it had better not, there will be pink slips issued." He gave the room one more sweep of the eyes. "Now, you're free to go." And that was that. Somehow Rob had found out about their little drinking party. It was bound to happen. And they were there to lead by example. It certainly eased the pressure a bit. Drinking was not as glamorous as everyone perceived it to be. She knew that lesson better than anyone else. Then again, she had been just as guilty as everyone else. Even after knowing that the punch had been spiked she had continued drinking right along with everyone else. Guilty as charged. And for that she was angry with herself.

Tracey pulled Julie aside. "Who was drinking last night? She whispered.

"A few people." She replied evenly.

"Jake." It was a curt statement. "That man never learns." She shook her head in disgust. "I'm surprised he didn't get a pink slip. If the Wiskles' were here he would have gotten the boot."

Julie didn't say anything but it seemed to her that Tracey had some kind of hang up where Jake was concerned. That man could not do anything right in her eyes. Julie wondered why. "I'm just glad that you weren't involved in any of that." Tracey went on. "Come on it's time for breakfast. At least we didn't have to run this morning. Every muscle in my legs is sore." They started in the direction of the cafeteria with Keith now sandwiched between them. "Just take my advice." Tracey said simply. "Stay away from Jake. He's nothing but trouble."

By the time the counselors were seated with their breakfasts the campers were arriving. Rob had not shown yet, at least not to Julie's knowledge. That was a blessing as the table was slowly filling up. That would mean that he would have to sit with the others. Kevin was once again sitting with Nancy, another fact that did not come as any surprise. Mike was on mail duty, which left Jake and Keith as the only two males at the table. "We're playing tennis today." Jake said from across the table. "I hope your girls can hit." He directed at Julie with a sly grin.

"Then you're really in for it." Tracey quickly spoke up in her defense. "Because Julie is a pro."

"I am not." She flushed.

"Yes you are, and why not? Your father's one of the best tennis coaches around."

"Your father's a coach?" Jake asked as he dug into his scrambled eggs. "I'm impressed."

"He was but that was years ago. Now he's coaching basketball." And she left it at that. Julie was never one to discuss her family life. In fact, it was a subject she avoided entirely. It was better that way.

"Some competition. I like that." Jake gave her a smile while Tracey shot her the knowing look. The look that almost seemed to say, 'beware of snake.' Julie almost cracked up. And would have, but being the lady she was, composed herself just in the nick of time.

They were to meet on the tennis courts at eleven, which gave Julie and her campers' time to brush up on the fundamentals. Besides, all they were going to do was hit the ball over the net. It wouldn't be a match, which was just fine with her. Besides, all she really knew about tennis were the simple basics. You hit the ball over the net. And that was enough for her.

Julie gave the pep talk back at the cabin. She knew that whole bit practically by heart. "It's only a game. It doesn't matter if we win or lose."

"Winning would be better." Ellen put in carefully.

"Yes, it would." Julie agreed. "But let's not lose sight of losing with dignity. You know that we do not throw the racquets down on the court. I don't want to see any sore losers. It's just a game. We're here to have fun. Does anyone have any questions?" She looked up but they too seemed to know the drill. "Just play a fair game and I'll be happy." She went to her night stand, opened her compact and proceeded to powder her cheek. "Is everyone ready?"

Obviously, as half of them were already out the door and jogging for the path. As Julie, Ellen, and Lorna were about to do the same Mike was heading in their direction. "Mail." He pulled a bunch of letters from a small blue pouch.

"Anything for me?" Lorna held out her hand expectantly.

"Not today." He flipped through the letters. "Just Nancy, Ellen, and Julie."

"Me?" Julie got a lump in her throat the size of a small grapefruit. Who would send her a letter?

"You have one letter here," he returned, matter-of-fact before handing her the whole bunch. "I'll see you Girls later." He gave them a wave as he headed back to the cafeteria which was off the lighted path.

"These are for you." She handed Ellen her mail before going back inside to put Nancy's on her bunk. Looking down she found that her hands were actually shaking. She could hardly believe her eyes, as the letter was from Scott. Her breath caught as she tore the envelope open carefully. She was almost afraid to read what he had written as she remembered all too well the way she had poured out her heart. Here it was the truth of the matter at long last. She took her time to read...

Dear Julie,

It was nice hearing from you. Although I couldn't believe it, your letter is sitting here in black and white. I wish everything could be this simple. But it isn't. After all, we haven't seen each other in a whole year. Things change. People change. We have changed. I sometimes wish it were last year and we could fix everything. But we can't. And I'm sorry. Maybe it's time we set the record straight. I wish you all the happiness in the world. I always have. I know in my heart that one day you will find the right guy just like I have found the right woman...

Julie's heart froze in her chest. How could he do this to her? How could he throw her love for him back in her face like that? With a little bit of effort she read on.

I suppose Matt has told you about my going away. I'm sorry I couldn't say goodbye in person. Actually the last time I tried to tell you I was leaving, you were really mad at me. We had something special, I won't deny that. I think it wasn't the right time. It wasn't meant to be but you will always have a place in my heart, Julie.

Goodbye,
Scott.

Going away! Scott was going away! You would think he was leaving the country by the way he had made it sound. Where could he possibly be going? And this was his final goodbye to her. He sent her a letter. He didn't even have the nerve to face her. Why? There were so many things racing through her mind. This letter told her next to nothing. Oh sure, she was special. Yeah, right. She was so special that he was now with someone else. Her letter, which he was never meant to see, had told him everything that she had felt. How she had fallen in love with him. Thank goodness he hadn't quoted anything from her letter. It had been her therapy and now it was her undoing because Scott had never loved her, and just knowing that one little fact was like a knife slicing through her tender heart.

Carefully she folded the letter and gingerly placed it back into the envelope. The girls were still waiting for her. She had a very important job to do. There wasn't any time for hysterics. She would not cry. Then again, how could she cry when all she felt was numbness where her heart had once been beating with hope.

"Are you okay, Julie?" Lorna's eyes were wide with concern.

"I'm fine." She forced a smile. "Come on. They're probably getting ready to send out a search party." She tucked the letter into the pocket of her camp tee and they started on their way.

Lorna and Ellen chatted all the way down to the tennis courts, while Julie lagged behind. It felt as though she were walking around in a dream. Someone else's dream because this simply could not be happening to her. Once they had arrived Jake and Nancy were on the court, and a game was already underway. They took their seats on one of the benches just outside the fence. All of the campers were patiently awaiting their turns. Some were talking while others were watching the game intently. Julie sat quietly staring off into space. Her mind was busy trying to make some sense of Scott's letter. But she couldn't because none of this made any sense at all. Then suddenly she was remembering when they had been happy just to be together. Slowly she found herself slipping back to another place in time when she had thought they had been so happy.

~ * ~

"You look beautiful." Scott looked her over, that hungry look in his blue eyes. "I'm a lucky guy."

She smiled going into his arms. Everything was perfect. Even more so now that she was safely in Scott's arms. "Did you have a problem getting out of the house?"

"Nope." She looked up at him, a glint of mischief in her eyes. "I'm spending the night at Tracey's."

"And how did you manage that?"

"It wasn't that hard. Matt was out with Janet, Dad was still at work and Mom was sleeping, so I left a note."

"Did you talk to Tracey? What if someone calls there?" He backed away from her. "What if they find out?"

"Nobody will find out. You worry too much. Tracey will cover for me."

"Okay." He relaxed slightly. "Let me show you how much I've missed you."

~ * ~

"Julie. Julie."

"What?" She looked up to find Jake looking down at her with a scowl. "You're next on the court."

"Can I skip it this time?"

"Are you kidding?" He laughed. "I want to see the pro in action."

"I'm not that good, Jake. And definitely far from a pro. You know Tracey; she makes a big thing out of nothing."

"I'll be the judge of that." He handed her a racquet.

There was no way out of this one. Why make a big deal out of it. Besides, physical activity sounded like just the medicine for an aching heart. She'd play one game so he could see for himself just how biased Tracey was.

"Your serve." He tossed her the ball with a sly grin.

All eyes suddenly were upon them and Julie could feel the tension building inside of her, almost like it had when she had been younger. The excitement of being on the court with her Dad. The thrill of the victory. With that thought in mind she whacked the ball over the net.

Jake was pretty good himself and kept her moving. They were only playing until they reached the score of eleven points. As Julie felt the adrenalin rush she could also vaguely hear the cheers coming up from the sidelines.

Finally Jake pulled ahead with the final score being eleven and eight. It could have been worse Julie reasoned and was actually pretty good considering the last time she had been on the courts had been more than two years ago. Not bad at all.

"Good game." He shook her hand with a smile.

"Thanks." She handed Lorna the racquet before walking off of the court with Jake. "You're pretty good yourself." She could always appreciate a good game.

"I wasn't completely honest with you." He began with a large toothy grin. "I do some coaching at the Y."

She hit him in the arm playfully. "But Tracey was right." He met her eyes evenly. "You're good."

She flushed. "I have to run back to my cabin. Can you keep an eye on my guys while I'm gone?"

"Sure." She went back to the benches as he took off in the opposite direction. Slowly she stretched her legs and flexed her arms for a few minutes before taking a seat on the bench. But no sooner had she sat down when Kevin approached her with a familiar envelope in hand.

"I think you lost something."

She met his knowing gaze evenly and knew at once that he had read the letter.

Seven

"Give me that." She tried not to snatch the letter from his grasp, while her heart was beating against her ribcage madly. "Where did you get this?"

"I found it on the ground. You must have dropped it."

She folded the envelope and put it into her pocket once again. "Thank you." She didn't meet his eyes. She couldn't. "You didn't read it, did you?" That was certainly a stupid question but she still felt the need to ask and Kevin hesitated.

"I didn't know who it belonged..."

He read it, as though she hadn't known that from the beginning. Honestly she had hoped that voicing it would have made her feel better but actually it made it all seem silly. Well, it hadn't made her feel any better. In fact, she felt even worse. He was probably laughing at her behind her back while calling her the love sick idiot that unfortunately, she was. For once she'd like to have the upper hand with Kevin. She needed to let him know, once and for all, who was boss.

"I read it." He finally admitted. "And I'm sorry."

She met his eyes then. And to her surprise, they weren't laughing. In fact, he looked rather serious. "I'm not as rotten as you would like to believe."

She wasn't too sure about that. Oh, part of her wanted so much to believe in him. But the other part, that was another story altogether. "Is it that hard to trust me?" He queried lightly. "Or maybe you just don't trust yourself."

Quickly she pulled her gaze away. She had no answer to that question, none that she was willing to give anyway. But it seemed to Julie that Kevin had all the right answers, some of those that she was not ready yet to admit. And that drove her crazy. "Think about what I've said Julie." He walked away then, leaving her speechless.

"Is it all right if we meet you at the cafeteria, Julie?" Lorna came up to her, racquet in hand. "I figured I'd help Nancy with clean up afterwards."

"Sure," she replied absently. "You can all go."

"Thanks." Lorna said before running back to the small shed where they stored all of the tennis equipment.

What a day this was turning out to be. Part of her wanted to run and hide somewhere. She longed to find a place where she could lick her wounds in private. Camp Wiskle was such a peaceful place yet she could not find peace. Scott had even followed her here. And there was no getting away from him. The memories invaded her every thought.

~ * ~

"When the time is right." Scott kissed her lips gently. "Just be patient with me, Julie." His blue eyes were pleading with her to understand. "That's all I've ever asked you for."

"Oh Scott." She leaned against his chest with a sigh because she didn't understand. "I know in my heart that it's right."

"If you do then give me some more time." He held her to him. "It will be worth it in the end. I promise."

~ * ~

She had to stop it! Remembering was only torture. She had so many unanswered questions and they all came down to one simple little why? Why couldn't Scott feel as she did? Did that mean that he had never felt anything for her at all? Had he been using her all along just to pass the time until something better came along? The questions came endlessly but she didn't have the time to muddle through them as she had a job to do.

The cafeteria was unusually quiet as lunch consisted of vegetable soup and a large leafy green salad. A dieters dream. The calm suited Julie's mood just fine. Once again Kevin and Nancy were seated at the table. It was almost a sickening sight as they looked like two little lovebirds. Tracey and Keith were also wrapped up in their own little world. This had to be the happiest that Julie could ever remember seeing Tracey. It was obvious that she was in love with Keith and that he felt at least something similar, if not the same, for her. And Julie was happy for her friend. Everyone deserved to be that happy.

It was just beginning to drizzle lightly as they were leaving the cafeteria. It didn't mean anything as they were heading back to the cabins for a rest before swimming in the afternoon. However, if it continued Rob would certainly suspend swimming for the day. Julie met up with Ellen, Carol and Maria halfway to the cabin. Nancy and Lorna had stayed behind as they were on clean up detail. "I guess we're not swimming today." Carol said.

"We'll have to see what happens." Julie replied as they fell into step together. "Don't worry we'll get our chance."

Just then, as though on cue, Rob's voice came over the intercom. "Swimming will be cancelled for this afternoon. Those campers will participate in arts and crafts instead. Please report to the dining hall at two o'clock. Thank you."

"It figures." Ellen groaned as they trudged into the cabin. "We have an hour."

"Might as well enjoy it." Julie fixed her bunk before taking a seat.

"At least we have the dance tonight." Maria remarked casually.

Julie had forgotten all about the dance. She and Tracey were supposed to go shopping in town before Rob had issued the punishment that all counselors were not to leave camp for the week. Now she was really stuck as she had nothing suitable to wear. Everyone was making such a fuss over a dance, a dance that she did not even want to attend.

The girls were talking amongst themselves while Julie pulled out the letter from Scott and reread it. Not only was the letter pure torture but she was tormenting herself by reading it over and over again. Maybe the words still needed to sink in before she finally understood what it all meant. Or maybe she was hoping that they didn't mean anything and that Scott did feel something for her. At this point she wasn't sure of much of anything.

Suddenly she felt the need to get away, if only for a few short minutes. As luck would have it, Nancy and Lorna were just coming in the door. "I'm glad you're back." She slipped on her raincoat. "I need to do something. I'll be back as soon as I can."

To Julie's complete surprise Nancy brooked no argument. In fact, she agreed with a smile while munching on an apple. "Take your time."

"Thanks." Julie forced a smile and quickly left the cabin. Although it was still raining it was only a light steady drizzle. The path was now muddy which was quickly turning her white sneakers brown. She paid no mind as her feet were absolutely soaked because she needed this walk. She needed the fresh air, the time to get away from everyone and everything. She could actually feel the tears as they were lying in wait below the surface just waiting to explode.

There were the haunting memories. How she longed to forget, but she couldn't and it was tearing her apart. The hurt went so deep, it was so intense. How naive she had been to believe that

Scott had ever cared, much less, loved her. What a fool she had been.

"Hey there, Brown Eyes. Where you going in the rain?"

Julie looked up quickly to find, Kevin, of all people, standing in front of her wearing a big smile. Or maybe it was a smirk. "On your way to mail a letter?" His voice had a biting edge and the tears finally rushed to Julie's eyes. She'd been fighting them for so long. It was too much to handle. Even Kevin was laughing at her. "Hey." His voice softened as she tried to walk past him. "Wait." Gently he took her arm and turned her around to face him. "I'm sorry. That was horrible."

"Yes it was."

"That letter upset you," he returned, matter-of-fact. "Talk to me, Julie."

Quickly she pulled away from him. "It's none of your business," she snapped. "Besides, you read it. Now you know everything."

"I didn't..."

"Who's the counselor here?" She demanded angrily. "Me or you? I don't appreciate the way you question me."

Kevin stepped back and stared at her as though he didn't know her. "Fine." His blue-green eyes blazed dangerously. "Shot down, huh?"

"Shut up!"

"How does it feel?" He sneered. "Not too good, huh?" Julie dropped her eyes. "I'm sorry," he apologized again. "I don't know what's the matter with me." He reached for her hand. "I had no right to talk to you like that." He moved closer to where she stood. "Come here." Gently he pulled her into his warm embrace. "No. Don't fight me."

Right away her body went rigid. "Shh." He crooned into her hair still holding her close to him. "Everything will be okay."

She could just imagine the makeup running down her face causing her scar to stand out even more. That realization only made her cry harder. "Hey," he lightly caressed her back. "I'm here for you, Julie."

~ * ~

"We've been through this so many times before." Scott threw his hands up in disgust. "Damnit, Julie!" He stood before her; they were close but not touching. "I'm not leaving for another three months. And I'm here now. Right?"

She nodded. "Okay then." His voice lightened considerably as he pulled her into his arms. "For you, I'll always be here."

~ * ~

It was like a bucket of cold water as Julie pulled out of Kevin's embrace. "What now?" He met her eyes evenly. "Had time to think about the situation?" He sighed wearily. "I like you, Julie, and I know that you like me..."

"The rules..."

"To hell with the rules!" he shouted. "You weren't exactly thinking about any of the rules when you filled out your application, were you?" he demanded. "Why don't you just let it happen..."

"No." She backed away from him the apprehension evident in her eyes. "I can't... We can't..." The words came tripping off of her tongue. "You don't understand..." she finished miserably.

"I understand all right." He folded his arms across his chest. "You're afraid of getting hurt. Damnit." He took a deep breath and let it out slowly. "Sometimes you have to take a chance. Sometimes you just have to get back on that horse. I'm not another Scott..."

"This has nothing to do with Scott," she cut in quickly.

"Yes it does," he said knowingly. "I don't know what else to tell you, Julie. I have some pretty heavy feelings for you. I want to be with you..."

"No." She turned away. She couldn't believe she was listening to this. "I don't expect you to understand. I really don't but I can't be with you when I'm in love with someone else..." There she'd said it. It was out in the open now.

"I guess the question is does he love you back?"

Julie didn't answer. She couldn't.

"Does he love you?" he asked again.

"I... I don't know."

"Of course you know." His voice was hard. "I think it's time you've admitted it to yourself." He went on. "I know it can be hard to admit the truth. And sometimes the truth can hurt. It can hurt like hell." He came up behind her. "But it still doesn't change the facts."

"Stop it," she choked out while fighting the tears that threatened to overwhelm her. She didn't want Kevin to see her cry. "It's none of your business anyway." She would try another tactic.

"No, it isn't," he agreed. "I just wanted for you to see the truth."

"And I suppose you think you know the truth." She swiped at her eyes angrily. "But you don't, Kevin. You can't possibly know anything about Scott, or me."

"I know how I feel about you." He placed his hands gently upon her shoulders. "I want to get to know you, Julie." He drew her against his muscular frame. "I've never felt this way before," he whispered into her hair. "I don't want to get hurt either. Sometimes love's a risk." He paused. "But it's a risk worth taking."

Love! What was he talking about? Love. Was it possible that Kevin was in love with her? No! Maybe. Her mind was spinning in reverse. Automatic rewind.

~ * ~

"I've never felt this way with anyone but you." Scott's blue eyes danced as they met hers. "It's almost like magic."

It was love. Julie felt it too. Oh Scott. Please say that you feel the same as I do. Just say it. But he didn't. And suddenly it didn't matter because Julie loved Scott with all of her heart. I love you. She thought silently.

~ * ~

Julie pulled away from Kevin as a blast of reality shook her to the core. "Do you always have to think things through?" It was obvious that he was angry. "Why can't you sit back and let things happen. Let it run its course."

"I can't think about this right now. I can't even think straight." That statement was certainly not a lie.

"Fine. Walk away. It's easier to walk away. Better yet." Kevin was rambling now. "I'll walk away. Goodbye."

It hurt more than she cared to admit. But it had to be done. Why couldn't Kevin see that? This was the best thing for the both of them. It was better this way. Better that it happened now before either of them could get hurt. Yet, it already hurt. It hurt like hell when she turned around and watched Kevin walk away.

~ * ~

The dance was in full swing by the time Julie and her campers reached the dance hall. The girls sure looked pretty tonight. They all wore different colored pastel miniskirts with matching short cropped shirts. All except for Julie who had borrowed a pair of white clam diggers from Lorna. She also wore a regular white tee shirt which looked pretty against her bronze tanned skin. She was certainly grateful that she and Lorna were the same size. Otherwise she would have worn just a regular pair of jeans.

The girls left her at the door which was okay with her. There was no sign of Kevin, thank goodness. Rob looked very distinguished in a gray suit and tie. It was rumored all around camp that he was dating Christine, another counselor who had to be in her twenties. Actually they made a cute couple. It was also rumored that Rob had been a widower for a number of years.

After making quite sure that the punch wasn't spiked she stood on the side lines watching the couples dance. Keith and Tracey glided by all smiles as though floating on air. They seemed oblivious to everyone but each other. As it should be when two people were in love. It was not that long ago when Julie had been floating on air as well. Magic, as Scott had called it. She also remembered when she had discovered that Scott had been dating one of Janet's cousins. How devastated she had been after learning that they had been seeing each other for months. Her name was Cheryl Walters. How Julie despised her. But even more than that, she had been hurt.

~ * ~

"You're seeing her again tonight." It was a statement. To her horror Julie had hit the nail right on the head. "Damn you Scott!" She was angry. But more than that, she was hurt. "Just give me an honest answer."

"Yes." He met her hurt brown eyes. "Are you satisfied now?" he demanded, blue eyes flashing angrily. "Maybe we'll even end up 'doing it'." He shouted furiously. "Is that what you want to hear?"

"I just... I..." She was fighting tears and quickly losing the battle. She was not going to let him see how deeply he had hurt her. "I don't care what you do." She left his room then, slamming the door behind her.

"Julie." He went after her but Julie didn't want to hear it. "Cheryl means nothing to me..."

She whirled around then causing him to stop short on the stairs. "Then break it off," she said simply.

"I can't do that."

She'd expected as much. "You know how I feel about you, Julie." His voice broke. "She means absolutely nothing." He paused. "And she never will."

~ * ~

"How about a dance?" Jake stood before her, smiling. "Come on."

At first she had hesitated. Actually the only reason that she had hung back was because of all that Tracey had told her. The next thing she did was throw caution to the wind as she stepped into his arms carefully. "You look pretty tonight?"

She smiled her thanks as they began to sway to a soft ballad. "That's nice." His blue eyes were serious and for a moment Julie was puzzled.

"What?"

"That smile," he said simply. "You hardly ever smile. And you have such a beautiful smile." His eyes widened. "Life is too short not to smile. Take this moment for example." He began on a light note. "In just one minute, one second, this moment will become a memory." For once his eyes were serious. "A fond one for me."

The music stopped but still he held her, smiling that most charming smile. Then suddenly it all seemed clear. It was like the clouds had suddenly lifted. Rather, the fog had been lifted and she could see something that she hadn't been able to see before.

As the music began again Julie realized that there was something that she needed to do. And she had to do it now before she lost her nerve. "Thanks, Jake." Now she was serious. "You've just opened my eyes to something." Gently she moved out of his embrace. "Excuse me."

As Julie weaved through the crowd the music picked up its tempo. Before stepping outside into the crisp night air she gave the dance hall one more glance. Her heart was skipping around in her chest. Jake had truly opened her eyes to something that had been happening all around her. Why fight it? Why deny the simple truth? She felt something for Kevin. She knew she had from the very first moment that their eyes met. Sure, Scott still had a special place in her heart, and most likely, always would. But it was time she got on with her life and stopped looking back. It was time she and Kevin created some memories of their own. And these memories too would last a lifetime.

As Julie walked the lighted path her spirits were lifted and she was even humming a small tune. The night was positively breathtaking with a full moon and millions of stars twinkling overhead. This was the first time, in a long time, that there was a spring in her step. Even the surrounding darkness couldn't touch her as she felt so light.

Then again, and as unfortunate as it turned out like most things that had happened in her life, it just wasn't meant to be.

That was when she first caught sight of them. She had been heading in the direction of the cabins when she thought that she heard soft voices. It seemed to be coming from just beyond the trees. She gasped as she caught sight of two silhouettes in the moonlight. She stopped short, and leaned against a giant oak tree. She couldn't believe her eyes. It was almost like getting physically winded. The hard cold truth stood naked before her. It was ugly and it hurt.

Just a little ways ahead, off the dimly lit path, Kevin and Nancy seemed to be immersed in some deep conversation. They seemed completely at ease with one another, as though at any moment he might sweep her off of her feet. They looked mighty comfortable. Before she could see him actually take Nancy into his arms or worse than that, be caught in the act of spying on them, she moved silently but quickly away. Although she felt completely numb she just couldn't bear to watch anymore. It was disbelief. It had to be. She refused to believe that this could happen twice in one lifetime. It was almost as though her past had suddenly become her present. Well, she wasn't going to allow it. But little did she realize that it was already way too late. From the moment her eyes had met Kevin's she had fallen. Her heart had known it even though her mind had refused to accept it.

Somehow she ended up at the lake. She knew she was going on automatic. And she knew how dangerous that could be but she wasn't thinking clearly. Maybe she was finally losing it.

After kicking her pumps off she sat at the edge of the dock and dipped her feet into the cool waters. With a sigh she leaned back on her arms and lifted her face up to the moonlight. Before she realized it her mind took over and she thought back on better days. Back to the first day that she had ever laid eyes on Scott. And what a day that had been!

~ * ~

"Matt." Julie tapped on her brother's door only once before flinging it open. "Daddy wants his tennis whites back and..." Her

breath caught as her heart catapulted into her throat. There, standing less than two feet away from her stood the most gorgeous guy Julie had ever seen. There he stood half naked, wearing only a pair of briefs, right in front of her.

"Hi." He smiled warmly and the first thing she noticed was his deep blue eyes. Eyes the color of the sky on a nice hot summer day. He did not appear to be embarrassed at all. "I'm Scott. One of Matt's friends from school." He had curly blond hair and he was built with strong muscled shoulders and biceps. He seemed to have muscles everywhere. Now he stood tall and proud. Like one of those Greek gods Julie had often read about. "And you are?" He cocked an eyebrow as he gave her a small flirtatious smile.

"Julie." She blurted out feeling like a fool.

"Matt's little sister," he said knowingly. "Not so little though." He regarded her solemnly. "It was nice meeting you, sweetie, but as you can see," he looked down then quickly met her eyes once again. "I'm in the middle of getting dressed."

"Uh... Yes." She reddened while backing out the door. "Bye."

He snickered. "Goodbye."

After pulling the door closed behind her she breathed a great sigh of relief. Scott was the man for her. And he most certainly was a man. From the first moment their eyes had met, she had felt that jolt of electricity. She had known then and soon he would know it as well. She could wait a lifetime for Scott.

~ * ~

With a deep heartened sigh Julie gazed out onto the waters surrounding serene Camp Wiskle. She had to stop remembering. She had to get her life back on track again. A year was a long time to wait for someone. The dream had worn thin some time ago. Scott didn't love her. In fact, he never had. It was time that she started living again. Time for her to be the woman that she knew she could be. It was time to move on.

"Hello, Julie." She knew it was Kevin before she even turned around. "I think we need to talk."

She couldn't have agreed more though she remained silent. Let him do all the talking. She would listen. "I said a lot of things I didn't mean before." He went on carefully. "And I'm very sorry. It was wrong the way I put you on the spot like that." He took a seat on the dock beside her. "Maybe I've been acting crazy because," he pushed out a short laugh. "I've never felt this way about anyone before." He sounded so damned innocent. So sincere, gentle and caring. There was something about him that touched her deep inside. Whenever he was around her pulse would begin to race. More than that even. He had that knack for making her smile.

"What?" Those blue-green eyes widened. "You're staring."

"I was just thinking." Quickly she averted her gaze.

"About us, I hope." He placed a gentle hand to her knee. "Just give us a chance, Julie." Their eyes met, collided actually. "It's no secret the way I feel about you." He edged closer. "You're funny, pretty, and I want to spend more time with you." He placed a careful hand to her scarred cheek. "And I know you feel something. Can't we..." He bent closer, placing a light kiss on her parted lips. "Let this happen without fighting it anymore." In the next breath he swept her into his arms, kissing her again with a passion neither could deny.

The stars shone down on them brilliantly. A breeze flirted with their hair. Lips touched lips. It was almost like magic. Almost perfect. Too perfect. He was carrying her to dizzying heights. Heights she had once been close to a long time ago. That realization had Julie scrambling to her feet.

"I'm sorry, Kevin." She could not meet his eyes. All she knew was that she had to get out of there before she lost it altogether. She needed time. "I can't do this. Not now." She knew she was rambling. Quickly she grabbed her shoes. "I have to go." And she was out of there. However, there was one mistake that she did make, for one brief moment she turned around and looked back. Kevin's hurt expression was now permanently imprinted on her mind just as he had made a gigantic imprint on her heart.

Eight

Rain pelted against the cabin noisily. This, in turn, ruled out all outdoor activities. However, to make it up to the campers, Rob announced, over breakfast, that a dance would be held later in the evening. That seemed to make up for the lousy weather according to all of the campers in Cabin Three. Julie, on the other hand, wasn't sure if she could make it through another night like last night. "Let's play truth." It was Ellen who suggested it and Lorna seconded it.

"I'm busy." Nancy was rooting through her suitcase in a frenzy. "I have to find something to wear for tonight."

Lorna groaned. "It's just a dance. Come on."

"Maybe later." She slammed down the case top angrily. "I have one skirt left. I can't even find my blue blouse. My sister is going to kill me."

"Who's your date?" Lorna asked as she shuffled a deck of cards. "Tonight's Ladies Choice, you know."

At that remark Julie pricked her ears. This would be her big chance. Then again, it all depended upon Nancy's answer to Lorna's question. "I don't know yet," she said, then shot Julie a knowing glance.

"We should be getting ready for arts and crafts." Julie composed herself quickly.

"Do we have to go?" Ellen asked. "I lost my stupid key chain last week."

"Don't worry about it. I think we're doing something different today."

"Good."

Julie gave her scar a little more attention because of the weather.

"It hardly shows at all," Lorna said as she pulled on her raincoat. "Are you going to ask someone to the dance tonight?"

Julie's hand froze in midair. Where had that come from? "Maybe." She smiled.

"You should," she said, matter-of-fact. "And I know the perfect guy for you."

"Really?" This time Julie laughed in spite of herself. "And who might that be?"

"If I tell you, will you ask him?" Talk about blunt.

"We'll see." She continued powdering her scar in the compact mirror.

"You have to say yes."

"Lorna."

"Come on, Julie. Besides, I know for a fact that he'll say yes."

"Who's the mystery man?" Nancy picked that moment to jump right into their conversation. "Come on, Lorna. Don't keep us in suspense."

Lorna shot her a disgusted look. "It's Kevin," she replied simply. As though it were that simple. Julie couldn't believe that Lorna had said anything at all. Especially considering how close she and Nancy were.

"She can't ask Kevin." Nancy returned flippantly.

"Why not?"

"Because he's a junior, that's why." Nancy said in her most sarcastic tone.

Lorna waved a hand aside. "So what."

"It's against the rules." Nancy went on.

"Who's going to tell?"

Julie could hardly believe what she was hearing. From the looks of things, Nancy couldn't either. "My mother is five years older than my father." Lorna went on in a matter-of-fact tone. "Age doesn't matter." She met Nancy's eyes evenly. "Unless there's another reason you don't want Julie to ask Kevin."

"Kevin can go out with whoever he wants," she said crisply but her brown eyes were blazing dangerously. "I thought I had told you that last night." She forced through clenched teeth.

"And if he decides to go with Julie..."

"Then it's fine with me," she said before storming out of the cabin, slamming the door behind her.

"Ask him, Julie." Lorna gave her a big smile. "It would be stupid if you let this chance get away."

Julie was definitely confused. After what she had witnessed last night she would have guessed that Nancy and Kevin were still involved. Then again, she was with him last night too. Maybe they weren't together. At this point she'd need a score card to keep up with all of the drama surrounding Camp Wiskle. "They're history." Lorna whispered. "I seen it coming a long time ago but Nancy wouldn't listen." She shrugged carelessly. "Everyone knows how he feels about you." Her brown eyes widened but were serious. "You must have noticed it." She laughed. "Everyone else has."

An indescribable feeling, she wasn't sure what, flowed through her veins. It made her feel light headed and giddy. Happy had to be the word to define what she was feeling. It had been a long time since Julie could truly admit that she was happy. This would be a night to remember. Of that, she was quite certain.

Everyone returned to the cafeteria after lunch for arts and crafts. Although it was quite noisy but for once, Julie didn't mind it. Lorna, who had suddenly turned cupid, quickly headed for the table where Jake and his campers were seated.

At each place setting on the table there was a ceramic plaque to be painted. Each white plaque was the same. It was a picture of a boy and girl, each holding a baby chick in their hand. The girls thought it was adorable. The boys, on the other hand, didn't care about painting a silly plaque one way or the other.

Tracey and Keith were conducting the class and were slowly making their way around the room to make sure everyone had the correct materials. "Would it be all right if I sit with Anne's group?" Nancy asked softly so no one could hear.

"Yes." Julie didn't meet her eyes. She already felt bad enough as it was. Kevin hadn't even arrived as yet and Julie could feel the butterflies in her stomach.

"Hello, Sweetie." Jake looked up as she and her group took their seats. "I'll have you know," he began on a serious note. "That tonight is Ladies Choice." He gave her a smile. "And wouldn't you know it, I don't have a date. That's not a hint." He hurried on to add. "I just figured you might like to know."

"Keep wishing, Jake," she returned his smile.

"No go, huh?" He shrugged. "I thought it was worth a shot." He paused then decided to change the subject as he wasn't getting anywhere. "Let's get this show on the road. I'll get the things we need while you get everyone here organized."

Getting organized meant helping everyone set up with old newspapers, which would keep the tables free of paint and other debris. Without another thought she grabbed a pile of the loose papers and started working her way down and around the table. Kevin chose that moment to arrive. On top of that, he took the only seat available, the one directly across from hers. After that, it was only a matter of time before she reached his setting. And as she did, they reached to lift the plaque at the same time and bumped hands. Kevin was the first to withdraw his hand as though her touch had burned him.

"Sorry," he mumbled carefully keeping his gaze averted.

"Kevin." She bit her lip. This wasn't going to be easy. Here goes nothing. "I'd like to ask you something..."

"And how are we doing over here?" Tracey would pick that moment to come over to the table.

"Good. Everything seems to be in order here."

She made her way around their table taking everything in. Everything, including the way Julie was standing over Kevin. That even warranted a small smile before she moved on to the next table.

"Yes," he said, the minute Tracey had gone and was out of ear shot, looking up with those magnificent blue-green eyes that could melt her very heart.

"What I'd like to know is..." How could she phrase this without being blunt? Thinking about it, there was no other way besides being blunt. "I was just wondering if you and Nancy were still..." She paused. "You know... Still involved?"

"No." That was simple enough answer, so she proceeded.

"I heard that tonight is Ladies Choice."

"Yeah, so?"

He wasn't going to make it easy for her. He was going to make her sweat it out until the very end. "I'd like to know if you would be my date tonight." There, it was said.

"Tonight, huh?" He was trying not to smile. "Isn't that short notice?"

Julie didn't know what to say to that. "Are you sure about this?" Without thinking of where they were he reached for her hand.

"Yes." She replied, although she wasn't, not really. Even more so considering that what they were about to do was definitely against the rules.

"I'd be honored." He gave her a warm smile which seemed to light up the whole room.

She moved past him then, and continued moving down the table, completing the task at hand. There was a new light shining. She could feel it burning from the inside out and she couldn't help but smile. In her heart she knew that this is exactly what she needed. Things would now get better. This had to be the beginning of something good.

Jake returned a few minutes later with the rest of the supplies. "Some of these projects that Rob picks to do are for the birds." He was now beginning to set up paper cups filled with water. Next, he passed out the brushes, lastly, the paints. "Let's not fool around with this." Jake tapped his brush on the table to get everyone's attention. "Just to let you guys know." He paused still waiting for everyone at the table's attention. "This is going to be a contest." He went on. "There will be first, second, and third prize ribbons awarded for the best plaque. The only thing I can say is that hopefully this table will win one. Good luck."

Although Julie and Jake had wanted to remain on the sidelines they soon found themselves caught up in the fun of painting. There was idle chatter at the table, nothing of any importance. They were there to offer assistance if it was requested but everyone seemed to know what they were doing. "I can't stand this weather." Jake ran a careless hand through his short brown hair. "But I hear that tomorrow is supposed to be a good swimming day."

"The girls have been complaining about the rain all day." She replied evenly while her eyes swept over Kevin. Something Jake did not miss.

"You asked him." It was a statement. "I guess I saw it coming." He chuckled and Julie met his eyes quickly.

"It's not exactly common knowledge," she whispered. "And I'd like to keep it that way, if you don't mind."

"I won't say a single word," he replied softly. "But what about tonight? Rob can be ruthless when he wants to be. He sometimes reminds me of a vulture, just waiting for the right moment to pounce."

Julie rolled her eyes. "I'll cross that bridge when I get to it."

His blue eyes were laughing. "Determination. I like that in a woman."

Julie laughed. "Give it up, Jake," she said before walking away. She was not in the mood for Jake's dry humor. Not today. She didn't want anything to spoil the way she was feeling happy on the inside.

The campers spent the remainder of the afternoon painting. All in all it had turned out to be a rather restful day. And it had finally stopped raining. That was definitely an added bonus. Now all that they had to do was clean up, have dinner, and return to their cabins before the dance.

Nancy had stayed with Anne's group all afternoon. Soon Julie would have to face her. She wasn't sure how she felt about that. Then there was the matter of tonight. Nancy was going to hit the roof when she heard about Julie and Kevin attending the dance together.

It took the counselors less than an hour to get the cafeteria back in shape. Even some of the juniors had pitched in to help as well. That made the job even easier, not to mention faster.

Dinner consisted of the famous Wiskle pot luck. This time Tracey had been absolutely right. It was awful. That was a fact that everyone agreed upon. Once again Nancy chose to sit at the other table. It was obvious that she was feeling left out and Julie didn't know what she could do about it. She would have to talk to her. She would have to somehow explain about Kevin. Explain what? What could she possibly say that would make any difference to Nancy?

Absently Julie pushed her food around on her plate. She too felt left out. Most of the conversation going around the table was centered on sports. That was what you got when you sat with a bunch of jocks and all they talked about was basketball. She and Tracey were the only women present. Even Tracey's junior counselor sat at the other table. "Nervous about tonight?" Kevin whispered close to her ear as he slipped into the empty chair beside her.

"No." She kept her eyes down still poking at her food.

"You're quiet." Tracey remarked from a few seats over. "I hope it has nothing to do with that letter."

Julie met her eyes quickly. Why would Tracey come out with something like that, and especially now? "You need to pick it up," she said, matter-of-fact. "I could have told you that he was never worth the effort."

Julie shot her friend a look which said more than words ever could. Leave it to Tracey to bring her down when she had been feeling on top of the world. And it wasn't that she knew what she was talking about either. "I'd rather not discuss it."

"I don't know." Tracey sipped her coffee waving a hand aside. "Then again what do I know anyway?"

Instead of replying Julie chose to sip her coffee instead. She especially didn't want to say anything that she might regret later. More than that even, didn't she see that Kevin was sitting right beside her? One of the problems that Tracey had was the fact that she had never known Scott very well. If she had, then maybe she could try to identify with the way Julie felt. All she had known was what Julie had wanted her to know. But there was nothing left to say. Coming to Scott's defense was a lost cause. Besides, it was over and she was trying to get on with her life. To drudge up the past now could only get in the way of her feelings for Kevin. It was the same scenario. One step forward and two steps back.

"Are you okay?" Kevin reached under the table for her hand. When he found it he gave it a small squeeze.

"Sure." She forced a smile that didn't reach her eyes.

"What do you think of Camp Wiskle so far?" It was Keith who presented the question to her.

"I like it." She stated simply while placing her folded napkin on her tray.

"Would you consider coming back next summer?"

"Are you acting as one of Rob's most recent recruits?" Tracey asked him.

"As a matter of fact, I am," he said most proudly.

"Julie?" He looked her way. "I'm totally serious."

"Well," she paused. "That all depends." She answered in all honesty. "Not everyone is free over the summer. And with school beginning in the fall…"

"You're right." He sipped his water while regarding her solemnly over the glass. "I almost didn't make it myself." He placed a gentle hand to Tracey's cheek affectionately. "But I'm glad I did."

Tracey giggled softly. "Me too."

At that moment Rob's voice came in over the loudspeaker. "I'm sorry to interrupt your dinner," he began hesitantly and Tracey laughed out loud.

"He should be." Keith said pointing to his plate. "This is a crime." That comment seemed to get a laugh out of everyone at the table.

"Will Tracey Collins please report to the main house?"

"What did you do now?" Keith jested and everyone's eyes were on Tracey.

"I don't know." Quickly she excused herself and left the table.

For some reason Julie could feel her heart rate kick up. It wasn't a good sign to get called into the director's office. It was like getting called into the principal's office. You knew that nothing good would come out of that. But Julie fought back the anxiety as it was probably nothing. It might just be one of her friends calling from back home. Tracey sometimes didn't realize how lucky she was. It seemed to Julie that she had forgotten just how upset she had been last year after returning from camp when she had thought she'd never see Keith again. Couldn't she put herself in Julie's place for one brief minute? The same held true for Julie when she and Scott had parted. Didn't Tracey understand that he had broken Julie's heart? And sometimes that pain came back hitting her with a force that was staggering. She was doing it again. She was thinking, getting lost in the past. She was sinking, as though caught in quick sand. And there seemed to be no way out.

~ * ~

"Come here." As Scott took her into his arms Julie sensed immediately that something was wrong.

"What?" She met his blue eyes evenly. Those beautiful deep blue eyes that were usually sparkling now seemed almost lifeless. "What's wrong?"

He held her to him tightly, almost as though he were holding on for dear life. "I need to hold you." And he did just that while Julie remained silent. "Oh Julie." He tangled his hands in her long brown hair pulling her closer still. "If only..." He muttered more to himself then to her.

"Tell me, Scott. Did something happen?" Suddenly she was afraid. Of what, she could not say. Her heart was jumping around wildly as her breath caught.

"I need to go away for a little while." He began lightly which caused Julie's heart to freeze. "But I'll only be gone for a few weeks."

"A few weeks?" Julie met his eyes evenly. "Where are you going?"

"There's something that I need to take care of. I'll call you every single night..."

"But, Scott..."

"Please, Julie." He sighed. "I can't handle a million questions right now." He still held her close. "This is something that I have to do. And I need for you to trust me. Okay?" He gave her a smile. "I need for you to wait for me."

She did not like the way he was talking. Not at all. Quite frankly, he was beginning to frighten her. "No more questions." He placed a gentle finger to her trembling lips. "I'm leaving tomorrow morning."

"That soon?"

"Yeah." He still held her. "But we have now, Julie. We have tonight."

~ * ~

"Julie..."

Mentally she shook herself into the present. "You were miles away." Kevin laughed. "Everyone's leaving." He was standing beside her chair waiting for her to gain her feet. "I guess I'll see you tonight then." They filed out together. "I can meet you at the hall. Unless you want me to pick you up..."

"No. No. I'll meet you there."

"You're not having second thoughts, are you?"

She forced a quick smile. "None." Although it was a bold lie, she would never admit that to anyone. Tonight she was going to have a good time if it was the last thing that she did. This was something that she had to do. She had to stop living in the past and thinking about Scott all the time and what they had shared was slowly but surely breaking her heart all over again. It had to stop. She had to gain control of her heart once again and put the past where it truly belonged, in the past.

Back at the cabin things were pretty tense all around. It was just as Julie had suspected. Although Nancy didn't come right out and say anything she didn't have to. Her actions did and they were coming through loud and clear.

Practically everyone was lined up at the bathroom door waiting for their turn in the shower. As Julie perused her closet Nancy chose that opportunity for confrontation. "Well, I'm glad you're happy." Nancy sputtered. "You've finally succeeded." She crossed her arms across her chest as her eyes were shooting daggers. "I can see that I was right about you from the start."

What did Nancy want her to say? "I'm sorry that you feel that way..." Julie could not find it in her heart to apologize for feeling something for Kevin. She hadn't planned it, it had happened. "I can understand how things didn't work out but it wasn't my fault that..."

Nancy snorted. "Not your fault!" She exclaimed. "It was all your fault. You knew about me and Kevin." Her brown eyes flashed dangerously. "I told you how he could never resist a challenge. And you went right ahead, behind my back. But you'll see. Kevin will dump you too. He's only after one thing."

Julie didn't know what else she could say to her. "And as soon as he gets it you'll get what you deserve." She turned away. "And one more thing," her voice was as hard as nails. "I've decided to go and stay with Anne and her campers."

"Nance..."

"Better than that even," she faced Julie again. "Maybe I'll tell Mr. Wiskle the whole story." She pushed out a short laugh that didn't quite reach her eyes. "I'm sure he'd love to hear all about the rule breaking going on." The words just kept right on coming. "But first I think that you should see for yourself what a slime Kevin really is. Then again, you both deserve each other."

"That's enough of that." Tracey said from the doorway. "What's going on in here?" She directed that question to Nancy. "I can hear you from halfway up the trail."

"Nothing that important." Nancy mumbled.

"Sounded real important to me." Tracey stood, hands on hips. "I think you need to come to a few realizations here, Nancy. The first being, that you are not the counselor here. What Julie says in this cabin goes. And it's that simple. Do you understand that? Because if you don't I can easily arrange for you to come and stay with me and that means that you will lose your title of junior counselor."

This was the first time Julie had ever seen Tracey so forceful or angry. It was so out of character. "Then she has to follow the rules like everyone else," Nancy returned, as she was not willing to let the subject drop.

"What rules are we talking about here?" Tracey dismissed the other girls with a wave of her hand. And from the way they hurried outside it seemed as though they could hardly wait to get out the door.

"She's not allowed to go out with a junior counselor, for one," Nancy pointed out.

"I've heard all about that. It's a dance for crying out loud." Tracey shrugged carelessly. "Nobody else seems to have a problem with it."

Nancy rolled her eyes. "If Mr. Wiskle..."

"You are not going to tell Mr. Wiskle." Tracey said simply. "Because if he does find out I can guarantee you that you'll get the boot faster than Julie will."

"I didn't make the rules."

"Save it, Miss Keller." Now Tracey was getting sarcastic. "You can just worry about your job and Julie will worry about hers. Okay?"

"That's fine with me." Nancy walked out of the door still mumbling.

"Thanks." Julie breathed a great sigh of relief but she was still a little bit puzzled.

"No big deal." Tracey waved a hand aside airily. "You don't exactly look ready for your big date."

"It doesn't bother you that I'm going out with Kevin?" Somehow Julie found this revelation a little hard to believe. Usually Tracey could find some kind of objection. And if she didn't, she'd find something to come up with. It was just her nature and sometimes Julie took what she said personally when Tracey didn't mean it that way at all.

"Actually, I think it will be good for you." She sat on the edge of Julie's bunk. "This has to mean that you're finally getting on with your life. If Kevin's the guy to help you get over what went on between you and Scott then I'm all for it."

Something wasn't right here. This did not sound like the Tracey that Julie knew. Besides, she could never understand that no matter what, no one could ever take Scott's place in her heart. It was now just the point of getting on with her life. It had been apparent for a long time now that she couldn't be with Scott. That it obviously wasn't meant to be. Why torture herself any further?

"Do you like Kevin?"

"I think he's nice." Julie pulled a black dress from her closet. "Do you think that this might be too dressy for tonight?"

"It's perfect." Her smile seemed weak, as though watered down. "I'm glad we finally could take the chance to sit down and talk." She laughed lightly. "Seems we've both been so busy..."

There seemed to be something that Tracey wanted to say but did not. In fact, she was babbling.

"Is everything all right Trace?"

In turn Tracey forced a smile. "You know me so well." Her hands were now twisting in her lap. She seemed edgy and nervous, and also on the brink of tears. It would have to take something very important to make Tracey cry. She was as tough as they came.

"Is everything okay with you and Keith?"

"Yeah." Her blue eyes were a bit moist. "Everything's fine with me and Keith."

"Then what's wrong?" Julie took a seat on the bunk beside her. "Talk to me, Trace." Suddenly it came to her and she remembered that Rob had paged her. "Does this have anything to do with Rob paging you to his office?"

At that moment she knew that she had hit the nail right on the head as Tracey actually shuddered. Something was dreadfully wrong; she just knew it.

"I have some bad news."

Julie's heart instantly began to constrict with fear. "Bad news." She repeated softly as her lips quivered. For once she just could not imagine what Tracey could honestly consider bad news. And what it would have to do with her. Julie was certainly confused.

"Yeah." Tracey breathed her hands still twisting in her lap.

"What?" Julie croaked expecting the very worse. There were not many things that could make Tracey upset to this point.

"I don't know how to tell you." Her voice caught and she didn't meet Julie's eyes.

"Just tell me." Julie jumped to her feet. "You're really beginning to scare the hell out of me." And she was scared. "Is it my dad?" It was Tracey's silence that really frightened her. Her heart was knocking painfully against her ribs as she waited for Tracey to continue.

"Julie." She paused once again. "It has to do with Scott..."

At the mention of Scott's name Julie's heart hit the floor like a ton of bricks. "Oh God." Her breath caught as she could feel the panic rising. "What..." She was afraid to ask, afraid to know, and afraid to hear what Tracey was going to tell her. And whatever it was she knew now beyond the shadow of a doubt that it was really bad. And then it hit her right between the eyes.

"He..." Tracy's voice caught and she sniffed before dropping the bomb. "He passed away last night."

Nine

Numbness gripped Julie's heart in its vise-like grip. She hadn't heard what Tracey had just said. She had to have misunderstood. It was too farfetched to even have one thread of truth to it.

"Julie," Tracey continued lightly. "Did you hear me?"

Julie's mind was taking off in a million different directions. At first she thought she might faint, or worse than that, throw up

"Here, sit down." Tracey took her arm but Julie moved aside. "Matt called the office and talked to Rob…"

"It's not true. It can't be true. And Matt would never call me here unless…" Her voice broke.

"And why didn't he ask to talk to me?" Her mind was still whirling in so many different directions. Julie sat back down as she was afraid her legs might give out at any time.

"He was really upset, Julie. Maybe he didn't want for you to know how upset he was." Tracey bit her lip. "When I went down to Rob's office I didn't know what the hell was going on. And Rob wanted to call you down there but I thought that I should be the one to tell you. I didn't want there to be anyone around when I told you in case..." She trailed off.

"In case of what?" Julie's brown eyes filled with tears. "In case I completely lost it." She began to rock back and forth as her mind continued to reel. "Oh God." She cried. How could something like this happen? "But why would Matt call here anyway he never knew about me and Scott..." The tears were steadily falling by now.

"He obviously knew something," Tracey said softly.

"I have to call home."

"We can use Rob's office phone."

Julie met her best friend's eyes evenly. "I need for you to tell me everything that Matt told you."

She nodded, her eyes filling with tears. "Like I said before, he was very upset. He said it would hit the papers in a day or two and he didn't want for you to find out that way." Tracey took a deep breath before going on. He said that Scott died about three a.m. and that he had some kind of cancer, he didn't say what kind, and that he was staying with his parents."

Cancer! What the hell is Tracey talking about? The very idea was positively preposterous. Did they all think that she was stupid? If Scott had cancer, had, being the key word, wouldn't he have told her? He was supposed to come home for summer vacation and then go back to college in the fall. In fact, next year would be his last before graduating with a degree in Business Administration.

"Julie," Tracey began hesitantly. "Nobody knows more than I do how you felt about him. And I'm..." Her eyes filled with unshed tears. "I don't want to be one of those people who go around saying I'm sorry. But I know why they say it now." She choked out. "Because there's nothing that they can say that will change anything. Nothing to make it better. Nothing at all."

Julie met Tracey's misty blue eyes. This was her best friend. In her heart of hearts Julie knew that Tracey would never intentionally hurt her. "I told Matt that he should have been the one to tell you. He said there's so much going on that he couldn't. And since he was calling from Scott's parents..."

It was too much. And Julie wasn't sure that she could handle it. Her insides felt like jelly. She felt as though she were floating on a cloud. She was positively numb. So numb, that she couldn't feel the pain in her heart as it was being slashed to ribbons. It seemed too far-fetched to be real. This wasn't the way that it was supposed to be. Things just didn't happen this way. And not to Scott. *Oh God...* Her mind cried. *Please let this be a bad dream. When I wake up I'll call him and everything will be all right. I'll tell him how I really feel. I'll tell him how I love him and need him. Please don't let this be true. Please.*

Julie squeezed her eyes closed and the tears continued to seep through. "Didn't Matt think that I'd want to be there?" she whispered. "Do you think that he knew how much I loved him?" She choked out as the tears chased each other down her cheeks. And they kept coming as though an endless parade.

"Yes, I think he knew. And if he didn't, he does now."

"What am I supposed to do?" She swiped at her eyes. "Am I supposed to not feel anything? Just pretend that I don't know? What?" Julie gained her feet and began to pace the cabin floor restlessly. "Matt should have told me himself." She continued to pace as it seemed to lessen the anxiety that was quickly building up inside of her. Although her heart was still rocking around violently and her breathing was quite labored she knew now what she had to do. "I have to go home."

"I don't know if that's such a good idea."

Julie stopped pacing and quickly met her best friend's eyes evenly. "I have to go home, Trace."

Tracey seemed to waver still. "Matt told me that you should probably stay here."

"Stay here?" she questioned. "How can he expect me to stay here? Stay here and do what? Pretend that I don't know anything. Pretend that I didn't love him. Pretend that it doesn't matter. Well, it does matter…"

"Of course it matters."

"I have to go home." Her breath caught and she stammered on. "I have to… I don't even know what I have to do…" She tossed her suitcase, which had been standing beside her closet, onto the cot. She was hurrying now as she felt the urgency building up inside of her all over again. At any moment she was going to lose control. She could feel it and there wasn't a damn thing she could do to stop it. With wild abandon she was tossing clothes into the suitcase. "I don't even have a way to get home. Maybe there's a bus that I can take…" She stopped and took a deep breath. "I don't even know what I'm doing or what I'm talking about."

Her hands were trembling as she pulled them through her hair. "I just have to get out of here." Her whole body was now shaking uncontrollably. This was it. "Oh God. Oh God." She was pacing the floor once again. "Why?" She cried brokenly as the sorrow washed over her in waves. "This cannot be happening." Her head was beginning to throb unmercifully. "I need some air." And then she was rushing out the door. For one heart stopping moment she thought that she might be ill.

The night air was balmy. Although it was still quite warm the humidity had dropped significantly. Julie inhaled the deep scent of the pines that lined the lighted path. She was going on automatic and that was dangerous. Tracey fell into step beside her as she was headed in the direction of the main house. She needed to leave now. She didn't think that she could wait until the morning.

They walked the path in silence. The only sounds that could be heard were the crickets tuning into the night. The tears had amazingly dried up and now Julie was hiccupping softly into a wad of tissues that Tracey had pressed into her hand.

"It's going to be okay, Julie."

"I can't even imagine what the funeral..." The tears suddenly returned. "I really should be there in case..." In case of what, her mind was screaming. "Just in case." Her voice was pathetically thin, as though it didn't belong to her. "I need to leave tonight. Now." She felt that she was going to hyperventilate at any given moment.

"I'm sure that it would be all right if you left first thing in the morning," Tracey said gently. "We'll work something out."

Her breath caught and she was weeping into the crumpled soggy tissues once again. "We'll talk to Rob and see what we can do, okay?"

Julie nodded as she walked beside her friend numbly. She'd never felt such grief in her entire life. The feelings shooting through her were indescribable. It was downright scary. Her heart felt as though someone had slammed it on the ground before putting it through a meat grinder. As they walked on, and had just reached the turnoff, they came face to face with Kevin. It was obvious that he too had heard the news.

"Is she okay?" He directed the question to Tracey as Julie wasn't in any condition to answer.

"I think she's in some kind of shock," Tracey whispered. "We're on our way to the main house to see Rob."

"I can see if he's still at the dance hall," Kevin offered his assistance.

"Thanks."

All these words that were spoken around her seemed to surround her but yet she could not respond. It was almost as though she were stuck in the middle of a fog that was thicker than pea soup. Her heart was slashed to ribbons and she didn't want to discuss it any further.

"Everything is going to be all right." Tracey led her up the stairs, into the house, and down the hall into Rob's office. Once inside she sat Julie down on a large red leather couch. "You just need to take a few deep breaths. Catch your breath," Tracey said before going into the bathroom and quickly returning with a wet face cloth. "Here. I think this might make you feel a little better." Carefully she took a seat beside Julie and proceeded to wipe her forehead gently. "Close your eyes and take a deep breath."

Julie leaned back and sighed wearily as the cool water was somewhat refreshing. "That's it. Good." She crooned gently as Julie closed her eyes. "Take a deep breath. We're doing good. Relax. Everything is going to be okay. I will talk to Rob and we'll find a way to get you home."

"Keith is probably waiting for you at the..."

"That's okay. He can wait. We have to take care of this first."

Julie shuddered as Tracey replaced the soggy tissues she held in her hand with a wad of new ones. That also seemed to trigger another bout of tears. Her mind was too busy screaming accusations for her to relax. She knew that if she didn't fight the tears that threatened to engulf her yet again that they may never stop.

"It's okay, Julie."

Was this what it felt like to have a nervous breakdown? If it wasn't, it had to be damn near close. "You just have to keep breathing deeply." Tracey gave her hand a quick squeeze for reassurance. "Deep cleansing breaths," she said and began to breathe deeply with her. "Doesn't that feel better?"

"Good evening, Ladies." Rob entered the office a few minutes later. "How are we doing tonight?" He looked from Julie to Tracey, than back again. "Oh Boy... Not that good I can see."

Kevin hovered in the doorway as Rob ventured over to his desk. "She doesn't look good."

"Maybe that's because she's in shock," Tracey whispered. "I don't think it was such a great idea to have told her tonight."

Rob went to Julie and knelt down in front of her. "Julie." He took her hand, the one that clutched the wad of tissues. "You're going to be fine sweetie. Everything is going to be fine." He glanced up at Tracey. "Get one of her family members on the phone."

Tracey went to the phone while Kevin entered the room and took a seat at the edge of an antique armchair. "I'll give her brother a call." She dialed the number and waited patiently for the call to connect. "Matt." The relief was evident in her voice. "It's Tracey... Yes... I'm here with Julie... No... No... She's not doing well at all." She coiled the wire around her index finger absently as she listened to what he was saying. "I think someone should come up here and pick her up." She paused for a brief moment. "I told her everything that you told me." She took a deep breath and let it out slowly. "You don't understand, Matt. It's obvious that you don't know how strongly she felt..."

Although Tracey was trying to be discreet it was also apparent that she was beginning to get agitated. Even her blue eyes that were usually sparkling with laughter seemed to now be shooting sparks. "What are you talking about?" Although she gave them her back her words were coming through loud and clear. "How can you say that... No maybe I don't." She sighed wearily while rubbing her temples lightly. "She loved him, Matt... Yes it really is that simple... Now, I can't stand here and argue with you all day... I need to get her home... Fine..." She replaced the receiver gently and took a deep breath before facing them.

"He can't come up to pick her up. There is so much going on with the wake... The funeral..." She stated simply. "I can't believe this is happening." Her voice broke as she turned away from them.

"It's okay, Trace." Rob waved a hand aside. "We'll work something out." He took a seat on the edge of the couch beside Julie.

"Is it possible for you to take her home?"

"That will leave you short-handed." Tracey was wiping the tears from her own eyes. "We can't just leave you with two counselors for the girls."

"Maybe we can promote Nancy…"

"Are you kidding?" She pushed out a short laugh. "She's not ready for it, and especially not under these circumstances."

Kevin cleared his throat from where he was now standing in the back of the room. "I can take her home." He met Rob's eyes carefully. "She doesn't live too far from me. I'm sure that Jake wouldn't have a problem if I took his car…"

"I don't know." It was Tracey who hesitated. It seemed she'd had a few minutes to evaluate the entire situation. "I don't know if it's such a good idea. At least not right now. I'm not sure if it's the right thing…"

Julie was still seated stiffly on the couch. They were all talking around her as though she weren't present. How she wanted to scream at them all to shut-up and leave her alone. Still remaining quiet she gained her feet and suddenly all eyes were upon her. Why didn't they give her the choice to do what she wanted to do?

"You know that I have to go home," she said simply, then directed at Tracey, "I thought that you, of all people, understood me. Understood how I feel. How I felt." That did it. Just thinking of Scott in the past tense was all it took to toss her right over the edge. Julie bit her lip as she held the tears at bay.

"I do understand…"

"No you don't." Julie shook her head. "I thought you did but you don't. You're just like Matt. The truth can be staring you in the face but still you refuse to see it." She turned away from them as the tears she forced back began to fall steadily. Suddenly the air in the room seemed to become stifling. It was becoming harder and harder to breathe never mind remain focused. Then it felt as though the walls were closing in on her from all sides. And then she was tumbling into a giant hole of blackness.

The next thing she knew was that she was breathing in this horrid odor. It was awful and she came up coughing and sputtering. It was ammonia. Someone was waving smelling salts under her nose. Slowly she opened her eyes to find herself lying on the leather couch with four faces peering expectantly into hers.

Keith had joined the crew. "You fainted."

Tracey placed a cool cloth to her forehead. "You'll be okay now." Her smile faltered as she met Julie's eyes.

Oh God! It hadn't been a dream, a horrid nightmare. This was real. This was really happening. She'd only continue to delude herself if she believed otherwise. This was as real as the constant pain in her heart. "Give us some time alone." Tracey looked to the guys for some support as Julie pulled herself to a sitting position.

"Not a problem," Rob said as he began to shoo Keith and Kevin from the office. "I really have to get back to the dance hall to check on things."

"I'll help you," Keith echoed.

"I'll be in the lounge." Kevin glanced at Julie again before leaving the room lastly.

When the door closed behind them Julie completely lost it. The tears she'd been holding back rushed forward in a flood. A raging torrent of emotion bursting free as it took down all the barricades with it. *Oh God*, she prayed. "Why?" She choked out, rocking back and forth. "Why?"

Tracey sat beside her with fresh tears in her own eyes. "I wish I had the answers, Julie."

"I never told him I loved him," she sobbed. "And now... He's gone. I'll never be able to tell him. Oh God." She buried her head in her hands and began to weep brokenly. "It's not fair. We never even had a chance..."

Tracey placed a comforting arm around her shoulders. "Talk to me, Julie. Let it all out."

"I just want to go home. I need to go home." She knew she must look a sight, especially with her makeup now long gone and that hideous scar shining through like a beacon. But for the first time since the accident it didn't matter. Nothing, but this tragedy she was facing, mattered. And it was a tragedy. Her world seemed to be slipping away. There was nothing left to hold onto. And she felt like she was drowning in her tears.

"Kevin is trying to get a car," Tracey said after a few minutes had passed. "We'll find a way to get you home."

Julie's breath was ragged. The tears had stopped but threatened to erupt again at any time. "Maybe a shot of whiskey will calm you down." Tracey got up and began to poke around Rob's desk. "I'm pretty sure he keeps a bottle around here somewhere."

While Tracey went through Rob's credenza Julie wiped her eyes and blew her nose. At this point she really felt as though her heart had been through a wringer and taking a shot of something didn't sound half bad.

"And here it is." She produced a bottle of Jack Daniels. "No glasses." She unscrewed the cap before handing Julie the bottle. "Take a sip."

At that point in time Julie didn't need much urging. Without another thought she took the bottle and took a long sip. And since she was never much of a drinker anyway she came up coughing. "Take it easy." Tracey perched herself on the arm of the sofa. "Give me a shot of that." She took the bottle and took a few sips herself. "Do you feel any better?" She shook her head sadly. "Forget I asked."

Julie took a deep breath and let it out slowly. No. She didn't feel any better and doubted that she would any time soon. "Take another sip." Tracey handed her the bottle back and Julie took it, no questions asked.

They must have sat in Rob's office for over an hour just drinking and talking quietly. They both learned things that neither of them had ever known before. And that gave them a new understanding as well as a new respect for the other. They created a bond which brought them closer than before.

Julie knew she was tipsy before she even tried to gain her feet but it didn't really seem to matter. Thank goodness the tears had dried up. Tracey put the bottle away while Julie tried to walk off some of the effects of the liquor. She needed to get her bearings before Rob returned. At this point she didn't need anything else to worry about. Life was complicated enough. She had to focus on what she had to do next. She was staring out the window into the blackness of the night with her arms wrapped around her middle when they returned.

"How are we doing in here?" Rob voiced the question lightly and Julie turned around slowly. "Come and sit down, Julie." He loosened his tie before taking a seat behind his desk. He looked as somber as everyone else did. "Come in and shut the door guys."

Julie did as she was told but knew she was having a tough time walking a straight line. "Now." He waited for everyone's attention before going on. "I'm going to give you three days." He paused. "Nancy will cover your position until you return. Kevin has offered to drive you home and he'll bring you back." He met her eyes evenly. "Unless you won't be returning in which case I will have to..."

"I will come back after the funeral," she promised.

"All right for now." He looked around the room. "I think everyone can do with a good night sleep. He gained his feet and waited for everyone else to do the same.

Keith went to Tracey and gave her a hug. "Are you all right, sweetheart?" He gazed down at her with love evident in his eyes.

Tracey hugged him fiercely. "I'm just perfect now."

Julie tried to swallow the lump in her throat but was having a tough time of it. "I'd better get my campers settled in for the night..."

"They'll be staying with Tracey tonight. This way you can leave at first light."

"Thank you, Rob." Her voice cracked. "For everything." And then she was out the door. She needed to be alone right now. Just seeing Tracey and Keith in each other's arms had her eyes stinging with tears. It wasn't safe to be around anyone while she felt like screaming until the pain in her heart subsided.

Just as she reached the bottom of the stairs Kevin had caught up to her. "Wait a minute." He took her arm and gently turned her around to face him.

"What?" She was blinking back tears.

"Let me walk you to your cabin." He still held onto her arm. "Please." He held onto her hand as they started through the dark heading for the lighted path. When they walked a little ways away he placed an arm across her shoulder. "You're cold." He caressed her arm and she shuddered. "Let's walk by the lake."

Julie remained quiet so Kevin did all the talking. "I missed you at the dance," he said softly. "This is my last year at camp. I know that the Wiskles' think that I'm coming back next year to be a counselor but I really don't think it's happening."

She knew that he was making small talk. And that was okay with her. She would listen.

"It's a great summer job," he continued. "But there's college to think about. And I don't think I'll have the time." He kicked at a few stones. "Julie." He began lightly as they reached the water's edge. "I just wanted to tell you how sorry I am."

She met his eyes. Although she still felt a little light headed and fuzzy she forced a smile.

"I mean that."

"I know you do," she whispered as he placed a gentle hand to her cheek. Their eyes met and locked as the full moon shone down in all of its brilliance. The soft breeze flirted with their hair as a frog croaked in the distance. The water lapped at their feet but they stood facing each other with just a breath separating them. It was obvious that he was going to kiss her. And she wasn't exactly sure how she felt about that.

As Julie closed her eyes she tried to remember what she was doing here. How had she gotten to this point in her life? The liquor seemed to be playing havoc with her emotions causing her to feel light and airy, as though she could just blow away on a gentle breeze.

Is this the feeling that had attracted her Mom to the bottle in the first place? Or had this been the feeling that had made her return to the bottle again and again? Had this been what had turned her into an alcoholic because if it was, Julie wanted no part of it. She didn't want to take such careless risks with her life. Like getting behind the wheel of a car and smacking head on into a tree. She didn't want to ever need something to make her feel good. She didn't want to crave something to the point of risking life and limb to get it.

"I just wanted you to understand that..." Kevin was saying softly and Julie's eyes flew opened. She'd been somewhere far away.

"It's not that I don't want to..." he continued softly.

"Want to what?"

Kevin traced her lips lightly. "Kiss you senseless." He breathed. "Because I do. But I know we can't..."

"Kevin." She stood on tiptoes and pressed her lips lightly to his. "Thank you for everything." Her voice was soft. "I wonder sometimes why you're so nice to me." Their eyes actually collided. "I just want you to know that it means a lot to me."

"You loved him." It was a statement. It was also like a cold blast of reality which had her stepping back. Their moment was now shot to pieces and Kevin cursed aloud as he realized what he had done. "I'm sorry, Julie. I didn't mean to bring it up again." He took a deep breath as she continued to move away from him. "Everything's going to be all right."

A shiver ran up her spine. "Let's get back." He sighed wearily. "We have a long trip ahead of us and it's already after twelve."

They headed back to the lighted path silently. The moment was definitely gone but it left Julie feeling shaky in more ways than one. It also brought memories of Scott back in full force. She almost felt guilty at some of the things she had been feeling for

Kevin. There was definitely something there. It had been something they had been fighting from day one; rather she had been fighting, as Kevin had made it quite plain that he felt something.

"Julie." He stopped her as soon as they were back on the lighted path. "I just want you to know that I will be here for you and that everything will be all right..."

"No, it won't." Her voice was small. "And I don't see how it can be."

"You'll get through this." He rested his hands on her shoulders. "I'll help you." He played with a strand of her hair. "I'll be with you every step of the way?"

"Why?" she choked out.

"Why?" His blue green eyes were smiling. "Because I've fallen in love with you." He took a deep breath after that. "Everything will be okay. I promise." He pulled her into his warm embrace and she rested her cheek against his green polo shirt.

"You can't love me, Kevin." Her breath caught. "Not now."

"All right." He still held her close. "Maybe now wasn't a good time to bring it up." He tangled his fingers into her long hair. "It's okay, Julie. I'm here."

~ * ~

They met under the bleachers after nine. It was their secret meeting place. No one, not even Tracey, knew where they met each night. "I missed you." Julie went into his arms laughing.

"Really?" Scott cocked an eyebrow. "Show me how much you've missed me."

She thought about that, but only for a moment, as she wasn't ready for that step. Maybe after he told her that he loved her, she might consider it. Until then, it had to remain a definite no. "Thinking about it?" His blue eyes were wide.

"No way." She flushed.

"Okay, so maybe now wasn't the right time to bring up that subject."

~ * ~

Julie pulled out of Kevin's embrace as she pulled herself into the present. "I'd better go inside now."

Kevin studied her intently as he took a step back. "I wasn't making a move on you. I didn't mean to tell you. But it's the way I feel." He paused. "But believe me; I didn't make a move..."

She had difficulty meeting his eyes. "I know."

"I just wanted to make sure you knew that." He gave her a small smile. "Sure you want to go in there alone?"

She hadn't thought about that. The cabin did seem quiet. The glow of the night light was of no comfort. "I was just teasing."

"I don't want to be alone," she said simply. And she meant that. "It's not that I'm afraid or anything..." She sighed. "I just can't... Can you... Would you stay for a little while?"

"How about I stay with you until you fall asleep?"

Julie breathed a great sigh of relief. "Would you?"

"I would do anything for you, sweetheart."

She shot him a look as they entered the cabin together. The screen door creaked behind them before slamming closed. Kevin took a seat on Lorna's bunk while Julie grabbed a nightshirt and headed for the bathroom. "You do realize..." Kevin's voice rose an octave so she could hear him through the wall. "That what we are doing is against the rules."

She came out of the bathroom a few minutes later with her face freshly powdered. "At this point I don't really care." She didn't look at him when she said it but instead went to her bunk, which was still a mess. She threw all the clothes that had been scattered on her bunk into the suitcase before moving it to the floor at the foot of her bed.

Kevin said nothing but watched her intently. "There have always been these rules," she began lightly while keeping her back to him. She was fixing the clothes that were hanging off the hangers. "All of my life there were these rules that sometimes you just couldn't live up to. Like going to the girls' school, I hated it. I wanted to go to high school just like everyone else." She gave the black dress a once over before returning it to the closet. That had been the dress that she had been going to wear tonight. "It just wasn't normal. My parents didn't let me be normal. There were never any dances. That's one of the reasons I never told them anything about Scott..." She stopped there. "We didn't follow the rules." She faced him then. "Now I know why."

"I can see what you mean." He smiled as he made himself comfortable on Lorna's bunk.

"Don't fall asleep over there." She climbed into her own bunk and pulled the sheet to her throat. "All I need is one more problem." She stifled a yawn as she closed her eyes.

"Sweet dreams, Julie." He whispered but she didn't hear him. She had already fallen asleep.

Ten

The next day dawned bright but cool and Julie awoke to the rays of warm sunshine on her face. She'd slept like a rock and thank goodness her mind had been too tired to even dream. As she stretched languidly she glanced over at the small travel alarm clock at her bedside. It was already nearing noon. Quickly she threw back the covers and got out of bed. That was when she first felt the effects of last night's memories of Jack. Boy, did Jack Daniels ever pack a punch. She had a hangover.

As she was pulling on a pair of faded jeans Tracey wandered inside. In one hand she carried the day's mail and in the other a glass of some kind of red liquid. "This should make you feel better. It's made with tomato juice, I think."

Julie smiled her thanks. "Kevin's waiting in the parking lot." She dropped the mail on Lorna's bunk. "He didn't want to wake you this morning."

Julie pulled a brush through her hair absently. "Don't forget to drink that. It isn't exactly a cure but it will help." She hung in the doorway. "Your suitcase is already in the car." Tracey forced a quick smile but it didn't quite reach her eyes. "Kevin took care of that too." She pushed out a short laugh. "I can see how much he cares about you." She paused for a brief moment. "You know that I would go with you if I could..."

"I know you would," Julie returned lightly. "Thank you."

"I didn't want you to think that I was deserting you." Her voice broke. "Because I need for you to know that I wouldn't do that."

Julie met her best friend's eyes evenly. It seemed Tracey was trying so hard to keep her emotions under control. She was walking on eggshells because she didn't want to bring up a painful subject, a subject that they both were not ready to address. "I packed you both a light lunch," she said while Julie proceeded to make her bunk. "I figured that you'd want to drive straight through." She paused as the small talk was beginning to wear thin but Julie remained quiet. "I'm running out of things to say, Julie. Please talk to me. Say something, anything."

What did she want to hear? Life wasn't exactly treating Julie fairly and never had. She was going home today, going home to a funeral. What the hell did Tracey want her to say?

"I know you're hurting right now," she continued. "This thing with Scott is... Well, it's..." She seemed to be searching for the right words. But there weren't any and even more so under these circumstances. "It's such a shock..." She got out finally. "I mean... No one even knew he was sick..."

"I have to go." Julie had to get out of there. This was hard enough as it was. There was no need to rehash any of last night. Just when she had thought she couldn't cry anymore. Well, she had been wrong. The tears were now just below the surface and they were fighting to burst free. But she couldn't let that happen. "I'll be fine, Trace." She forced a smile before taking a swallow of the red liquid. She came up choking and sputtering. "What's in this?" Hot tears squeezed past her eyelids. It was almost like she had peeled a whole bag of onions.

"It's one of Jake's concoctions," Tracey returned simply. "All I know is that it begins as tomato juice. Don't even ask about the rest because you probably don't want to know."

Julie grabbed her handbag and quickly perused the cabin to see if she had left behind anything of importance.

"Are you coming back?"

She stopped short just outside the door. "Of course I'm coming back. I still have a job to do." She held the door for her friend. "I'll be back in a few days.

They walked silently on the lighted path which was basked in glorious sunshine. It was amazing how things could go from one extreme to the other. It was either all or nothing. Just as it had been all of her life. They walked on quietly. There wasn't anything left to talk about. It surely wouldn't change anything if they did, so why bring up any further pain. Besides, Julie was all talked out. There wasn't anything to ease the pain, nothing short of being in Scott's embrace again, and since that was no longer a possibility she had to resign herself to the hard cold truth. One of life's hardest facts had to be dealing with the death of someone close.

Kevin was waiting in the parking lot wearing a pair of jeans with a striped green tank top. It was unusual to see him in anything but cut off shorts. As she walked closer to the small black sports car she met Kevin's eyes evenly. Those magnificent blue-green eyes that had shone with affection last night now seemed distant in the morning light. "Good morning." He simply acknowledged them before sliding in behind the wheel.

After everyone exchanged their goodbye's they were soon on their way. Julie pulled on a pair of sunglasses as Kevin maneuvered the car away from Camp Wiskle and they began their journey. Since it was mostly highway driving, once they got out of town the ride should be clear sailing for the remainder of the trip.

They rode in silence with Kevin playing with the radio dial as he couldn't seem to locate a station without any static. He finally switched it off and Julie breathed a sigh of relief as she was still fighting off that lingering headache. The quiet stretched through the miles and Julie leaned her head comfortably into the head rest.

"Did you sleep okay?" Kevin questioned lightly as soon as she closed her eyes.

"Yes." She gazed out of the window forlornly. "I know that you went out of your way for me." Her breath caught. "And I want to thank you for that." She paused. "And especially for driving me home."

He stole a glance in her direction. "You know." He began thoughtfully. "It's about time that you gave up on all that makeup."

Julie's breath caught and her hand went to her scarred cheek automatically. With everything that had been going on she had actually forgotten to powder her face. Quickly she pulled down the visor while digging in her handbag at the same time. Her trusty compact was never far from her grasp. "You don't need that." Kevin placed a gentle hand over the one that held the compact. "You're a very pretty girl, Julie," he said simply. "I think you're even prettier without all that makeup."

Julie flushed. "Don't put it on." He still held her hand but she wavered. "Please."

"This time." She agreed returning the compact to her bag.

"We have three days." He turned the topic towards the reason they were here. "And that isn't a lot of time." He gave her hand a brief squeeze before returning it to the steering wheel. "Do you think it will be enough?"

"I think so." She took a deep breath and let it out slowly. The further they traveled away from Camp Wiskle the more apprehensive Julie became. It was like facing the fear of the unknown and she found herself praying to God as she had never prayed before. Sure, she had attended church services with her parents all the time, but had she really been listening? If there would ever be a time when she needed God this would certainly have to be one of them.

"How does it feel? To be going home?" Kevin cut into her thoughts.

"Okay I guess." She kept her eyes straight ahead and on the road. "You make it sound like I'm not coming back."

"Are you?" he asked bluntly.

"Of course." She got out in one breath. "I have a responsibility." She stole a quick glance in his direction.

"Good." Was his simple reply.

After they had been on the road for a solid three hours Kevin pulled into a complete service station situated right off of the highway. "I know Tracey packed us sandwiches but how about some real food?" He pulled the car up to the gas pump. "We'll fill up and get a bite. I'm starving." He then turned to the gas attendant who had stepped up to the window. "Fill it please." He then turned his attention back to her. "Is that all right with you?"

Although she really wanted to keep going she could see that Kevin was tired. "Sure." She studied her reflection in the mirror above the visor. "But I'm really not all that hungry."

"You have to eat something." He handed the attendant a couple of bills and waited for his change. "Even if you only order a cup of tea and a sandwich." He put the car into gear and headed towards the restaurant on the other side of the parking lot. "This looks like a cozy little place." After parking the car he cut the motor then faced her. "Give me a half hour and then we'll be back on the road."

Before Julie could draw a breath he had locked up the car and had her ushered inside. Once they were seated in a secluded booth in the back of the restaurant Kevin reached across the table for her hand. "You're looking pretty good."

What did that mean? And how could she look good on the outside when she felt so terrible on the inside?

"I guess it's that natural glow that you have." He met her brown eyes evenly. "Just one of the many reasons that I fell in..." He had been about to say love but stopped himself just in time. And it was a good thing as the waitress had suddenly appeared with their place settings and two glasses of water.

"Good afternoon." She gave them a big smile before setting their placemats and silverware before them. "The special of the day is on the front page of the menu." She began poised with pen and pad. "I can come back if you need a little more time..."

"We'll have the special." The special of the day was cheese steak and fries. "Coffee too."

"Coffee comes with that."

"Good." He took Julie's menu as well as his own and handed them to her. "That will be it for now."

She took the menus and headed to the kitchen with their order. "Now where were we?" Kevin met her eyes evenly. "Oh yeah... I think getting away from camp will be good for the both of us. You know, I could have come in as a counselor this year. I chose not to only because..." He stopped as the waitress came back with two steaming mugs of coffee. "I guess that doesn't matter, what matters is that we're not at camp now so I guess that the rules no longer apply."

How could he bring up this topic now? Even more so now. Her whole world felt as though it was slipping away and he was suggesting.... She didn't even know what he was suggesting.

"I think that you know how I feel about you," Kevin continued as he poured sugar in his coffee. "It's different now that we're away from camp. Away from all the rules..."

Julie fixed her coffee silently, anything to divert her attention away from the conversation at hand. It was too soon to talk about any of this. Didn't Kevin realize that she was going through a tough time? She had to come to terms with Scott's death. Her heart felt as if it had been slashed to ribbons. Didn't he see that? Or was she slowly losing her sanity?

"I know that this news must have come as a shock but..."

"But what, Kevin?" She demanded meeting his eyes evenly.

"Well, it's not like you were going out with him and he suddenly died."

Julie just looked at him. It was almost as if she were seeing him for the first time. "I mean," Kevin went on. "It's been over for a while. It's not like you were with him yesterday and he's gone today."

Suddenly she was seeing Kevin in a whole new light. And she didn't like it one bit. "I'm sorry," he murmured as the waitress came back with a smile.

"Your food will be out shortly. Can I refill your cup?" she offered with a smile.

"Thank you," Kevin answered his eyes never leaving Julie's.

"If you need anything..." she left the invitation opened before walking away.

"I didn't mean to come off sounding heartless." Kevin said the minute the waitress was out of earshot.

"But you did." Julie returned softly.

"What I meant to say was..." He paused as though searching his mind for the right words. "I just meant that you hadn't been together for a long time." Julie sipped her coffee. "I said I was sorry," he continued. "I shouldn't have said that. It was very insensitive."

"You're right."

Their waitress was back with their food and plucked it down before them without missing a step. The tension at the table was thick enough to cut with a knife and she wasted no time getting out of there. "I'm sorry, Julie," he said again softly. "Let's talk about this." He picked up his sandwich and took a big bite. "It's delicious."

Julie pushed her plate away. She really couldn't eat. Her stomach was wreaking havoc with her ability to sit still. "You haven't eaten a thing all day. Please try and eat a little something."

"I can't." She got up from the table and made a beeline for the door. Not only did she need fresh air but she needed to be alone, if only for a moment, to collect herself. Thank goodness Kevin let her go. She didn't want to make a scene in the restaurant and she knew Kevin didn't want to either. Hopefully he would give her some time to get her emotions in check, which at this point felt next to impossible.

As she left the coolness of the dimly lit restaurant the sunshine seemed awfully bright. She took a deep breath as she moved away from the steady stream of customers milling about. Before heading back in the direction of the car she noticed a newspaper stand off to the side of the building. She was close enough to home to be able to purchase the county paper. Without another thought she wandered over and looked at the selection of papers offered. Sure enough it was there. After digging in her bag for a dollar bill she picked up the newspaper on the top of the pile and handed her money to the little old man who was sitting in a corner chewing a short stubby cigar. He handed her change over with a toothless grin.

As she meandered back in the general direction of the car she leafed through the first few pages with shaky fingers. After locating the car she leaned against the door frame, shakily she continued turning pages until she reached the section she had been looking for. The death notices. The column seemed awfully long. Her heart was beating furiously as she quickly scanned the names. Remy, Rhodes, Riley, Rourke. Oh God. Rourke, Scott, age 23. But that was as far as she got as a pain like never before engulfed her heart.

"Julie." Kevin was walking towards her carrying a brown paper sack. "I had everything wrapped..." He forced a small smile as he realized what she had been reading. "I figured we could eat on the road. We'll get there faster."

~ * ~

Julie followed him silently back to the car. There was nothing to say. Nothing at all. She felt as though she were walking around in a dream. This constant dream state. And it was beginning to frighten her. Even the tears had receded into the background. There were so many things to take into consideration. One of those being, how she was going to face her brother. Matt was going to demand some answers. Was he prepared for the truth? "Hopefully we can find a decent radio station." Kevin cut into her thoughts as he was playing with the radio dials. "We're still high up."

Julie pulled on her sunglasses silently. "I guess you're angry with me," he said as they pulled back onto the highway. "You're not going to talk to me?" It was a question. "Julie?"

"What would you like to talk about, Kevin?" At that moment she knew she sounded snippy but she didn't care. "Anything besides us because there is no us."

"Okay," he said softly. "Why don't you tell me about Scott."

Julie looked at him as though he had lost his mind. "All right." He sighed wearily. "Tell me about you."

"Me? What would you like to know about me?"

"Whatever you'd like to tell me." He handled the car with ease a small smile playing on his lips. "Anything at all."

She thought about that. There was nothing interesting going on in her life now aside from this crisis that she didn't even want to think about. There was nothing of any importance. "My father wants me to go to college in the fall," she began with that as it was the first thing that came to mind. "But I'd rather get a job."

"What kind of job would you get?"

"Probably not a good one." She pushed out a short laugh. "I'd like to work with children. But I'm still not sure. Maybe I'll do both."

"My parents are pushing for the State University." He made a little face. "But I'd rather go to County."

"Why?"

"I guess because it's closer to home. And now it's closer to you." He stopped suddenly. "Hey, we're supposed to be talking about you, not me."

"I have a brother, Matthew, Matt," she went on. "He's twenty-three. He's been married for about two years. Janet, my sister-in-law, is a very straight forward person. She'll tell anybody anything, including my father. Last year he had brought up the issue of grandchildren and Janet told him right where it was at."

Kevin snickered. "What did she say?"

"She said that she'd let Matt know when the time was right." She laughed. "And if he wanted he could let his father know."

"That takes guts."

"Yeah, I suppose. But that really hurt her."

"What did?"

"My father saying that. In my opinion she should have told him to mind his own business. But instead she made a joke out of it." She sighed wearily. "The truth of the matter is that Janet can't get pregnant. She and Matt have been trying for over a year now. They even went to different doctors. And they're not very optimistic."

"I'm sorry to hear that."

"They haven't given up yet." She smiled.

"They shouldn't."

Julie rested her head against the seat. "Don't stop now. Tell me more. Is Matt your only brother?"

"Yeah. It's just Matt and me. Of course, Matt has always bossed me around. Maybe because he's older. Maybe because I'm a girl." She shrugged. "I don't really know. We never really fought. Probably because we had nothing to fight about. His friends were his friends, and my friends were my friends." She stopped suddenly. That put Scott right in the middle. Funny, she had never looked at it in that way before.

"You never dated any of his friends? That I find hard to believe."

"Why?"

"Did he have a lot of friends?"

"Yeah, so?"

"I can probably guarantee that half of them came over to see you."

"I doubt that."

"I don't. I happen to know from experience."

"Really." She snickered.

"Sure. All my friends from school used to come home just to see my sister. Not that I blamed them. I guess it's human nature. Jake had warned me but I didn't believe him." He laughed. "I'd say, at least, half of them had asked her out."

"And you didn't mind?"

"Nah. As long as they didn't get fresh with her I didn't mind."

"What's your sister's name?"

"Lindy," he said simply. "She's a year younger than I am. She'll be sixteen next month."

Julie nodded as he continued. "She came to camp last year. But this year she had to go to summer school so my parents put their foot down."

Julie knew that feeling well. "I can admit that my parents are harder on Lindy because she's a girl. But I can see why they have to be too."

Julie agreed with him to a point. In her family it had been the same way. "You were in a car accident?" He changed the subject completely.

"Last year."

"How did it happen?"

Julie took a deep breath before taking the plunge. "I was with my Mom when it happened. And she'd had a little too much to drink." She paused. "To make a long story short, we hit a tree. And the windshield hit me."

"So, it was pretty bad then."

"Bad enough, I suppose." She paused. "My Mom was fine, she didn't have a scratch. I ended up with all the scars." She knew that she sounded bitter. But she had the right to feel that way. She had been through a lot with that damned accident. She had lost everything. More than that, she had lost Scott.

"You're fine now though."

"In case you haven't noticed, Kevin," she began on a lighter note. "I'm scarred for life."

"At least you have a life," he pointed out.

"And I suppose my scars don't have any effect on you."

"Not at all," he returned.

"That's only because you haven't seen the rest of them," she quipped. "If you did, you would be singing a different tune."

"You think so?"

"I know so."

"Prove it."

"How can I prove it?" she demanded. "I know you would."

"You're wrong, Julie." He shook his head.

"I think not, Kevin."

"Is that why you and Scott broke up?" he asked bluntly.

"We're not talking about Scott."

"We weren't," he said simply. "Is that a closed chapter in your life?"

"Yes."

"Oh really?"

They were reaching the city limits now, which meant that they were almost there. Fifteen minutes at the most and they would reach their destination. Julie's heart began to pump anxiously. What would everyone say when they discovered that she had come home for the funeral?

"Julie," Kevin spoke gently. "What would you like me to do?"

"About what?"

"Do you want me to come to the funeral parlor with you? I can pick you up and…"

"That won't be necessary but thank you." She pulled out her compact and began to powder her scar with a somewhat steady hand. "I'm sure my dad will take me with him."

"All right." Kevin made the turn onto Evergreen. "Can I see you tomorrow?"

"I don't know." She studied her reflection with a critical eye. "I might not be home."

He sighed. "I'll leave you my number. This way you can get in touch with me."

As he pulled onto Maple, Julie got a lump in her throat.

"Is it fifteen?"

"Fourteen," she corrected as he pulled to the curb. "It doesn't look like anyone's home," she said swinging open the car door and getting out.

"They might be at the funeral parlor now." Kevin got out of the car as well. As he popped open the trunk Julie looked around. "I can wait with you." He pulled her suitcase out of the trunk then placed it at the curb. "Let me carry this up to the house for you." He locked all the doors before picking up the heavy suitcase.

Julie led the way up the walk and up the four front stairs. After finding her key, at the bottom of her handbag, she opened the door. "Would you like to come in?" she asked as Kevin stood on the threshold, suitcase in hand. Kevin followed her lead as he stepped inside.

"Dad?" she called as they walked down the foyer and into the living-room. "Dad. Matt," she called out again when no one had answered. "I guess they're out." She sighed taking a seat on the beige love seat. "Sit down, Kev."

"I should go," he said, placing the suitcase at the foot of the stairs. "But I'll leave you my number. I'll call Rob at camp so you don't have to worry about that. If you have a pen and pad.

"On the desk." She pointed to the desk just beyond the living-room, where the foyer and living-room met.

"You can call me any time, day or night," he said, matter-of-fact, as he jotted down the necessary information. "I'll let my parents know what's going on so they'll know to tell me when you call." He handed her the piece of paper. "Call me, Julie."

Julie walked him to the front door. "Thanks, Kevin." She placed a gentle kiss on his cheek before he walked out the door.

"Just call me."

Julie leaned against the door frame as he walked away. She went inside only after he had driven away. It was already early evening and it looked like she was in for a long night ahead. She'd make herself a light snack and wait. At this point there was nothing else she could do.

Eleven

It was creeping towards eleven when Julie succumbed to sleep. She had been dozing on the couch for well over an hour when exhaustion overpowered her and she finally gave in. The key in the lock was what had her sitting bolt upright on the couch with her heart racing madly. Upon hearing familiar voices she relaxed slightly. "Dad," she called out tentatively.

"Julie." He hurried into the room with Matt and Janet following close behind. "What are you doing home?" He went to her as she wearily gained her feet. "Camp isn't over for another month. At least that's what I thought…"

For a moment the room became completely quiet. "I took a few days off," she replied simply finding her voice at last.

"How convenient." Matt snorted as he took a seat on the matching love seat.

"Good." Her dad gave her a warm smile. "We've missed you."

"Yes." Janet sat beside her husband carefully. "It's been too quiet around here."

"You have a whole stack of mail from different colleges. Even from State University." He seemed happy about that, which was something that wouldn't last long. He'd most likely hit the roof when he discovered her plans for college. "When did you get in?" He waited for her to take a seat on the couch before he did the same.

"A few hours ago," she replied evenly while glancing in Matt's direction. His eyes were cold and angry. At that moment she knew that his reaction hadn't been kindly. "Since no one was here I just took a nap and waited."

"Cut to the quick, Julie," Matt countered frostily. "We all know why you're here."

Julie willed her resolve to remain strong. "Really?" She met his eyes evenly. This time she wouldn't look away. She'd already come this far and she wasn't about to back down for anyone. It was too late now. The sad part of it was that Matt would never know half of the truth.

"Matt," Janet nudged him gently. "This isn't the time or the place..."

"When is the right time?" he forced through clenched teeth. "I'm sick and tired of keeping my mouth shut." His brown eyes were actually spitting fire. "My father deserves to know the truth too."

"What truth?" Jackson Finch met his son's eyes evenly. "What are you talking about?"

"Never mind," Janet said softly. "It's not important right now." She shot Matt a look before meeting Julie's eyes carefully. "How was camp?"

Suddenly Matt shot up from his seat and stomped out the room, slamming the front door behind him.

"What was that all about?" Jackson directed at Janet.

"He's upset," she replied softly. "This whole business with the funeral coming up has him saying things that he doesn't mean."

Julie bit her lip as Janet continued. "I think I should go and talk to him." She gained her feet with a small sigh. "I'll see you both later."

"And stay off your feet." Jackson called after her.

"Yes, Dad." She smiled softly as she took her leave, following in her husband's footsteps. And finally Julie and her dad were alone.

"How are you doing, Julie?" Immediately he pulled her into his embrace and held her close. Just as he had done when she was a little girl and had scraped a knee, or had fallen off her bicycle.

"I'm okay, Dad."

"Are you now?" Jackson held her at arm's length. "The camp director called this afternoon. I believe his name is Robert."

Julie didn't meet his eyes. She couldn't. "We had a nice long talk." He went on. "You don't have to talk to me about it." He paused drawing a deep breath. "And I won't ask, but I want you to know that I'm here."

"Thank you, Daddy." Her voice broke as tears threatened.

"You're not all that grown up yet. And you're still my little girl."

Julie fell into his opened arms again, this time the tears coming forth in a rush. All the pain she had so carefully concealed came forth in a torrent of emotion. "It hurts so much," she cried.

"I know." He held her tight. "I wish I could take away the pain."

Julie clung to him as the tears fell. It almost reminded her of all the thunderstorms they had battled together when she had been a child. How he had held her close, read her stories, made her laugh until the storm had passed. He had made it better. But this was something completely different. This was something he could not make better. This was something that he had no control over. This was the one battle she had to face alone

"Just remember that God is still in control and He knows what He's doing. Sometimes we don't know the answers as to why things happen and maybe we never will, but through all of it God knows. You have to believe that things will get better and continue to have faith."

It felt as though God had deserted her and faith was just a word. Jackson wiped the tears from her eyes. "Scott had been in pain for a while. I'm just relieved that his suffering is over. He is in a better place, Julie. I believe that." Julie sniffed. "And I know he wouldn't want to see you cry."

The pain in her heart would be there for a long time. There was nothing that anyone could ever say that would make a difference. That much she did know. However, her dad's wisdom made it a little better. "Matt's taking it hard," he continued. "I know he tries to put up a good front. Outside he's as hard as nails, but on the inside he's a mess." He sighed. "Maybe you could talk to him. Janet isn't in any condition to handle this now."

Before Julie could voice a question he went on. "She's three months pregnant." So, that was why he was beaming. "She doesn't need this kind of strain. I told her not to go to the funeral parlor tonight, but you know Janet." He made a little face. "She has a mind of her own." He stifled a yawn. "You and Matt need to talk. I think it will do you both some good." With that said he got to his feet. "This tension in the house is not good. Not now. And especially with Mom coming home in another week..."

Talk about a bombshell! This was certainly news. Whether it was good or bad, she wasn't quite sure. Julie met his eyes quickly. "She's been alcohol free for eight weeks," he returned with a smile.

"I'm happy for you, Dad." And she meant it. Maybe now Jackson could get on with his life as it had been on hold for so long. For everyone's sake, she hoped so.

"Remember what I said, Julie." He started for the stairs which led to the master bedroom. "Talk to your brother. You need each other now. He's hurting just the same." After that was said he left her alone.

For a brief moment silence filled the house. Julie knew that deep down inside her heart that this hurt was something that she and Matt shared. And it was something that they both had to face head on. There wasn't time for secrets as the truth was now out in the open. It was time to stand up and face the world. With that thought in mind she picked up the phone and dialed Matt's number. Janet picked it up immediately, as though she were expecting the call. "Is Matt still up?" She decided she may as well get straight to the point.

"He just got into the shower."

"Oh," Julie hesitated.

"Why don't you come on over?" Janet said. "I'll make some coffee and we can talk."

"Are you sure it's not too late?" It was well after midnight.

"Don't be silly. Come over. I'll leave the back door unlocked for you."

"Thanks, Jan," she said then hung up.

Sometimes it was so convenient that Matt and Janet lived in the apartment over the garage. But at other times, they seemed almost too close. Julie knew that she'd have to face Matt sooner or later. She couldn't avoid him forever. As attractive as that sounded sometimes, it was not plausible.

Carefully Julie combed her hair and applied a light coat of powder to her scar in the downstairs bathroom. Then before she could change her mind she went out the back door and across the lawn to their small garage apartment.

It was wonderful to be home. It was the circumstances that brought her home that she disliked. It also felt odd, especially knowing that she had only left Camp Wiskle for just three short days. She still had to return to finish out another month.

The green grass was damp beneath her feet. But it was a short walk before she reached the pavement. As she climbed the stairs located behind the garage her heart began to beat a little faster. This was the confrontation she had avoided for so long. The confrontation that should have taken place a long time ago. It had been inevitable, only she had hoped that the circumstances could have been different. In fact, they should have been different.

Janet opened the door as soon as she had reached the top landing. "Hi." She gave Julie a warm smile. "Matt's in the living-room."

Julie ventured into the kitchen, which was just inside the door. The living-room was just beyond the kitchen and the master bedroom after that. "Daddy told me about the baby." She gave Janet a big hug. "I'm happy for you."

"We're pretty excited about it too." Janet actually had this glow about her. It must be true that all expectant mothers had a special glow, because Janet was certainly one of them. It was a glow that seemed to emanate from deep within.

"Julie," Matt acknowledged from the doorway.

"Hi, Matt." She faced him forcing a smile. It was a weak smile at best but at the moment it was the best she could do. But that didn't last long. Not with the way he was glaring at her.

"I'm surprised you came," he said curtly. "You've got nerve. That much I'll give you."

Julie did her best to remain unruffled. "Julie didn't come here to look for a fight." Janet said softly.

"I know why she's here," he growled, coming further into the kitchen. "And it isn't a social call." He opened the fridge and took out a bottle of beer. After twisting open the cap he took a seat at the kitchen table.

It was as if Julie was rooted to the floor. All she could do was watch him in complete and utter amazement. It didn't take long for him to hit the nail on the head. "She came to ask us about Scott. Why do you think she came to congratulate us about the baby?"

"Maybe I should leave."

"You'll do no such thing." Janet interjected. "I don't care why she came. All that matters is that she's here."

"I am happy about the baby." Julie looked at the floor. "But I came to see why you're so angry with me."

Matt snorted before finishing off the beer. "You mean you don't know why?"

"No, I don't."

"I think I'll go and put my pj's on." Janet looked like she wanted to bolt. Julie could certainly identify with that.

"Please, Honey." Matt gave his wife the hint of a smile. "I don't want you getting upset." He went to her and gave her a kiss on the forehead. "Why don't you put your feet up and relax and I'll be in shortly. You look tired."

Janet looked at Julie. Only when Julie nodded did she comply. "Good night then." And she left them alone.

"Now then." Matt got himself another beer. "Where were we?" He paused. "Oh yeah, you wanted to know why I'm angry with you." He popped it open and drank that one as quickly as the first. "Where should I begin?" He took a seat at the table and gestured for her to do the same. "I guess we can start with the lying."

She took a seat as he was waiting for an answer. But she honestly didn't know what to say, so she said nothing. "You lied to me. My best friend lied to me..."

"It wasn't my idea." Julie found her voice at last. "I wanted to tell you..."

"Then why didn't you?"

"Because Scott asked me not to."

"Damnit, Julie!" He slammed his fist down on the table with such force. "Why Scott?" He demanded. "Out of all my friends, why Scott?"

Julie fought sudden tears. "It doesn't matter..."

"The hell it doesn't!" he bellowed. "I want to hear you say it. I want to hear it from your mouth."

Finally the tears came and slipped down her cheeks. "What do you want me to say, Matt? It won't change anything." She swiped at her eyes. "I know he was your best friend and I respected that..."

"If you respected that you wouldn't have lied to me."

Julie took a deep breath not meeting his eyes. "I'm sorry I lied to you. I didn't want to and I know that I shouldn't have..."

"I told Scott three years ago." He hit the table for emphasis. "That he was to stay away from you."

Julie looked up quickly. "Now that I have your attention." His brown eyes were as cold as ice. "I had seen it coming. I knew that he liked you." He took a deep breath, and then let it out slowly. "Scott found out that he had leukemia when he was fifteen." Matt paused briefly. "He moved here about a year later."

Julie sat silently and listened. "We started hanging out in my senior year." He went on. "Scott had always been a loner. No one ever knew why, and no one questioned it either. I think that they probably thought he was a snob." Matt shrugged carelessly. "We became good friends from day one. Do you remember?"

She nodded numbly. "He didn't tell me about his illness right away. I never even suspected that anything was wrong. One night we had a few drinks and he told me everything." Matt shuddered. "I couldn't believe it. I was shocked. I didn't even know what to say to him. Then again, what could you say? But he was still my friend. He was my best friend and I would have trusted him with my life." He sighed wearily. "I trusted him with everything. That was up until he started looking at you."

Julie bit her lip. She didn't know what to say to him. The only thing she could do now was listen. "Then I really flipped," Matt went on and she believed him. There was a fire in his eyes that she had never seen before. "I always told him that I would stand by him no matter what. And I did, Julie. But I wouldn't allow him to hurt you."

Tears formed beneath her eyelids one again. "I told him to stay away from you. I knew what would happen once that illness took over completely. He did too. And I knew that he would hurt you. And especially if you fell in love with him..."

By now the tears were falling faster and Julie's breath caught in her throat. In her heart of hearts she knew that Matt had only tried to protect her the only way he knew how. But he could have done it differently. And he should have. In fact, he should have left well enough alone. "And I was right, Julie." He went on. "The one time I had prayed to God I was wrong, I was right." He reached across the table for her hand, but Julie wasn't budging. Not this time. "I had to protect you, Julie. He wasn't the right guy for you. There would have been no future..."

"You lied to me too, Matt." She gained her feet in one quick motion. "So, I guess that makes us even."

"You're not going to leave now." It was not a question, but rather a statement.

"Does it matter?" She threw back at him. "After all this, does it even matter?"

"It does to me." He went to her. "When I found out about everything I was mad as hell." He stood in front of the kitchen door, seemingly blocking her path, which was so typical of Matt. "And I was hurt. But I don't think what I did was wrong. I had to protect you."

"Well Matt, for once in your life, you were wrong. Don't you get it? Don't you understand?" Her voice cracked and her lips trembled. "You could never protect me from Scott because I fell in love with him." The words tumbled from her lips and she couldn't believe that she had actually stood up to Matt. For once in her life she had actually told it as it was and had not painted a pretty picture or skirted the real issue. She had just come right out and said it and the relief was tremendous.

"I know you did," he said softly. "I know."

Now what? Where did they go from here? What was there left to say? "Tomorrow is the burial." Matt turned the topic to the present. "I've asked Janet to stay home. And I want you to stay with her."

"Why?" Her voice was but a whisper.

"Because I'm asking you." His eyes were filled with hurt. "It's hard enough the way it is. I'm begging you, Julie. I can't explain why now, but I will."

"I'll think about it," was all she would commit to at that moment.

"I have something for you before you leave. I wasn't going to give it to you yet but I will." He paused then left the room quickly only to return seconds later. In his hand he carried a long white envelope. "No, I haven't read it." He began lightly. "I have no idea what's in it. But Scott asked me to give it to you when you came back from camp, after the funeral... But I'm going to give it to you now."

Julie took the letter with trembling fingers. "Thank you," she said as she opened the door. Then Matt said something he hadn't said in a long time. "I love you, Julie." It was a statement that stopped her in her tracks. "And I'm sorry." His voice broke and she turned around to face him. "Maybe what I did was wrong. I honestly don't know anymore. All I wanted was to do the right thing. I wanted to protect you. That's all."

She couldn't remember the last time she had ever seen Matt cry. That's how long ago it had been. But he was crying now. Losing his best friend had really hurt him deeply. She could see that now. "I'm sorry too, Matt." She went into his arms and hugged him tightly. And as she did they battled the pain together. It was something they would always share. For the moment, all they had was each other. That and the many fond memories that Scott had given to the both of them.

Twelve

By the time Julie reached the safety of her room the tears had become a tangible ache. The emotions were so overwhelming that she knew it was just a matter of time before she lost complete control and then what? The dam of emotion would be free. But not her heart. Never her heart. With trembling fingers she still held onto the letter. She was almost afraid to open it for fear of what could be inside. So many thoughts were racing through her mind as to what this letter could possibly mean. Was it just a final goodbye? Did it reveal anything about Scott's feelings? There were so many possibilities.

She paced the confines of her room anxiously. The only way to know was to open it and read it. She would no longer allow fear to control any part of her life. Slowly and carefully she tore opened the envelope. The letter was typewritten and folded neatly. It showed that he had taken time to write this letter to her. He didn't just scribble something short and sweet. Time had definitely gone into what she was about to read.

Dear Julie:

Here I am again. Sitting in my room, at my desk, pen in hand. Still, the words will not come. After all, what is there left to say? I think maybe we've said it all. I'm listening to the radio. Tonight they're playing a flash back collection of love songs. Songs that make me think of you. It's Monday night. July 17th. You'll receive this letter after I've gone. It's not that I wanted it this way but in the long run I do think that it's better this way. Please don't be angry with Matt. He loves you very much. I would have done the same if I had been in his shoes.

There were things said. I hurt you. I know that now. And if you hate me, then I reached my ultimate goal. But I know you, Julie. You're not capable of hating or hurting anyone. I guess that's why I'm writing you this letter now. I can admit it's the chicken way out. But right now, at this point in time, I just can't face you. I'm having a tough time even facing Matt.

I'm dying, Julie. I couldn't tell you that when we were together. I was too busy trying to ignore it. And I did ignore it for a long time. Every time I was with you my condition didn't exist. And if you ever wondered why I was away a lot, that's why. There wasn't any other girl. I was away a lot because of this illness. And you know how much I hate hospitals. I think that's one of the things that you do know about me. I've been in and out for a while now. So, now I have to face some facts. I've done some soul searching in the last year or so. I've done a lot of praying and you know what, I'm not afraid. It sounds strange, even scary, but I'm not afraid of dying. The doctors all seem to be optimistic. They think I'll go into remission. But I know better. And I'm handling it. I'm running out of time.

Matt and I got into an argument today. Not our first, but hopefully the last. I told him everything. Remember when I promised that when you turned seventeen I would tell him? Well, today I did it. And it felt good to finally tell someone, anyone. I know that it really hurt him. And it hurt our friendship. In time maybe he can forgive me. We've been through so much already. I also told him about the letter I was going to write to you. I hope he gives this letter to you. Deep down I know he will because no matter what, Matt has always done the right thing. He's one in a million. And he's so lucky to have Janet. They have what only I can ever dream of having. They're two lucky people.

Now, it's down to business. Yes, Julie. I'm referring to you and me. I've always had a problem with finding the right words to say. I'm telling you now because I never had the guts to tell you before. And I know now that you deserve this much from me. Please understand that I've never in my life told a woman I loved her before, because I never thought I would. I never got close to anyone because I knew it couldn't last. And I accepted that. At least I thought I had. Then I fell in love with you. I don't even remember when it happened. I told myself I had to stay away, that Matt was my best friend. I tried to stay away from you, I really did. But it didn't work. I knew you were too young for me. And I knew I was falling in love with you. I tried to run away from it all. I was mad at the world. I was even mad at Matt for having such a pretty sister. I was mad at my parents for moving here in the first place. I was mad at this damned leukemia. And I was mad at you for making me feel this way. Through it all what I didn't realize was how much I was hurting you. And I'm so sorry, Julie. If I could do it all over again I would, but I can't. I know deep down that this is the way it has to be. You deserve to find someone who can love you forever. And as much as I'd like to, I just can't do that.

I need for you to do a few things for me. You don't have to, but I wish you would. Please don't come to the wake. The funeral either. Remember me the way I was. You know I was always partial to my blond curls. They're gone now. The chemotherapy took care of that. But that's okay. I can handle it. But I don't think I could handle knowing you would be there.

Second, I want you to be there for Matt. Don't let bitterness drive a wedge between you both. That would only cause more pain.

Third, I left something for you. It's in Matt's possession. He'll give it to you when he feels the time is right. Don't ask him about it. If he doesn't give it to you there's probably a reason.

Fourth, in time you will find the answers to all the questions you'll have. Believe that. Believe that part of me will always be with you. I need for you to trust in God. He will always be there for you. He will comfort you. Don't question Him. No matter what, God knows what He's doing. Have faith. God bless you, Julie.

Love always,
Scott

Julie held the letter to her chest as the tears coursed down her cheeks. Scott had loved her! It was just as she had always suspected but was afraid to hope for. The realization of it all was now staring her in the face. How could something be so simple yet so complex? Although she found it to be some measure of relief there was still the funeral to deal with. And with that reality really took hold of her. Scott may have loved her but now he was gone. There was no going back to fix that. It was gone. Never again would she talk to him, hold him, or laugh with him. That was all gone. Scott had left her forever.

Carefully Julie returned the letter to its original envelope. She'd keep this letter always. It had been Scott's final words. The words she had longed to hear for so long. The words which had kept them apart. He had loved her enough not to say them.

After Julie put the letter away for safekeeping she climbed into bed. As she lay on her back she found herself drifting as she had done many times before.

~ * ~

"I've never felt this way with anyone but you." Scott's blue eyes danced. "It's almost like magic." It was love. Oh Scott. Just say it. Please. But he didn't. And it didn't matter. Julie loved Scott with all her heart. I love you. She thought silently.

~ * ~

Julie awoke to the bright rays of the sun streaming through her window. It looked to be a beautiful day ahead. But looks could be deceiving. And they were because today was Scott's funeral. She wasn't so sure she'd be able to get through it. One thing was for certain, she wouldn't be there. The least she could do for Scott was to honor his final wishes. She owed him that much. And she would grant him that.

Time seemed to drag unmercifully. At first she thought she'd stick it out in her room but by eight o'clock she felt she'd go stir crazy. She knew Matt and Janet were downstairs as she could hear their voices floating through the hallway. They were probably waiting for her. She'd have to face them sooner or later. It may as well be now she thought as she pulled a brush through her hair. Besides, she still had to give Matt an answer to the question he had presented to her last night.

In the end, it was Matt who sought her out. She knew it was him before she opened the door. "Hi." He stood in the doorway wearing his finest suit. He looked so tired. And it showed in his eyes. The dark circles were definitely noticeable. "We're leaving in ten minutes." He took in her appearance but said nothing.

"I'm not going to go after all," she said simply. As though it had been her idea from the very beginning.

"Okay." He paused. "Janet is downstairs. She's not going either."

Julie nodded. It was all she could do at the moment. "Are you going back to camp?" He met her eyes evenly.

"Tomorrow."

This time he nodded. It was almost as if they were afraid to speak to one another. Maybe, in part, that was true. "I'd better get downstairs. Dad's waiting." He turned away then.

"Thanks for giving me the letter, Matt." That seemed to make him stop short. "I know you didn't have to…"

He kept his back to her. "I hope it helped."

"It did." Her voice cracked. *More than you'll ever know,* she finished silently.

"Good," he said before walking away.

~ * ~

As the day slowly moved on, Julie decided to keep to herself. Matt and Jackson still hadn't returned which meant they were probably visiting with the immediate family. Janet had been in and out all day. At one point she had even suggested that they go shopping. Julie gave her a look and the subject was closed.

Julie did her best to keep busy. She was too tired to think, much less want to think about Scott. All she had left now were the memories. And they seemed intent on torturing her. At this point, she didn't want to remember all the good times they had shared. Not when they could have shared so many more. And they could have. If Scott would have been honest from the very beginning, Julie would have stood by him no matter what. In her heart she knew that to be true. Why hadn't he given her the choice instead of taking matters into his own hands? That had been one of their biggest problems. Scott had never let her decide anything. That was probably why he and Matt had gotten along so well. They had almost the very same viewpoint on everything. That was a scary thought.

The clock was slowly ticking off the seconds. As she placed the dishes in the dishwasher the phone rang. She grabbed for the phone. "Hello," she said breathlessly.

"Julie." It was Kevin.

"Hi, Kev." She tried not to sound disappointed. After all, she had been the one who had forgotten to call him. Then again, her mind wasn't exactly functioning as well as it should be.

"How are you doing?" His voice seemed distant.

"Fine."

He paused. "What time can I pick you up tomorrow?"

Talk about right to the point. "Whenever it will be convenient for you." It was better left up to him.

"Is ten too early?"

"Ten will be fine." The conversation was stilted and they both knew it.

"How are you, Julie? I mean, really?"

"I'm fine," she lied. And thank goodness, for once, Kevin didn't push the issue.

"Can I take you out for a bite to eat?" He asked then hurried on. "You probably haven't eaten a thing all day..."

"Thanks, Kevin but I'm waiting for my brother to come home. I really should stay here."

"Okay. Then I'll see you tomorrow."

"Goodbye." She hung up just as Janet came in through the back door.

"I have a chicken roasting in the oven," she began as she closed the door. "Matt called and said he'd be home in an hour." She met Julie's eyes evenly. "Have you had anything to eat today?" Her gaze narrowed.

"I'm not hungry." She went back to loading the dishwasher. "I still have some packing to do." This was a half-truth. She may as well lessen the load as there were only four weeks of camp left. Then Camp Wiskle would be just another memory. As for attending next year, that was something she'd rather not think about. Besides, next year seemed such a long way off.

"You should rinse those dishes first," Janet said suddenly which brought Julie back to the task at hand.

"That would be nice." She pushed out a short laugh. "I guess I wasn't thinking..."

"Julie," she began on a light note. "You don't have to put on a brave front."

Julie remained still while the water ran onto the dishes and down the drain. It was almost the picture of her life. That too resembled water running down the drain. Out of reach. Out of control. "I'm pretty sure that Scott told Matt close to everything." She went on carefully. "So, it would only be natural for you to..."

"To what?" Julie turned around quickly. "To feel sorry for myself." Her voice caught.

"I didn't mean that at all." Janet lowered hurt blue eyes. "You need to let it out. You can't keep it bottled up inside."

"It doesn't matter anymore." Tears stung the back of her eyelids. "It wasn't as if things had worked out between us." She had promised herself she would not cry. And that was one promise that she intended to keep. "They probably wouldn't have." As she closed the dishwasher with a bang she realized just how angry she was. "Then again, I'll never really know that."

"Scott was a hard person to understand." Janet took a seat at the kitchen table. "You, of all people, should know that. He never told anyone how he felt..."

"No one, except Matt," she put in bitterly.

"You're right," Janet said simply. "He didn't want to hurt you, Julie. He may have gone about it the wrong way, but to him, it seemed right. You have to respect him for that."

Maybe Janet was right. She wasn't sure. Then again, she wasn't too sure of anything right now. "It's going to take some time," Janet went on. "But you have to get on with your life. Close that book and begin a new one."

The way Janet put it, it sure sounded simple. Just close the book. Throw it away. Throw the memories away. Just forget that Scott had ever existed. Forget everything and begin again. If only it were that simple. But it wasn't. And it hurt. It hurt like hell. "I'm going upstairs to pack."

"Okay." Janet's voice was soft and gentle, as was her nature. "Dinner will be ready in about half an hour."

Julie could only nod as she walked slowly away.

~ * ~

By the time Julie realized it, the three days had come and gone and it was time to go back to camp. Much to her surprise she was happy to be going back. She needed those few weeks to get herself together. To get her life back on track. As though, at this point, that was possible.

Instead of going to the Y, as was Jackson's usual custom, he had opted to stay home to see her off. It was not quite ten when she had barricaded herself in the bathroom to fix and powder her face. In less than ten minutes she'd see Kevin and although her heart felt heavy she had missed him.

"You're friend's here." Jackson tapped on the door softly.

"I'll be right there," she called back as every nerve began to jump. She didn't know why she was so nervous about seeing Kevin again. Maybe anxious was a better word. Julie stared at her reflection in the mirror. This was definitely not the same Julie Finch who had left for camp only four weeks ago. Somewhere along the line she had changed. She had grown up. That hurt frightened little girl had turned into a woman.

Before stepping out of the safe confines of the bathroom Julie washed her face. The powder rinsed off quite easily and she watched it run down the drain with a small smile. After that chore was complete she threw the compact into the garbage can. That closed one chapter in her life. Now, there was the rest of the book to contend with.

Thirteen

Julie dozed off and on as Kevin drove them back to Camp Wiskle. It was such an effort to keep her eyes opened and by half past ten she had seemingly given up the battle. Kevin had remained quiet, as though he had a lot of pressing issues on his mind and that was fine with Julie. Something was different. They were going back to camp two different people.

The minute the radio began crackling with static Kevin switched if off with a scowl. "I have to admit," he began on a light note. "That I'm a little surprised that you're coming back. I thought you were going to bail on me at the last minute."

"I promised that I would," she replied evenly.

"I know." He gave her a sideward glance. "But I thought you were just saying it to shut me up." They both laughed.

"It's my job." She sighed. "And I gave Rob my word. He was nice enough to give me the time off..." She was wistful and she felt as though she were leaving a part of herself behind. The part that was hurting more than words could ever express.

"I want you to know that you look much better," he said, matter-of-fact. "Better than you looked when I dropped you off a few days ago."

She didn't know what to make of that. "Definitely better without all that makeup." He changed the subject almost as quickly as he had brought it up. "I hope things went well."

She knew he wanted to ask but probably didn't know how. "I didn't go to the funeral, Kevin," she said softly.

"Oh." His voice was light.

"At first I was going to," she began. "But after I got the letter I..." She bit her lip as she suddenly realized that she had revealed too much.

"What letter?" Kevin picked up on that slip of the tongue immediately.

"It was a letter that Scott had written before..."

"Uh huh." He gripped the steering wheel tightly. "Is everything okay, Julie?" he asked. "Are you okay?"

"I think so," she answered honestly. How did one define okay?

"Good." He sighed keeping his eyes straight ahead. "And you're picking up the pieces?" That was a question.

"I'm trying," she answered softly. She could almost guarantee where he was going with this line of questioning. Idly she wondered how long it would take him to cut to the quick. This had been inevitable from the beginning. At this point in time she wasn't ready to jump into anything and she could only hope that Kevin would understand.

"And us?" he queried softly.

"I... I can't say right now, Kevin." She didn't look his way. This was one person she didn't want to lose as a friend. And she didn't want to hurt him either. "I think it's good that we're friends right now and..."

"Friends." He nodded his head knowingly with a small smile.

"I like you a lot, Kevin but…"

"Friends." He repeated. "I thought we were just a little bit past being friends."

"I'm not ready for anything more right now," she stated. "I would hope that you would understand that."

Kevin took a deep breath and let it out slowly. "You're right." He agreed, forcing a smile. "I didn't mean to push the issue. Friends is good," He snickered. "It's a start." He reached across the leather seat for her hand. "Yeah, I think I can handle that."

~ * ~

They pulled into the long driveway leading up to the main house just as a group of campers were heading down to the lake. As Kevin pulled out her two small overnight suitcases they were suddenly surrounded by Keith and Tracey, both of whom had been on their way to the basketball court. "It's so good to have you back." Tracey gave her a big hug. "We missed you both."

Keith was patting Kevin on the back looking serious. "Your brother is in a meeting right now with Rob and Nancy," he said simply.

"Is everything okay?" It was Julie who posed the question, her brown eyes wide.

"They were caught in, let me see, a compromising situation," Keith returned.

"A compromising situation. What would you call a compromising situation?"

"Why don't you walk Julie to her cabin and we'll talk later," was all Keith would say.

"Go on you two." Julie laughed. "I can make it back okay."

"I'll go with her," Tracey offered, taking one of the two small suitcases and the argument was settled as Julie took the other and they started on their way.

"This almost feels like the first day," Julie said as they started for the lighted path. For a brief moment she almost wished it were. Then maybe, miraculously, she would be granted one more chance.

"You look good." Tracey carefully avoided her gaze. "I noticed you lost the makeup."

"Is it that obvious?" Her hand went to her cheek involuntarily.

"You look great. I always told you that."

"I know. It feels different that's all." Julie paused for a moment. "I want you to know that you've always been a great friend, Trace."

"How was it?" she asked softly. "The funeral?" As though she needed to clarify that.

"I didn't go," Julie said simply. As though it were that simple, when of course it wasn't. It just seemed so much easier when the decision had been taken out of her hands. In some ways it had been such a relief.

"Maybe it was better that you didn't go." Tracey shuddered. "I don't think I could have gone under the circumstances."

"Tracey." She stopped suddenly and faced her friend. "I have to tell you something. And no, it's not a secret." She couldn't help but smile when she thought of that letter, Scott's last letter of love. "Scott left me a letter," she began. "He gave it to Matt some time before..."

"A letter." Tracey's blue eyes were wide.

"I brought it with me."

"You're going to let me read it?"

"Why not?" Julie shrugged carelessly. "You're the only one who really knew the whole truth about me and Scott. I want you to read it."

They started walking again. "Did you and Matt straighten things out?"

"I think we did." Julie sighed. "I finally understand a lot of things that I didn't understand before. I see things differently now."

"Does he know everything?"

Julie giggled softly as she nudged her friend. "I hope not."

"You know what I mean." She smiled as her cheeks flushed.

"I don't really know. Scott told him a few days before..." She just could not bring herself to say Scott's name and the word death in the same sentence.

"Are you okay, Julie?" Tracey put the question to her bluntly. "I mean really?"

"I'm trying to be," she answered in all honesty. "It isn't easy, Trace." By now they had reached the cabin. As they went inside Julie couldn't help but notice how everything was so neat and tidy. It was also very quiet. "Especially after reading the letter."

"And Kevin?"

"What about him?"

Tracey pushed out a short laugh. "Where does this leave you and Kevin? Almost everyone knows how he's crazy about you."

"I... I don't know. It's too soon." She tossed the suitcase she had been carrying on her bunk. "Sometimes I feel so empty inside. And sometimes I feel like somebody's ripping my heart right out of my chest." She took a deep breath. "I can't even begin to explain it.

"That's understandable. This was a shock."

"It was. And now..." Her voice broke. "I don't feel anything." That realization frightened her even more than the pain.

"You need time to sort out these emotions."

"That's what I told Kevin." She opened up the suitcase and began to pull out her clothes and place them neatly in the closet. "I'm not ready for something major like a relationship. I don't think I can handle it, not now anyway."

"What did he say?" Tracey took a seat opposite her bunk, which was Lorna's bunk.

"He said he'd handle it."

"That's good. At least he's not being pushy."

Julie met her best friend's eyes evenly. "But what if I'm never going to be ready?"

"You'll be ready." Tracey smiled. "Right now you need time to grieve. You need time to remember. After all, you loved him. What you're feeling is completely normal. You need time."

Julie forced a small smile. "So, what's been happening around here?" She changed the subject entirely.

"You would never guess in a million years." Tracey's blue eyes were sparkling like little sapphires. "Nancy and Jake got caught skinny dipping."

"No?" Julie was shocked.

"Rob hit the roof. The whole camp was up in arms. I thought all hell was going to break loose." She shook her head sadly. "I expected Jake to get a pink slip."

"He didn't?"

"Not yet." Tracey shrugged. "I would have given him one without thinking twice."

"What gives?" Julie faced her friend, hands on hips.

"What do you mean?"

"You hate him." It was a statement.

"Hate is a very strong word. Let's just say that I dislike him."

"Whatever." Julie met her eyes evenly. "Love and hate run a very fine line you know."

"He's a jerk," she returned simply. "He takes advantage of people and I don't like that."

"Okay, so what did he do to you?"

"Nothing—"

"Come on, Trace." She laughed out loud. "Whenever his name is brought up you get this fire in your eyes. You should see yourself."

"It's nothing, Julie."

Although Julie knew there was a lot more to this subject she let it drop. When and if Tracey wanted to tell her then she would be there to listen. "So they were caught skinny dipping," Julie said. "Should we be surprised?"

"They got real close after you and Kevin left. Almost inseparable." Tracey said with wide eyes and Julie knew there was more, as though that weren't enough. "There was talk about them actually doing the deed, if you know what I mean."

"No." Julie's eyes were wide.

"That seems to be the talk," she replied. "It can be serious." Tracey continued, "But right now they're both denying it. So it can't be proven."

Julie couldn't believe it. "You always miss the good stuff." Tracey laughed out loud. "But I have a feeling it isn't over yet."

"Why?"

"I don't know. But if Mr. and Mrs. Wiskle had been here there would have been pink slips. Who knows, there still might be."

"That's what I call taking chances." Julie breathed.

"It's downright disgusting," Tracey said simply. "They should both get the boot. There's no excuse for it." She paused momentarily. "The Wiskles' had a death in the family so they won't be here this year." She turned the subject around. "But they'll be here next year and you can meet them then."

"I don't know if I'll be coming back next year," Julie said honestly.

"Why not?"

"I'm just not sure yet."

Tracey nodded. "You have plenty of time before making a final decision." She smiled. "Now, let's get down to the lake and back to work."

The rest of the day went rather quickly. The girls were happy that Julie was back, all but Nancy, who was deliberately staying away from her. That was okay as Julie had enough on her mind without any other problems.

After lights out Rob had called a meeting which all senior and junior counselors were to attend, no exceptions. She could only imagine the topic.

Her mind was running in different directions as she changed into a pale pink short set. This was one that she had brought from home. Actually, it had been one of the many outfits that she had carelessly tossed to the back of her closet, vowing to never wear it again. That was another chapter closed. She was really trying to change things. At this rate she would be rid of that book by the summer's end.

"Not wearing any makeup tonight? Nancy raised a delicate eyebrow in question. "That's a first. Then again, I guess there's a first time for everything."

Julie pulled a brush through her hair. "I left it home," she returned simply. And at this point in time it was just that simple. She refused to let Nancy ruffle her feathers and her new found composure.

"Are you sure that was smart decision?" They stood in the bathroom sharing the same mirror. "I mean, what would Kevin think..." She paused as though searching for the correct phrase. "Of such a thing?" she finally added.

"I'll be sure to ask him," Julie said as she walked past her and headed for the door. "Please remember to leave the night light on," she directed at Lorna on her way outside.

"Okay." Lorna didn't look up from the book she was reading.

Julie decided to meet Tracey at her cabin. After all, it was only around the bend and not that far away at all. Tracey was sitting on the stairs just staring off into space. In fact, she didn't see Julie until she was upon her. She gained her feet with a smile. "I remember that outfit." She snickered. "Brought it out of retirement?"

"I guess you can say that."

"It looks great. As good as it did when you bought it."

"Yeah?" They fell into step heading for the main house. "Be honest with me, Trace..."

"I'm serious, it looks great."

"No. I'm talking about my scar." She paused. "My face." As though she needed to elaborate. "I shouldn't have thrown out that makeup..."

"You look good, Julie. The best you have looked in a long time." Tracey took a deep breath. "Believe me. I see a big difference. That scar is small potatoes." She paused. "You never needed all that makeup and powder. And everyone knew that. The only reason your parents agreed to let you get it was because it made you feel better. It was like a crutch..."

"Seriously, Trace. Don't give me a line of bull. Just give it to me straight." They had just reached the turn-off. "I can handle it, one way or another."

"You don't need it. You never have." They proceeded through the darkness heading towards the main house in stride. "And I've never lied to you before, right?"

"Right."

"And I'm not lying now."

Julie took a deep breath and let it out slowly as they started up the stairs. "Do we know what this meeting is about?"

"After what's been going on," she laughed out loud. "This should be a piece of cake."

~ * ~

The meeting lasted well over an hour. At one point Rob had actually pulled out the rule book and read a few chapters aloud while Julie tried her best not to fall asleep. He placed special emphasis on the rules regarding the counselor and camper relationship. She could almost feel Kevin's eyes upon her. Deep down inside she knew that this meeting was not meant for them. But it was still wrong. This rule applied to everyone and not a select few. It was something that they both had to face.

As Rob began to close the meeting he made the mistake of asking if anyone had any comments or questions. Of course, Nancy was the first on her feet. "I don't think it's fair when you single out one person and let another get away with the same thing."

Rob raised an eyebrow thoughtfully. "And is that what you think I'm doing?"

"Sit down, Nancy." Jake said from the other side of the room.

"No, I won't." Her eyes were shooting sparks. "And you know I'm right Jake. And you know where I'm going…"

"It's not the same thing." He forced through clenched teeth. "Now sit down."

Nancy remained standing. "I don't think we should get into this now." It was Rob who spoke. "And we're not here to make comparisons. We're going to move forward on a good note from here on."

"So it's okay for Julie and Kevin to meet after lights out but it's not okay if someone else does it."

Julie couldn't believe what Nancy was suggesting. "It's okay if they're off the lighted path kissing somewhere." She went on. "And doing who knows what else."

"Just hold on right there." Now Kevin was on his feet. His green eyes were blazing dangerously as he squared off with Nancy. "That's a lie and you know it…"

"That's enough." Rob slapped his hand against the rule book with a startling crack. The whole room became silent. "We're not going down this road. This is done. Sit down, the both of you." He directed at Kevin and Nancy. "This has gotten completely out of hand now. There will be no mudslinging. I will not stand for it." He took a deep breath and let it out slowly. "Now, let's get back to camp business. Keith has a few announcements before we close."

Julie had been mortified to hear the lies that had spilled from Nancy. Did she hate Julie that much that she would tell such horrid lies? Did Nancy want her position that badly? Well, if this were the penalty, she didn't want it. In fact, she wanted no part of it at all.

As Keith droned on about camp business and the arts and crafts awards to be presented in the next week or two, Julie turned her thoughts to other matters. She wasn't interested in basketball competitions or art awards. Her mind was on Scott, and the many clues he had dropped. If only she had realized the situation then. If only she had known.

~ * ~

Scott had certainly changed in the last year. He had lost some weight. But that was probably because he was too busy with his social life to find the time for something as simple as eating. His blond hair was really short, as short as a buzz cut. Gone was that thick curly hair she had once run her fingers through. But he was still as handsome as ever. With those deep blue eyes that could always look right through her and always had.

Then there had been the confrontation. The very last time she was to see him. If only she had known it then. Although, he hadn't said a word concerning his condition he sure had left some kind of signs, clues that she should have picked up on and questioned. But at that time she had been too busy feeling sorry for herself to notice, and now it all came back in a rush.

"You're looking good," he said the minute Janet was out of ear-shot.

"Thank you." Her voice was crisp, tense.

"It's been a long time." His tone was light. "Almost a year is it."

"Should I be honored that you remembered." Her brown eyes flashed. At that moment she was sorry she had opened her mouth at all.

"Still mad at me, huh?" He was trying to get a rise out of her. Not that he had to try that hard. "I thought that the situation..."

"There was never any damned situation," she hissed cutting him off. "You wanted it all, Scott. Why can't you just be honest enough to admit that?" She met his eyes evenly and was rather taken aback at what she found lurking there. It seemed to her

that in the past year he had, in fact, changed. He looked older and tired. However, she would not soften. He had hurt her deeply and she wasn't ready to forgive and forget. Not yet.

"Maybe I wasn't honest with you." He started towards her with a purpose. "But you always knew how I felt..."

"Disgusted," she finished for him. "Everything changed after the accident." She promised herself she would not get upset. And she wouldn't. It was over and had been for a long time.

"You're still hung up about those scars." He shook his head sadly. "It's amazing how some things never change."

"I don't want to discuss my scars with you." She found herself backing away. "You've already made your feelings clear."

"You never gave me a chance..." He broke off suddenly as Janet came back into the room suitcase in hand.

"I think this is the biggest out of the three. I'm sure Scott wouldn't mind carrying it..."

"That's okay." She hedged backing towards the door. "I'll pick it up later." Then she got out of there as though the devil himself were chasing her.

~ * ~

Julie came back to the present with a start as everyone around her was milling about. They were either leaving or getting ready to leave. As she gained her feet she noticed Kevin heading in her direction with a smile.

"Hi." His blue green eyes were shining. "I didn't know you painted one of those things." He shook his head and Julie had no idea what he was talking about. "I thought it was a stupid project from the start..." He paused. "The plaques that we painted before... You won first place." He was grinning from ear to ear. "Come on, I'll walk you to your cabin."

Fourteen

All night Julie tossed and turned as Scott's image chased her from one dream to the next. At one point his blue eyes openly mocked her as his voice called out from a pale white mist. She tried to tell herself it was only a dream. She tried to pull herself awake but could not...

~ * ~

Before she realized what was happening she was standing alone in a darkened room with a polished white casket standing just a few feet before her. An opened casket with a flowing white silky material cascading down the sides. Although she could not see inside she knew what it meant. "Please." She choked out dropping to her knees and offering a silent prayer. Anything to avoid looking inside. She didn't want to see him. Not like this. "You're dreaming, Julie." She spoke aloud and it echoed throughout the large room. "You're not here."

"I told you not to come." It was Scott's voice. "But since you're here you may as well finish what you started. Come here."

"No," she whispered keeping her head bowed.

"Come on, Julie." His voice was low and quite soothing. "This is what you came to see. I'll tell you everything you want to know. All you have to do is come over here."

To her horror she found herself getting to her feet. She seemed to be going on automatic because her legs suddenly had a mind of their own. With wide eyes she began to walk, the pristine casket still just a few feet ahead...

~ * ~

The clanging of the bell had Julie sitting bolt upright on the bed, her heart hammering in her chest. It had been a nightmare! Just a horrible nightmare! Her nightgown was clinging to her shaken form and her breathing was labored. Shakily she ran a hand through her tangled hair as the girls were stretching and yawning. It was time to get ready for another fun filled day at Camp Wiskle. In another four weeks it would all be just another memory, just another chapter in a book. A chapter she could hardly wait to close. It couldn't come soon enough.

They met down on the baseball diamond. And another day was born. Julie threw herself into the regimen with pleasure. She could feel her muscles working. It was great to feel them straining with each movement. It was a pleasure to feel something besides numbness. "Slow down, will you," Tracey mumbled. "You're making the rest of us look pretty lame."

Julie forced a smile but pressed on. When the whistle blew for breakfast she was disappointed. As everyone started for the dining hall she chose to remain behind. Just a few more toe touches, maybe a few stretches, and she'd be finished. But when she looked up she found herself looking into Rob's deep questioning eyes.

"I didn't mean to startle you." He stood erect, while swinging the whistle string around his index finger. "How are you doing?" he asked candidly.

"Fine."

He nodded while his gaze was concentrated. "We haven't had a chance to talk since you got back." He declared simply. "How about joining me for breakfast in my office." It wasn't a question but rather a statement. "This way we can have a little privacy while we talk." And the matter was settled.

As he started in the direction of the main house Julie had no choice but to follow, which of course she did. "It has turned out to be a rather nice day." Rob turned the conversation to the weather. A safe topic she supposed. "We were due for rain. And who knows." He shrugged carelessly. "We still might get some."

Julie remained silent as she followed him up the stairs, down the hallway, and into his office. Breakfast was already waiting for them. "You can sit here." Rob held a chair for her.

"Thanks." She sat down and waited for him to do the same.

"Would you like a cup of coffee?" He held the pot.

"Please."

He sat down after pouring them each a cup. "Smoke?" He withdrew a package of cigarettes from his top drawer.

"No thanks." She concentrated on fixing her coffee while he lit up.

"It's been a rough summer." He began lightly as he leaned back in his chair. "For all of us." He paused while puffing on his cigarette. "My parents had an immediate death in the family, which is why I took over this year."

Julie was quiet. "Here." He piled scrambled eggs and a few pieces of toast on her plate. "Breakfast is the most important meal of the day." With that he placed a glass of orange juice beside her plate as well. "Death is something of a mystery." He went on putting out the cigarette. "Sometimes it can be one of the hardest things that people can accept. And there are so many phases of grief."

Julie pushed her food around the plate with the fork absently. "My wife passed away about three years ago."

Julie looked up quickly. That revelation had taken her aback. He seemed like such a strong man. Almost as though there was nothing that could touch him. But obviously something had. "I've been there." He took a bite of his toast meeting her eyes evenly. "You're not eating." He observed with a small smile.

How could she eat after discovering such a thing? For once she didn't feel like she was alone. She wasn't the only one to experience this pain. This emptiness. "Ask away." He put his fork down and leaned back in his chair.

"I couldn't." She dropped hurt brown eyes.

"Julie." His voice was soft. "It's okay to talk about it. You can ask me any question you want. Believe me; I will try to answer as honestly as I can. And I don't bite either."

She smiled in spite of herself. "Go ahead." He poured himself another cup of coffee.

"When does it stop hurting?"

"The truth?" Rob pushed out a short laugh. "Never." Julie's eyes widened and he continued. "Time seems to dull the pain a little but it never really goes away. You can't forget someone that you loved. Someone that you shared memories with. You can't and you won't." He shrugged. "Deep down inside, I believe that we don't want to forget. We want to remember everything. The good times and the bad."

She gave up pushing the eggs around her plate with the pretense of eating. "It's different for me, Rob."

"What's different?"

"Everything. Being married is different. Me and Scott... Well, we... It's just different."

"Did you love him?"

The question was straight to the point. No beating around the bush. "Yes."

"Then I can't see the difference. I know the pain. It's something I wouldn't wish on my worst enemy. The pain is still there. I still feel it. Some days it's stronger than others. Some days I'll walk into my apartment in the city and I'll see her everywhere. Sometimes a particular place brings it all back. Like the little bench in the back of the public library where we used to meet every Monday night." He took a deep breath and released it slowly.

"I still think it's different."

"Fair enough." He leaned back in his seat. "Tell me about Scott." He declared suddenly turning the conversation in her direction and Julie bit her lip. "Tell me the first thing that pops into your mind."

She looked at him as though he had lost his mind. "Come on," he urged. "I'm sure you can think of something."

She could think of many things. "He was fun to be with."

"Fun?"

"He knew how to make me laugh. Even when things at home were terrible he could always make me smile." She leaned back in her chair. "He had the brightest blue eyes I have ever seen." She smiled warmly as Scott's image sprang to mind. "With blond curly hair." Instantaneously she was remembering, just what she had promised herself that she would not do.

~ * ~

"Matt." Julie tapped on her brother's door only once before flinging it open. "Daddy wants his tennis whites back and..." Her breath caught as her heart catapulted into her throat. There, standing less than two feet away from her stood the most gorgeous guy she had ever seen. There he stood half naked, wearing only a pair of briefs, right in front of her.

"Hi." He smiled warmly. He did not appear to be embarrassed at all. "I'm Scott. One of Matt's friends from school." His eyes were as blue as the sky. He had curly blond hair and was built. He had strong muscled shoulders and biceps. He seemed to have

muscles everywhere. Now he stood tall and proud. Like one of those Greek gods Julie had often read about.

"And you are?" He cocked an eyebrow as he gave her a small flirtatious smile.

~ * ~

"Julie?" Rob called out gently. "Earth to Julie?"

She came back to the present with a start. "What."

"You were miles away."

"I'm sorry." She sighed. "I really should be going," she said as though she had just realized the time. It was getting late. They had already lingered over breakfast for well over an hour.

"Everything has been taken care of. Jake has your campers on the tennis courts this morning."

"Oh," was all she could think to say.

"Relax and have another cup of coffee." He poured her a fresh cup. "There's nothing wrong with remembering. It even helps sometimes."

But she didn't want to think. At least not now. It hurt too much to remember. It was torture. Pure torture. "My wife died in a car accident." Rob completely turned the conversation around. "A little over three years ago." He munched on a piece of toast absently. "We had been married for a year. We met at college, fell in love, and got married." He pushed out a short laugh. "There were a few times I wanted to just pack it all in." He met her eyes evenly and Julie could see the pain buried deep within. It was almost like looking into a mirror. It seemed to reflect the same pain. "But I loved her."

"What was her name?" Julie asked softly.

"Laural. Her name was just as different as she was." He sighed as though deep in thought. "She died instantly. There was no time to say goodbye. It happened so fast. One minute I was kissing her goodbye and the next... She was gone."

Julie blinked back sudden tears. She honestly didn't know what to say. Somehow saying that she was sorry seemed too impersonal. Besides, being sorry didn't make the pain lessen. Not in the least. "So," he pulled himself up with a smile. "I think it's fair to say that I can identify with what you're feeling."

It was at that moment that she knew how much it had cost him to share that personal information with her and she was grateful. "Thank you, Rob."

"If you ever need to talk." He left the invitation opened. "I think you know where to find me." He gained his feet slowly. "Now, I'll let you get back to your campers."

Julie left the main house and headed straight for the tennis courts where she was sure to find her campers. It was time for work. And she knew that if she lost herself in some kind of physical labor that there wouldn't be time for anything else. And right now that was exactly what she needed.

~ * ~

The next two weeks were truly hectic ones. There was so much to do and almost all of their activities were held outdoors as the weather had been truly wonderful. They had even gone as far as holding chapel outside by the lake. The surroundings had been so serene that it eased Julie's heavy heart.

The campers were suddenly caught up in the many festivities. And so was Julie. Kevin had kept his distance as he had promised. So there wasn't any pressure in that area of her life and that was a load off Julie's mind. Although deep down inside she missed him, she wasn't ready to acknowledge it. Time had seemed to soften Nancy's disposition and she no longer seemed moody or angry all the time. It was almost as if she had come to accept the way things were. It was certainly a change for the better. In the two weeks since Julie had returned she could honestly see that Nancy had matured. However, there was no room for perfection. It wasn't exactly common knowledge but Julie suspected that Nancy and Jake were still seeing each other on the sly. But that was Nancy's business and Julie would not stick her nose where it didn't belong. There were some rules that were meant to be broken.

There was a dance scheduled for later in the evening, or as Rob insisted on calling them, a mixer. Talk from his old college days. Although Julie did not feel like going, she had missed the last one. This time the girls were not letting her off the hook. Lorna was looking forward to this one as she had a date. "You need to loosen up, Julie," she said simply. "Have some fun. It's not a sin to have fun," she said, matter-of-fact. "And it's just another boring Friday night dance. I'm sure that Kevin will be..." She bit her lip thoughtfully. "He didn't have a date last week."

"I thought we had this discussion about match-making..."

"I wasn't match-making." Lorna returned evenly. "I was stating the facts. You don't have a date and Kevin doesn't have a date. Even if you went as friends..."

"Forget it." Julie turned away. There were so many different emotions racing through her at just the mention of his name. She didn't trust her feelings at all and she mustn't as her feelings for Scott remained just below the surface.

"Hi, Girls." Tracey chose that moment to enter the cabin. She was smiling and her bright blue eyes were sparkling like little sapphires. It was obvious that she was happy with her life. And Julie knew that Keith played a large part in that happiness. "Are we almost ready in here?" She gazed around the room quickly then her eyes came to rest upon Julie. "You know what I realized on my way over here." She began on a serious note. "We haven't had a night off since we'd been here. Everyone has done their own thing and that's fine but I say we need at least one night away. And this week we're doing it." Her eyes were wide. "Just the two of us. We'll go out for dinner. Then maybe we'll take in a movie, or maybe we'll go shopping. Anything to get away for a few hours."

"We don't have to..."

"No we don't have to." She agreed with a shrug. "But why not? We deserve a night out. And we're entitled to have one night out once a week and since we haven't we're going to do it."

"You should," Nancy chimed from the bathroom. "I know I would take advantage of it if I could." She stuck her head out the door. "Don't worry Camp Wiskle will be here when you get back. We'll all be here."

"What do you say?" Tracey was waiting for an answer and Julie couldn't help but smile.

"Okay," she finally agreed.

~ * ~

The dance was already in full swing by the time they arrived. The music was lively and it seemed that almost everyone was out on the dance floor. The girls left Julie at the punchbowl with the promise to meet at ten sharp.

Julie stood on the sidelines watching the couples dance after getting herself a glass of punch. She didn't want to make it obvious that she was cautiously seeking Kevin out. For the tenth time she had to tell herself that she was only curious to see who he was dancing with. But from the looks of it he was nowhere to be found. It was probably just as well. At least he had respected her wishes. For that, she was somewhat grateful.

As the music slowed its tempo Julie wandered about. She seemed to be drifting along in a fog as she walked around the refreshment table. Thank goodness that the last two weeks had been busy ones. It was good for the mind as well as the heart. It was the nights that were unbearable. Those were the times when Scott would creep into her mind and leave his mark on her young heart. Julie must have walked around the table a few times before Jake approached her with a smile.

"Hi." His blue eyes were wide. "How about a dance?"

"No thanks," she refilled her glass just for something to do.

"I get it." He rocked back on his heels with wide eyes. "I take it you're waiting for my brother," he said knowingly.

"No," she returned evenly.

"Then you can dance with me." It was a statement this time. "Please."

Hesitantly Julie agreed only because she didn't want to cause a scene. But after this dance she would find Nancy and place her in charge while she skipped out.

"Cheer up, sweetie." As he took her into his arms she stiffened. If Jake had sensed it he said nothing. As they swayed to the music Julie could not relax. It was the longest ten minutes she had ever spent. Once the music broke she was out of Jake's arms. As she pulled away she knew it was time to take her leave. The festivities were just too much. It was too soon. She was having a horrible time and was afraid that it showed. She had to leave now before her resolve crumbled and then she completely lost it.

She found Nancy in the ladies room fixing her makeup. Quickly she explained that she had a terrible headache and was turning in early. "Are you sure that's all?" She met Julie's eyes evenly in the mirror.

"I'm just tired. Meet the girls out front at ten."

"Sure." She glided a lip tint across her pouting mouth. "Hope you feel better."

As she walked the lighted path she carefully kept the tears at bay. It wasn't easy as the pain seemed to continuously slash at her heart. Soon there would be nothing left. At least now she was shielded from everyone's watching eyes. The memories were intent on tormenting her. They were everywhere she turned. There was nowhere to run to escape the pain. That, as well as everything else, was everywhere. If only she could forget for a little while.

'I'm dying, Julie.' Those written words replayed in her mind over and over again. Just three words. Only they hadn't been the words she had wanted to hear. Not when he had finally come close to admitting to loving her. Life just could not be that cruel. She didn't want to believe that Scott could have known and not have trusted her with the truth. *'You deserve to find someone who can love you forever. And as much as I'd like to, I just can't do that.'* Scott's letter came to mind in little bits and pieces. The pain

was still there despite the act of covering it up, which she was doing pretty well. *'I'm running out of time.'*

Well, they had both run out of time. All that remained now were just the memories. She had to remember all of the good times that they had spent together. All the times she had snuck out of the house so they could meet for just a few minutes, the times they had been in each other's arms. It had been real. Their feelings had been real. So real, in fact, that it almost seemed as clear as yesterday. If only she could get that time back. Do it all over again. She'd do things much differently this time.

"Hello, Julie." At the sound of her name she came to the present with a start. It was Kevin and he was standing just a few feet away. Where had he come from? "I didn't mean to scare you. I thought you'd seen me."

Julie's heart was still beating furiously. "How was the dance?"

"It was fine." She forced a weak smile as her voice caught. At that moment she knew that he wasn't buying any of it. She could feel the tears stinging her eyelids but she swallowed them with some difficulty.

"Then why did you leave early?" He cocked an eyebrow.

"You weren't even there," she said, then flushed.

"You noticed." This time he smiled. He had gotten her to admit something she hadn't wanted to think about.

"I noticed," she said softly. "Why didn't you go?"

He paused briefly. "I had a few things to do."

"Oh."

"How have you been?"

"Fine," she lied.

"Fine enough to get this mess straightened out." He edged forward. "I've missed you."

She didn't meet his eyes. She couldn't. She wasn't ready for this confrontation. Not yet. "I'm not going to put the pressure on." It was almost as though he had read her mind. "I know you're not ready for that. I'm not that heartless. And I think I'm a pretty patient guy."

She could think of nothing to say. Absolutely nothing at all. Her mind went completely blank. "I'll see you around, Julie," he said and then he walked away.

~ * ~

Instead of going right back to the cabin as she had first planned she somehow ended up down at the lake. The moon was full and hung in the sky like a giant orange night light, holding true to the age old promise of a hot day to follow in its wake. The crickets had already tuned into the night. Although there was a small breeze it was just enough to cause a whisper among the trees.

Julie kicked off her pumps before taking a seat at the edge of the dock. As her feet slipped into the cool waters she gazed up at the millions of stars twinkling overhead. They were utterly breathtaking. It was a beautiful night. A night meant for romance. But not for her. It just wasn't meant to be. It wasn't written in the stars. Maybe it never had been. For once she didn't have all the answers. The little bit that she had thought she had known had somehow slipped away. Like water going down the drain.

She could have stayed there forever just gazing up at the stars. Lost in the only thing that was real enough to touch. Two weeks and Camp Wiskle would be over. She'd be going home again. Her mother would be back at home, where she belonged. Her dad had to be happy about that. Matt and Janet would be wrapped up in their own lives and preparing for their new addition to the family. But Julie had no more hopes. No more dreams of one day walking down a flower-strewn aisle to where she would become Mrs. Scott Rourke. That was all gone. All her dreams had been cut to the quick leaving nothing but hurt in its wake. She was going home to nothing.

As she closed her eyes Scott's image burned her eyelids. She opened them quickly. But this time her eyes burned with unshed tears. She refused to cry. Crying would solve nothing. It was too late and she had to accept that. Whether she liked it or not, whether she accepted it or not, Scott was gone. In her heart she knew that she would love him forever. There wasn't anything that would change that. But he was gone. And there wasn't a damn thing that she or anyone else could do about it.

Fifteen

The following week at camp was the most strenuous one yet. There were the final games that seemed to be another pleasant ending for Camp Wiskle. Julie threw herself into the task of cleaning out the cabin to make it suitable for the next year. Many things that had been lost were suddenly found and returned to their rightful owner. There were cots to be folded and stored in the back of the cabin. Those had been the few cots that hadn't been in use for the season. That task could have waited until the last day but Julie decided to get that done early. There would be plenty else to do on the last day.

Tracey was winterizing her cabin as well. They had wanted to jump in and finish the job by taking down the screens, as the weather was turning cooler at night but Rob had been against that idea. It was a chore that he wanted the guys to tackle within the week.

The days seemed shorter and the nights were longer. At least that's how it felt to Julie. She found it easier to fill her days with activities. But the nights seemed almost endless. There were a few nights when she was lucky if she slept an hour all-told. Unfortunately it showed. There were dark circles beneath her large brown eyes that would not go away.

Late one afternoon Tracey came in during rest hour smiling like the cat that had finally captured the mouse. "It's all set." Her blue eyes were shining. "Tonight we're going out." She hurried on before Julie could protest. "There's this nice little country inn..."

"I don't know." Julie wavered.

"It's too late; I already cleared it with Rob. We both need some time away."

"Why don't you go with Keith? I'm sure..."

"Because this night is for us."

Julie fell silent and Tracey went on. "We'll go out, have a few drinks, and just have fun." She shot Julie a big smile. "And it's on me. What do you say?"

"I can handle things here," Nancy said from where she was sitting on her bunk polishing her nails a flamboyant, jazzy, pink.

"Okay," Julie agreed finally. Maybe all she needed to get back on track was a night out. She was warming up to the idea as it was starting to sound better.

"Great!" Tracey exclaimed. "I'll meet you in the lot around seven. Now I've got to dash." She scowled. "I have Dance in about fifteen minutes." With that said and a quick wave she was already out the door. She probably wanted to get out quickly before Julie had the chance to change her mind.

The rest of the day went rather quickly. They were in the middle of a serious softball game with Keith's campers when the dinner bell sounded. Julie's campers were not ready to give up as they were only behind by just one run, which they were determined to get as they had only gotten up to bat in this last inning. Although Keith gave the go ahead to continue with the game his campers didn't want to do that. "They have to have their turn at bat," he yelled to Johnny who was pitching. "If not, it's a forfeit, and they win." He shrugged. "I'll leave it up to you to decide." He turned towards Julie with a knowing smile. "They won't give up this game," he said knowingly. "Not when they still have a chance to win it."

Right on cue Johnny announced that, of course, they would continue. Julie knew this was going to be tough on the girls but they seemed determined. This win would definitely boost their confidence. Then Ellen struck out after Lorna hit a fly ball. Two outs. Julie was almost holding her breath as Maria stepped up to the plate. Maria, who was a very graceful dancer, but did horribly in sports and hated them with an equal passion. All season she'd struck out. But she had never really tried either. Julie could see that Nancy was already giving up. "Give her a chance." Julie whispered before going out to where Maria stood holding the bat with tears in her eyes. "Remember our motto." She began gently. "We can give it our best shot. Do your best Maria. Don't choke the bat. Easy. Watch the ball. Watch. Concentrate." The tension on the field was mounting. "Swing." Julie said above the shouting and Maria swung. The crack of the bat hitting the ball was almost deafening.

Maria was so excited she forgot to run, which in turn had the girls on their feet and yelling. Then she was off like a shot fired from a cannon. First base, second, third, and finally home base. To everyone's complete and utter astonishment Maria had hit a home run! All they needed now was another run scored and they would win the game.

Carol came up to bat with a fierce determination blazing in her bright blue eyes. The girls were still on their feet shouting. With Carol they knew that they still had a chance. She was involved in many different sports and definitely had that competitive edge. She hit a double and that brought Nancy up to bat. Nancy who was famous for her high flies. Julie was now down to biting her nails. This time it was the silence that was deafening. She was holding the bat with tension in her stance.

"Strike one!" Keith yelled and Nancy shot him a disgusted look. "Strike two!" They couldn't lose the game now. Not when they had worked so hard. The tension was almost stifling.

Johnny pitched and Nancy swung, rather she bunted. It was a complete surprise to everyone, including Johnny who had been expecting another high fly. The ball slipped out of Johnny's grasp as Nancy took off like the wind for first base and Carol sprinted for home plate. They had won the game! Never before had Julie witnessed such team spirit as she did today. It didn't matter that it was their first win all summer. The team spirit was what mattered. They had all worked together for the win. It may have been their first win, but hopefully not their last.

Both teams headed for the dining hall, all in good spirits. That left Julie and Keith to walk behind. "Good game." Keith gave her a big smile.

"It was great." She breathed. "I was getting a little nervous there towards the end."

"I didn't notice a thing." He snickered as they fell into step together. "Haven't seen you around much lately." He acknowledged simply. "How have you been?"

"Fine."

"Settled anything with Kevin yet?"

Talk about straight to the point. "No," she returned softly.

"I hear you and Tracey are having a big night out."

"I guess you can say that."

"You both deserve it," he said as they reached the dining hall. "Sometimes you have to get away. Just forget everything and have a good time."

Julie gave him a small smile as they got in line for dinner. Maybe he was right. Dinner consisted of pot luck, which when simply put were left-over's. It was something that didn't look appetizing the first time around, never mind the second time. All Julie could get down was a buttered roll and a cup of coffee. She wasn't hungry but needed something solid in her stomach.

Kevin was seated at the other table, which was just fine with her. He was giving her the space she needed. Although there were times when she missed his company terribly she was not ready to admit that. So she sat with Tracey, Keith, Christine, Ann, and Rob. There was a lot of laughing and joking which made it generally a light atmosphere as they were truly a colorful bunch.

As the clock was nearing seven Julie began dressing for her big night out. The girls were also getting ready to go see a movie that was scheduled to be shown in the dance hall. Keith and Rob were setting up the projector for the big event. Tracey breezed into the cabin just as the girls were taking their leave. "Have fun," she called after them before facing Julie. "You look nice."

"Thanks." For the evening Julie had chosen a black mini skirt with a hot pink blouse. Unfortunately, which she soon had come to realize, had been one of Scott's favorite colors.

"I didn't think tonight would ever get here." Tracey's bright blue eyes shone with excitement. "We should have done this a long time ago. Are you almost ready?"

"Just about." She put the finishing touches to her makeup. "I'm ready."

"You look great."

"And so do you." She truly admired Tracey's blue skirt set. "It goes great with your eyes."

"Thanks. Now let's get out of here."

Tracey drove her little efficient Chevy on the lonely country road. The road seemed as though it could go on for miles and when they entered the nearest small town Julie could hardly believe her eyes. This wasn't what she had expected. It could hardly even be considered a town. It looked to be about four city blocks long. "This is it?" she asked as Tracey parked the car.

"This is it. Small, isn't it? But it's cute." She cut the motor and turned towards Julie with a grin. "We can go to a movie if you'd rather."

"No."

"This pub is called The Firefly. Wait until you see the inside."

After carefully locking up the car they ventured inside the dimly lit pub. Tracey had been right. The Firefly was something you had to see. It was true to its name. There were little blinking bulbs dangling from the ceiling that actually resembled flitting fireflies. It was definitely a festive place. There was plenty of food, liquor, and dancing. There was even a small light show playing on a full dance floor. After finding a small booth, out of the way, they ordered their drinks. Tracey ordered a diet soda and Julie a double scotch. Although Tracey shot her a look she said nothing.

They talked about camp in general but didn't touch on any major topics, which was just fine with Julie. After all, this was their night to get away from everything. After ordering a small pizza they ordered another round of drinks. The liquor seemed to be going straight to her head. Although she considered it a diversion from reality she drew the line after that as she was feeling just a little bit fuzzy.

They returned to camp well after two and although Tracey insisted on walking with Julie the rest of the way to her cabin Julie assured her that she was fine. She was only a little tipsy and wouldn't have a problem getting back alone. She'd be all right and a few minutes later was well on her way. Mentally she noted that a few bulbs were out along the lighted path. A few more than that as she reached the bend. That had to be one of the reasons that she had tripped over the roots of a big tree and landed flat on her face. That warranted a small giggle. Now to get up she thought as she rolled onto her back. The sky was dark. There weren't many stars to light the way she thought as she gazed upward. She was comfortable right there. Although the grass was a bit damp where she lay she didn't seem to mind. That was probably due to the liquor she had consumed. This was the first time in a long time that she felt somewhat warm on the inside.

After she had remained where she had fallen for a few minutes a voice came out of the darkness. "What are you doing?"

"Who's there?" Her voice caught as she slowly sat up.

"It's me." Kevin stepped out of the shadows.

"Hi, Kevin." She giggled softly as she struggled to her feet. "I tripped over that tree over there." She bit her lip as she met his eyes. "But I'm fine, as you can see."

Kevin snickered. "Sure you are." He took a hold of her arm which had her swaying slightly towards him. "Take it easy."

Julie smiled up at him. "You're drunk." He sounded surprised and acted as though she weren't human like everyone else.

"Just a little bit," she confessed with wide brown eyes.

"What did you have?"

"I had..." She held onto his arm for support. "Just a few drinks." She finally got out after a soft hiccup.

"Of what?"

"Scotch," she stated. "I only drink the best."

He shook his head. "And they served you?"

"Why not?" She met his eyes evenly.

"We won't get into that right now."

"Oh Kevin." She smiled up at him. "Since when are you so high and mighty?"

"Since I know better."

Their eyes collided and Julie's heart began to race wildly. "Do you?" She breathed, her heart shining within her eyes.

"Yeah." He was going to kiss her. Even through the haze she knew it. And this time she was going to be ready. As his lips touched hers lightly she wound her arms around his neck pulling him closer. Before she realized anything else Kevin was easing her back down onto a soft bed of moss kissing her all the time. She would not fight the feelings this time she vowed. She wanted this.

She wanted him as much as he wanted her. Why fight what was inevitable? The time was right and she was ready.

As Kevin's body covered her lightly his lips trailed sweet kisses all over her face. Over and over he kissed her until she was breathless and quivering beneath him. The kisses began gently but soon turned to an urgency and Julie arched her back as passion assailed her in waves. Their hearts beat as one as she clung to him. At that moment nothing existed but what she felt for Kevin. She wanted him, needed him, as she had never needed anyone before.

Then, as suddenly as it had begun, it was over. "We can't do this." It was Kevin who pulled away and scrambled to his feet. "This isn't right."

Julie remained as he had left her. This new rejection was like a slap in the face. "You'll thank me in the morning." He held out a hand to help her up but she turned away from him. "Let me help you..."

"Go away." Her voice broke.

"I can't leave you here, Julie..."

"Just go away." She choked out as she slowly gained her feet.

"But..."

"I'm fine. I can get back to my cabin just fine..." Carefully she avoided his eyes. "Good night, Kevin."

"Don't walk away like this." He called after her but she kept on going. "Julie." He caught up to her. "I'm sorry, please don't walk away mad."

"I'm not mad." She kept her back to him. "I just thought... I thought..." What! Her mind was screaming at her. What did she think?

"I didn't mean to hurt you."

"You didn't," she lied.

"This isn't like you. It's the liquor." He seemed to be selecting his words carefully, but not carefully enough. "If anything were to happen tonight you'd hate me for it in the morning. Our relationship would be shot to hell." He gently rested his hands upon her shoulders. "It's not you," he said close to her ear. "I want you real bad." He groaned. "You know that."

"Then what?" She whirled around angrily. "Did you finally come to your senses?" The tears came then. "Leave me alone, Kevin." With that she stormed off into the night.

Thank goodness Kevin didn't come after her. She didn't know what she'd say if he had. Had Nancy been right about him all along? Had he been looking for a conquest? All these questions raced through her mind as she made her way back to the cabin. Had he been baiting her all along only to turn her down when she came to him willingly? None of this made any sense at all. Couldn't he see how much he had hurt her? Her pride was now torn to shreds and her heart slashed to ribbons. Kevin had just added the final topping to the cake.

The cabin was in total darkness as the girls had forgotten to turn on the night light. But that was quite all right. At least no one would see her like this. For just a moment she was safe from everyone's prying eyes. She was safe from everyone except herself.

After pulling on a nightshirt she climbed into her bunk. As she pulled the blankets to her throat she squeezed her eyes closed against all the pain and humiliation. Never again would something like this happen to her. Nothing or no one could hurt her now. She would not allow it. She didn't need Kevin. She didn't need anyone.

Only after she had reached that realization did she fall asleep. And that was only out of sheer exhaustion.

Sixteen

Julie awoke to the early morning sounds of a large thunderstorm approaching. Although the rain had yet to begin the sky looked like it might open up at any time. In another minute Rob's voice would come over the loud speaker with the morning agenda. The girls were already up and getting ready for the day, which seemed to hold a little promise for anything. It took most of Julie's will power just to get out of bed. "You look terrible." Nancy gave her a scowl. "I hope it was worth it." She then scurried off in the direction of the bathroom.

Worth it! There was nothing that could be worth this. Although she wasn't sure if *it,* was the booze or the rejection that had followed, one thing she did know for sure was the fact that she would not let Kevin see how much his rejection had hurt her. That would prove to be an even greater mistake. One rejection was enough.

"Good morning." It was seven a.m. and right on cue Rob's voice filtered through the intercom. "Please be advised that all outdoor activities will be cancelled for the day. Instead, everyone will be teamed up for a volleyball tournament after breakfast in the dance hall. All teams have already been chosen and will be posted in the dance hall. It is mandatory for everyone to participate and that means counselors too." He laughed lightly. "Good luck everyone."

"Volleyball," Lorna snorted with contempt. "Who wants to play volleyball? I can see this now."

How bad could it be Julie wondered? It was better than having a tennis tournament. Maybe it would even prove to be fun. Her main goal for today was to stay away from Kevin. It sounded manageable enough at this point in time.

"Julie," Nancy called from across the room. "You're on clean up beginning next week."

"Okay." She pulled a brush through her hair absently. "And I thought they had forgotten about me."

"No such luck." Nancy laughed as she powdered her nose thoughtfully. Usually the counselors are last on the list." She made her way over after clicking her compact closed. "Are you feeling okay?" Her gaze narrowed. "You don't look too good."

Julie forced a smile that didn't reach her eyes. "I'm okay." Just one more week to go and then she would be going home, never to see Camp Wiskle again. That fact in itself was a comforting thought. There would be many things to occupy her time. Her Mom would be at home by the time she got back. But that was something she'd rather not think about yet. However, amidst all of the grief she was feeling now she was looking forward to it. They would be a family again. And that had been something that she had missed.

The breakfast bell sounded and Julie wasn't even dressed. "Girls," Tracey acknowledged with a small smile as she came inside. "Go on to breakfast. We'll meet you there. Stay together please."

She called as they were already out the door. "I brought you a little fixer upper." In her hand she held that famous red liquid. "I thought you might need this."

Julie didn't meet her eyes. "Thanks. I just have to get dressed." She picked up her jeans and headed for the bathroom.

"Why don't you drink this first?" She held out the glass and Julie took it. "We still have a few minutes."

In a few swallows she had the drink down. "Thanks. It hit the spot," she choked out.

"I bumped into Kevin this morning." Tracey plopped down on Julie's unmade bed. "He's on mail call." She swung her legs back and forth while staring at the floor. "He told me what happened last night."

"Nothing happened," Julie got out in one breath.

"He told me that too." She sighed wearily. "He thinks that you hate him," she said simply. "Which I told him was untrue."

"Don't be too sure." She muttered more to herself than to Tracey.

"He's worried about you. And so am I." She paused. "I didn't think about it until this morning." Again she hesitated. "You were always very much against drinking. And I understood that, especially because of your mother's drinking problem. I still understand that." She met Julie's eyes evenly. "But now I think that you're drinking to forget. And you know that it isn't the way to..."

"I had a few drinks last night just to unwind. I don't do it every day."

"Don't get defensive. I'm worried about you, that's all." She tapped her foot on the wooden floor lightly.

"Can we change the subject?" Julie could feel the tension thickening in the room.

"Sure." She shrugged carelessly then blurted out. "Keith asked me to marry him."

That statement surely stopped Julie in her tracks. What did you say?" She met Tracey's eyes evenly.

"Keith asked me to marry him."

"I heard that part." Julie rolled her eyes. "What I want to know is your answer to that question."

"I said," she paused momentarily. "Yes."

"I'm so happy for you." Julie's smile faltered. She knew she was only feeling false cheer. But Tracey was so high up on cloud nine that if Julie had been bawling her eyes out she probably wouldn't have noticed. At this point it was better than the third degree she had been receiving. "When's the big day?"

Tracey gained her feet her blue eyes shining happily. "A year or two. We're not in a hurry. We still have a few things to work out."

"That's good, Trace. I'm happy for you both. Now," she started for the bathroom once again with her clothes in hand. "I'd better get moving." At that moment she'd do almost anything to get out of there.

~ * ~

The cafeteria was definitely nosier than usual. At least that was how it seemed to Julie. After following Tracey through the short line they went to their usual table. As she looked around the room nonchalantly she was happy to discover that Kevin was nowhere to be found. She didn't think she could handle seeing him this soon. In fact, she didn't want to see him at all.

But she also knew better, as that was wishful thinking. Sooner or later he would approach her. And that she knew was an inevitable fact.

Only Keith, Rob, Christine and Ann were seated at their table. Everyone seemed to be in a cheerful mood despite the dreary weather. As Julie sat beside Tracey, Mike joined them. "Everything is set up at the hall." He took the seat across from her.

"Good." Rob sipped his coffee thoughtfully. "That should keep everyone busy through most of the day."

As Julie picked at her breakfast absently he went on. "I don't think the campers enjoyed arts and crafts this year."

"We only made key chains. Last year we had leather goods. The girls made hot plates and jewelry," Tracey supplied. "This year they would rather go swimming and who wouldn't?" she asked. "How is the weather supposed to be tomorrow?"

"So far it's supposed to be partly sunny." Rob shrugged carelessly. "But then again, your guess is as good as mine."

"About those screens, Rob," Tracey went off in another direction.

"I'll get the guys on it today."

"Good. It's starting to get colder at night. Last night I was freezing."

"How is it in your cabin?" Rob directed at Julie.

"It's fine." Julie took a few sips from her orange juice carefully not meeting his eyes.

"Did you ladies overdue it just a little last night?" Keith asked with a smile. "A few drinks too many perhaps?"

"That's right; you went out on the town." Rob cocked an eyebrow with a grin. "How did it go?"

"It was fine," Came Julie's simple reply. And soon after that the conversation fizzled out completely. When breakfast came to an end there was only enough time to run back to the cabin for sneakers before they were to report to the dance hall. Since the girls were wearing their sneakers Julie would run back to secure the windows against the rain that had just begun. Of course she got completely soaked in the process. But it was good that she had come back as someone had left the window opened in the bathroom and there was a large puddle in the middle of the floor. As she struggled to get the window closed she heard a small knock at the cabin door. "Come in," she called out as she still struggled with the window.

"I have your mail." It was Jake.

"Thanks." She came into the room wiping her hands on a damp towel. Didn't Tracey say that Kevin had been on mail call this morning? He was probably avoiding her the same way she was avoiding him. That was all right with her. Two could play that game she supposed.

"There's quite a few." He handed her a bundle.

"I guess that's because we're pretty popular." Absently she leafed through the pile. "Nancy, Nancy, Nancy, Ellen, Lorna, Lorna, Nancy," She mumbled as she continued sorting. "Nancy, Carol, and Julie. A letter for me. Now that's a surprise." She placed the pile of letters, minus her own, on the night table.

"Don't you have to report for the big tournament?"

"Yeah." She ripped open the envelope containing her letter. "I had to come back and close the windows." It was just a letter from her brother. It was nothing of any major importance. It went on to say how Janet was beginning to show. How excited they both were. How Marie had come home as though nothing had ever happened. How she and Jackson were so happy together. Not a word about Scott. Nothing. Then again, it may be just as well. Wait. There was something after all. The very last paragraph. 'I have a few things that belonged to Scott. Nothing big. I'll give them to you when you get home. Love Matt.'

"Earth to Julie," Jake called gently.

"What?" She returned the letter to its envelope before meeting his blue eyes.

"Come on. It's tournament time."

~ * ~

The dance hall was packed. Julie didn't know how Rob was going to organize any kind of tournament with so many people. Then she realized what the confusion was all about. Everyone was pushing towards the front of the room so they could read the sheet that listed all of the names.

A few minutes later a sharp whistle permeated the air. "Can I have your attention please?" Rob sounded agitated. "Since we can't get any cooperation I will read the teams aloud." He paused for a moment as the dance hall quieted down considerably. "There will be five teams. They are as follows…"

Julie wasn't really paying attention. After all, she wasn't going to play. Maybe she'd supervise the team. That sounded more her pace this morning. On and on Rob went as the list seemed to be endless. There had to be at least eight or nine people per team. "…The red team players are Lorna, Belinda, Marc, Kevin, Ellen, Julie, and…" Julie didn't hear the rest of it. Of all the teams, she would have to end up on the same team with Kevin. What did she do to deserve such a fate? Today would be another day to remember.

It took most of the morning just to get the teams organized. There were to be two games played simultaneously. The next team in line would then play the winner, and so on and so forth. The winners would then be chosen by the highest number of games won. It sounded logical enough. The first two games were scheduled immediately following lunch. They had plenty of time to warm up if they chose.

By lunchtime Julie was still trying to come up with a good excuse to get out of playing in this tournament but so far no luck. All the teams were getting together before lunch and because Julie was the only counselor on the team that automatically made her team captain, which in turn, made Kevin co-captain. This day was just getting better and better as the day moved by.

Kevin, on the other hand, seemed cool and indifferent. He acted as though last night had never happened, while on the inside, Julie had been shaken right to her core. She refused to let it show. She'd never admit how much he had gotten to her. Not now. Not ever. All she had to do now was get through this last week. Then she'd never have to see Kevin ever again. She'd close that book as though it had never been opened. "Aren't you going to give us your famous speech?" It was Lorna who had presented that question.

"Sure." Julie forced a quick smile as her team gathered around. "It's important to remember that this is only a game. All I ask is that everyone do their best. If we win that would be great and if we don't..." She shrugged her shoulders. "Then we will lose with dignity. Do your best and have fun." She gave them a big smile. "I'll meet you all back here after lunch." And with a wave of her hand she dismissed her team for lunch.

"Julie," Kevin called out to her just as she was about to walk away. "Can I talk to you a minute?"

"Yes." She faced him slowly while forcing a smile.

"I wanted to talk to you about last night..."

"Forget it." She waved a hand aside airily. "I can hardly remember it at all."

"But..."

"It's okay, Kevin." She almost choked. It's okay Kevin. She sounded like an idiot.

"Is it?" His blue-green eyes met hers evenly. "Are you all right?"

No! She wanted to scream. *I'm not all right damnit! You took my heart and stepped all over it. When I thought that I could finally trust someone else you turned me away.* She could hardly look him in the face. And he knew it. She could deny it all she wanted but Kevin knew the truth. "I'm perfectly fine, Kevin." She was lying through her teeth. "I had a little too much to drink last night and got carried away. You were so right when you said I'd thank you in the morning." Her heart hammered in her chest.

"I just thought," he paused, eyes intense. "I thought that maybe you needed more time to get over your feelings for Scott. I don't know."

She'd never get over her feelings for Scott. Didn't anyone understand that? She had given up trying to get over him. It was impossible. All she had left were memories. But at least she had something. Not many people had even that.

"I never intended to hurt you Julie," he continued on a softer note. "And I'm sorry if I did." He was saying that they never stood a chance. He was saying that he didn't care like he had before. Or maybe he had never cared at all. Although the words weren't coming out that way Julie could read between the lines.

"It would never have worked, Kevin." Her voice caught and she hoped he hadn't noticed. "And I don't think I'll ever get over Scott." With that she walked away with her dignity intact.

~ * ~

Before Julie had realized it, the day was over. Unfortunately the rain was not. However, the weather forecast sounded rather promising for tomorrow. They would have to wait and see.

There was a meeting scheduled following lights out. It was to be one of, if not, the last, of the season. Although it was something Julie would have liked to miss, she knew she had to be in attendance. Nancy had already taken over much of the routine which had been a relief to Julie who seemed to be tired all the time.

By ten o'clock she was ready to venture outside. Only this time she was prepared, wearing her yellow slicker with matching rain hat. She would meet Tracey at her cabin and they'd continue on from there. After giving Nancy her usual pep talk she started on her way.

The rain was slowing to a steady drizzle. The bulbs that had burned out on the lighted path had been replaced. Not that Julie really cared about that. Ever since the light had burned out of her heart nothing mattered. She was walking around in a haze most of the time now. It was a wonder she had noticed anything at all. Then again, she had. Only it had been too late and had been cruelly snatched from her grasp. When would she learn that love was nothing more than another word, a simple little word, which meant absolutely nothing?

Seventeen

At last Julie was at home again. It seemed as though she had left a lifetime ago. So much had changed over the summer she could hardly believe it. Even she had changed.

Marie had met her at the door upon her arrival. Tears had filled their eyes as they had embraced. It had truly been a joyous reunion. Even Jackson looked a little misty. He too had hugged her close.

However, Julie found that she wasn't quite ready to let go of Camp Wiskle so completely. Not yet. The last memory she could recall vividly was saying goodbye to Kevin. And what an experience that had been.

~ * ~

"That's the last of it." Keith placed Julie's suitcases beside Tracey's in the trunk. "Call me as soon as you get home." He took Tracey into his arms while Julie walked away. They needed a little privacy. As she leaned against the car she spotted Kevin out

of the corner of her eye. They had hardly spoken a civil word since that awkward moment on the volleyball court. Now what? Was he going to hurt her one last time before they said goodbye?

"Hi." He gave her a weak smile. "I couldn't leave without saying goodbye." He rocked back on his heels his blue-green eyes wide. Almost the very same stance as the day she had met him. Only this time they were saying goodbye. "I'm going to miss you." If only she could believe that. "I'd like to call you sometime if that's okay?" he added quickly.

"Why?" She couldn't help but ask. After all, he hadn't exactly gone out of his way to see her. Not like before.

"I'm sorry, Julie." He sighed. "I don't know what to say. It wasn't the right time. You were hurting. Getting over Scott. I didn't want to get in the way of that."

Just then Tracey got in behind the wheel and it was time to go. "Maybe it just wasn't meant to be." She joined Tracey in the car. "Goodbye, Kevin."

"Can I call you?" he shouted over the motor of Tracey's car. "Please?"

What should she say? Yes? No? She wasn't sure. So instead she said absolutely nothing at all. "Are you sure you want to do that?" Tracey questioned lightly.

"It's for the best." Not that she believed that. Not for a minute.

~ * ~

Julie came back to the present with a start. That had been almost a week ago. If Kevin had really wanted to talk to her he would have called. It was that simple. Marie was busy downstairs preparing dinner. They were having a family get together. Matt and Janet were to join them. All in all everything seemed to be coming together. Marie hadn't had a drink since Julie had returned. At least, not that Julie knew of. And she certainly looked much better. Before she had looked older and was tired most of the time. Now she seemed younger at heart and smiled a lot. It felt good to be a part of a normal family once again.

At five thirty Julie went downstairs to set the table, as she had done since she'd turned twelve years old. She and Marie chatted about camp in general and the many activities she had participated in. "Sounds like you enjoyed yourself," Marie said as she placed the roast on the dining-room table.

"It was fun," she admitted. "And I got paid for it."

"You can't beat that." Marie laughed. "Were you interested in doing it again?"

Julie didn't have enough time to answer as Matt and Janet were coming in the back door. Matt had been right in one respect, Janet was certainly beginning to show. Never before had Julie remembered seeing them so happy and so much in love.

Dinner ran smoothly, unlike so many dinners which had come before. Afterwards Jackson and Marie were going for a drive while Matt and Janet were meeting some friends for dessert. Julie was going to sit home and wait for Tracey to come over. She had just received her engagement ring the day before and couldn't wait to show it off.

"Leave the dishes, Mom," Julie said as they cleared the table together. "I'll load the dishwasher before Tracey gets here."

"Thank you, Hon. We won't be late." She kissed Julie's cheek.

Five minutes later they were all heading out the door. However, Matt remained behind. "We didn't have a chance to talk all night." He gave her a small smile. "I have something for you." He withdrew a small box from his jacket and handed it to her. "It was Scott's. I thought he would like for you to have it."

Julie opened the box and peered inside. There nestled on the cotton lining was Scott's college ring on a thick silver chain. "There's an inscription inside the ring."

Her heart almost fell at her feet as she read the tiny fancy writing. It was simple and so sweet and it meant the world to her. All it read was: 'Julie. Love Scott'. Tears filled her eyes as words failed her. "I have a few other things at home. I haven't had a chance to go through the whole box yet."

Julie nodded as the words still would not come. "It's been hectic since the funeral."

"You better go. Janet's waiting," she finally got out breathlessly. But she still didn't look up. She did not want to see the mirror of her own pain reflecting in his eyes, as it was still quite fresh.

"Take care," he said as he headed out the door to where his wife was patiently waiting.

And a few minutes later Julie was alone. The only way to hold onto her sanity was by being busy. With that thought in mind she headed straight for the kitchen and a pile of dirty dishes. She worked diligently for a good hour. Instead of loading the dishwasher she washed the dishes by hand. Next, she scrubbed the oven range. There were so many things that could be done. Little things, such as straightening up the pantry. She had always wanted to do it but never had the time. Tonight she'd make the time. All the canned goods she placed on the bottom shelf. That included all vegetables, fruits, and gravies. Next, she organized all the boxed items according to size. Those had ranged from cereal to rice. After placing the last box on the shelf the doorbell sounded. It had to be Tracey. And of course, it was. But she wasn't alone. She had Keith with her. The happy couple together again. The only thing missing were their smiles. "Hi." She moved aside to let them enter.

They walked into the living room but did not take a seat. It seemed they came on some mission of great importance. Maybe Kevin had sent them. Now that was wishful thinking. "What's going on?" Julie decided to come straight to the point.

"Why don't you sit down?" Keith said gently.

Whenever someone asked you to take a seat you knew it was something major. "What?" She perched on the arm of a chair as her heart jumped wildly in her chest.

"Jake called me tonight," Keith began on a light note. "It seems that Kevin was in a car accident."

"Is he all right?" she choked out, brown eyes wide.

"He was banged up pretty bad."

"Oh God." Julie jumped up and began to pace the living room. "He's going to be all right though, right?"

"We came to take you to the hospital," Keith went on.

"But only if you want to go," Tracey supplied.

"Of course." Julie grabbed a light jacket and her purse from the hall closet. "I should leave a note for my parents." She yanked open the desk drawer which gave way easily sending all of its contents spilling all over the floor. "Damn..."

"I'll leave the note." Tracey dropped to her knees and began to pick up what had fallen. "Take her out to the car." She shot Keith a look. "I'll be right out."

Keith took her arm and led her outside into the damp night air. Not that Julie could feel it because she could not. In fact, all she felt was numb. The ride to the hospital was a complete blur. Her heart felt as though it were being torn in two while her head was screaming all kinds of accusations at her. She would not lose Kevin the way she had lost Scott. That couldn't happen. She wouldn't let it.

Julie followed after Keith and Tracey as though walking in a daze. They met Jake in the waiting room. "Thanks for coming, Guys." He looked like hell. His blue eyes were bloodshot and glassy. "My parents are in with him now." He took Julie's hand. "I know that he'll be especially happy to see you."

Julie squeezed his hand as there was nothing she could think of to say. "Thank you," Jake said again and they took their seats in the waiting room. Ten long minutes later two people plus a doctor came out of the room. Immediately Jake went to them. They talked for a little while before the doctor took his leave. Then Jake came over with his parents. "Mom and Dad," Jake directed toward his parents. "These are some friends from camp. Tracey, Keith, and Julie." He introduced them one by one.

"It's nice to meet you." Tracey stepped forward. "How is Kevin doing?"

"He's doing as well as can be expected." It was Jake's mother who spoke. "With all the medication he's been in and out." Her blue-green eyes were still moist as it was apparent she had been crying. It wasn't a mystery where Kevin had gotten those magnificent eyes from.

"You can each go in for five minutes." Jake's father added. "Because he's scheduled for surgery shortly."

"Surgery." Julie's eyes were wide as her breath caught.

"They have a reason to believe there may be some internal bleeding." Jake's father answered evenly. "Go see him." He dropped hurt blue eyes.

"We don't want to exhaust him." Tracey began lightly. "We'll wait for you in the waiting room." She gave Julie a small smile.

"Come on." Jake took her arm and began to lead her down the hall. "Before we go in I think you should know something." He stopped short in front of the door. "I know all the hell you've been through this summer." He met her eyes evenly. "And I can't even begin to identify with the way you feel. But Kevin loves you, Julie. I know he does. I've seen it at camp and I've seen it when we came home. He wanted to call you. But all he kept saying was how it just was not the right time." Jake paused his blue eyes blinking back tears. "But when is the right time before you run out of time?"

Julie bit her lip. She wished she had the answer to Jake's question. Really, she did, but she didn't. Deep inside, however, she did know the truth of the matter. Somewhere along the line she had lost sight of what was real. She had lost sight of love. Instead of feeling anything but anguish she had given up. She didn't want to chance the fact that she might get hurt again. Especially not the way that Scott had hurt her. So, instead of allowing herself to feel anything for Kevin, she had locked herself away, while at the same time she shut everyone else out.

All was quiet as the hospital door swung open noiselessly. In a bed, less than five feet away, Kevin lay. From a distance he appeared to be sleeping. He was so still. As they ventured inside the small room he turned his head towards them and Julie's heart constricted in her chest. She was beside the bed instantly, not even realizing how her legs had gotten her that far without buckling.

"Hi, Kev," she got out breathlessly, while at the same time, forcing a watery smile.

"Hi." His blue-green eyes widened in surprise. "I'm happy to see you." His voice was so low that Julie had to strain her ears to hear him. "Do I look okay?" He directed at his brother.

"You look fine, Kev." Jake stood at the foot of the bed while Julie remained at Kevin's bed side.

"I missed you." His blue-green eyes were soft.

"I missed you too." She placed a trembling hand to his swollen cheek and he winced. "I'm sorry." She withdrew her hand quickly.

"Why did you come?" Although the question was direct, it was serious as well. Julie didn't know what to say. "Were you afraid for me?"

Tears pooled in her eyes. "I had to come," she whispered.

"I'm not Scott," he stated simply.

"I'll just step outside," Jake said before leaving them alone.

"I know that." She held onto the iron bars on the side rail of the bed so tightly her knuckles turned white.

"Good." He tried to shift his position slightly and called out in discomfort. "Damn," he cursed viciously.

"Are you all right? Maybe I should get a doctor or…"

"I'm fine." He took a few deep breaths. "And I didn't mean to throw Scott up in your face like that."

Tears slid down Julie's cheeks. She knew he hadn't meant to hurt her. It seemed all they did was hurt each other.

"Don't cry, Julie. I'm going to be fine."

"I know." She swiped at her eyes.

"Then stop with the water works." He gave her the faintest of smiles. "Women."

"Julie." Jake poked his head in the door. "The doctors' are scrubbing up…"

"I have to go now." Julie stood beside the bed looking down at him. "But I'll see you after…" The rest of the words got caught in her throat.

"Is that a promise?" His eyes widened a little.

"Yes." She patted his hand gently before turning away. Something told her that this was going to be one of the longest nights of her life. Walking away from Kevin was one of the hardest things she had ever had to do. "Kevin." She paused at the door keeping her back to him. "Kev." She called out once more.

"Yeah." His voice sounded so far-away.

I love you. The words were right there. All she had to do was open her mouth and say them. It was that simple. "I'll see you later," she said as she fled from the room.

~ * ~

After two hours of pacing the waiting room floor Jake came over to her. "He's going to make it just fine." Only minutes before had Jake convinced his parents that it would be all right if they went down to the cafeteria to get something to eat. He had assured them that he'd call them if the doctor came out before they returned. "Maybe you should call your parents."

"I took care of that already," Tracey said from where she was seated beside Keith while glancing through a magazine.

"Why don't you sit down?" Jake took her arm but she shrugged him off. "Before you fall down."

"I'm fine," she snapped. This waiting was beginning to get to her already fraying nerves.

"Jake's right," Keith pointed out. "By the time he comes out of surgery you're not going to be good for anything, or anyone."

As though it had been her own idea Julie perched herself at the edge of a chair. She knew she was in for a long wait and this was only the beginning.

Eighteen

Kevin's surgery had taken nearly five hours. It had taken almost all of Julie's strength not to scream. Although it had been against Jake's better judgment, Julie decided to wait it out. After all, she had promised Kevin she would be there when he came out. And she wasn't going to break that promise.

The night seemed to stretch out unmercifully. The hospital was quiet with an occasional call from the different nursing stations. They had been moved out of the emergency department and placed in another waiting room as the emergency room was filling up with the usual broken bones and mishaps. At least in the family waiting room they had some peace and quiet. The small room was equipped with a small television and on a side table a telephone. There were four regular straight backed chairs as well as two lounge chairs that were almost as large as a bed when in the reclining position.

Tracey and Keith had left when the doctor had told them Kevin was now in the recovery room and doing just fine. But Julie decided to remain behind and see that for herself. She then had phoned her parents and spoke with her Dad, who had been half asleep. At first she thought he'd demand that she'd come home. When he didn't she said she'd talk to him later then hung up.

"Let's go get something to eat." Jake was standing in front of her. "We'll only be gone a few minutes."

Julie followed him saying nothing. At that point she didn't have the strength to argue with him. The cafeteria was nearly empty. There were only a few nurses sitting together taking their coffee breaks. Jake took a tray, placed it on the iron rail, and started down the line. On the tray he dumped a few assorted cakes, two cartons of milk, a few bags of chips, and two cups of Jell-O. While he paid the cashier, an elderly woman, Julie slid into a booth. "I'm glad you came." Jake said as he took a seat opposite her. "I know Kevin is too." He placed a carton of milk with a Danish before her. "It's been one hell of a summer."

Julie agreed. "What happened?" She decided to get right to the point. "How did the accident happen?"

"They hit a tree." He bit into his own Danish. "Kevin hadn't been driving but he wasn't wearing his seat belt either."

The fact that he hadn't been driving really didn't come as any great surprise. Was that the way things happened? Did the innocent always have to suffer? "Who was driving?"

Jake sipped his milk. "Some girl."

Julie felt as though she had been winded, kicked in the stomach. Would she ever learn? What had led her to believe that Kevin was any different? "His ex-girlfriend," Jake added, as though he had to elaborate.

"Oh." She took a sip of her milk not meeting Jake's eyes.

"It's been over a long time, Julie."

If it had been over, as Jake was claiming, then Kevin had no business being out with her in the first place. But was anything ever really over? Wasn't she having a hard enough time dealing with Scott's death? "He has some pretty intense feelings for you," Jake continued carefully. "He just thought you needed more time."

Julie sat silent and Jake continued. "He knew you'd been through a lot. He had seen what Scott's death had done to you. He was going to call you..."

"Don't make excuses, Jake," she began lightly. "Kevin is free to see whoever he wants." She paused. "It's okay."

"You love him, Julie." It was a statement. A statement which brought Julie's eyes up quickly. "And he loves you too. I think he was cutting all ties with Lorrie." He took a long sip of milk his eyes intent on hers. "She isn't the type that likes to let go."

"Why isn't she here tonight?"

"She was here," he said. "She left before you came." He snickered and Julie was taken aback. "When they first brought Kevin in he was out of it. He kept calling her by your name. I don't think she liked that very much."

Even Julie had to smile at that. So, he had really been thinking about her. The question remaining now was what she going to do about it. As the minutes continued to tick slowly by Jake polished off a bag of potato chips while watching her intently. "Are you coming back to Camp Wiskle next year?" He changed the subject entirely. "And will it be legal this time?" He shot her a knowing smile.

"What do you mean legal?"

"You know what I mean," he said simply. "It wasn't exactly common knowledge." He waved a hand aside. "But I know my brother and he usually knows his place. And this time he wasn't budging an inch." He shrugged. "Kevin's only headstrong when he knows he's right."

Julie didn't know what to say so instead she sipped her milk.

"You're not going to deny it?" His blue eyes were wide.

"No," she returned, matter-of-fact. "I needed a job. Actually I needed to get away for a while. Tracey came up with the idea so..." She smiled. "We pulled it off."

"How old are you anyway?"

"Seventeen."

He nodded knowingly. "I should have figured as much." He leaned back in the booth smiling. "So how did Kevin find out?"

"I don't really know how he found out. I think he was eavesdropping."

Jake cracked up laughing. "You have to admit it's good. Blackmail at Camp Wiskle. News at eleven. I love it." He grinned. "I can't believe that no one else caught on."

"I'm glad it's over." She rested her chin in her hand, her brown eyes wide. "While we're on the subject of truth here, what happened between you and Nancy?"

Jake met her eyes evenly. "The truth?"

"Yes, the truth." She smiled.

"I don't want to call it a fling. I guess that's kind of cheap."

"Did you..."

"I know that was the talk around camp," he said simply. "And it's what Nancy wanted everyone to believe." He paused. "She didn't want Kevin. She just didn't want for you to have him. If that makes any sense." He waved a careless hand aside. "I don't get it."

"What about the skinny dipping part of it?"

Jake threw his head back and laughed. "You wouldn't believe me if I told you."

"Try me."

Jake took a deep breath and let it out slowly. "It was hot on that night we went swimming. And we were not skinny dipping. I had on a pair of shorts and Nancy had on a bikini. The bottom part anyway."

Julie gasped. "She lost the top in the water. And that's the truth. We spent a good half an hour looking for the damn thing. Rob and Christine just happened to be walking by and you guessed it. Rob knew the truth of the matter. Especially considering Nancy had no problem getting out of the water even without her top." Jake laughed lightly. "That girl would do anything for attention. It's amazing." He shook his head sadly. "And the rumors are even worse. Once she gets her nails into you there's no letting up." He met Julie's eyes. "She's hurt a lot of people. It's amazing that she has any friends at all."

"I can't help but feel bad for somebody like that."

Jake shrugged. "You're a special person, Julie. My brother's a lucky guy."

Julie stifled a yawn. "Let's go see Kevin. Then I can get you home."

~ * ~

It took almost another hour before Kevin was out of the recovery room and settled comfortably in his own room. By this time Julie's nerves were almost, if not, completely shot. His parents were getting ready to leave as they had already spent some time with him in the recovery room. "I doubt they're going to let you see him tonight," his father said. "But I'm sure if you come back in the morning..."

"In the morning..." She repeated absently.

"Come on." Jake grabbed her arm. "I'll see that she gets home safely, Dad. I'll see you both later." He blew his mother a kiss and steered Julie down the hallway.

"What are you doing?" She pulled away from him. "I'm not leaving until I see Kevin."

"That's where we're going,." he whispered, leading the way.

Thank goodness it was a small hospital. They made it to the third floor without incident as everything was quiet. It didn't take long for them to locate Kevin's room. And once they did, quietly they crept inside. While Julie remained by the curtain Jake went to his brother's side. Only when he motioned for her to come forward did she join him beside the long white bed. "He's sleeping," Jake whispered. "But he looks good."

Julie looked at him closely catching sight of the bandage spread across his forehead. His left leg was resting atop two pillows while his right arm was wrapped in a sling and lying on his chest. Although his sleep was fretful his eyes remained closed. Tears burned her eyelids as she caressed his uninjured hand gently. "The worst is over." Jake placed an arm across her shoulders gently. "He's going to be fine."

Julie nodded as words were impossible. "And now I'd better get you home." But Julie hung back. There were so many things she was feeling. So many words she hadn't said. Would she ever get the chance to say them?

"Are you ready?"

"Julie?" Kevin's eyes fluttered opened as a small smile crossed his face. "You stayed."

"I told you I would." Her voice broke and she bit her lower lip to stop its trembling.

"I'm glad you stayed," he whispered breathlessly. "Jake." He acknowledged finally.

"Hey, Bro." Jake smirked. "Looks like that tree won the fight."

"Looks that way." His voice was low. "Is Lorrie all right?"

"She didn't have a scratch."

Kevin breathed a sigh of relief. "Good." His blue-green eyes sought Julie's. "I want for you to know how much I've missed you."

"I missed you too."

"I didn't think you'd come."

Julie placed her hand inside Kevin's, softly. "I had to come." Her brown eyes were wide and filled with unshed tears. "I'm glad you're all right."

Kevin took a deep breath and let it out slowly. "I'm not going anywhere, Julie." He met her eyes evenly. "Not for a long time." He looked to Jake then back to her.

"Is this my cue to leave?" Jake pushed out a short laugh. "Cause if it is..." He threw his hands up. "I don't know where to go. We're not even supposed to be up here." He looked around the small room as though searching for some great escape. "Guess I'll go and check out the bathroom."

"Good idea." Kevin gave him a wide grin, then winced.

"Does it hurt much?"

"Not that much." He moved a little but the pain seemed too great, so he remained in the same position.

"I'm sorry." She still had her hand in his.

"I'm the one that's sorry, Julie." He squeezed her hand for emphasis. "I should have called you. I wanted to. I just didn't think we stood a chance. Not with Scott always in the shadows." He sighed wearily. "I was jealous. I can admit that. But I honestly didn't know what to say. I still don't." He paused. "I am sorry that things had to happen that way. I know how hard it must be..."

"Shh." Julie placed a finger to his lips to silence the rest of his words. "I didn't come here to talk about Scott." Her voice shook.

"Why did you come?"

Because I love you. Before tonight the thought took her completely unawares. Deep down she had always known it even though her mind had refused to believe it. Somehow her heart had known the truth of the matter.

"Why did you?" he questioned again. "And don't say anything out of pity."

"Kevin." She bent down over the side of the bed and kissed his cheek softly. "I came to see you because I..."

"I can't stay in there any longer." Jake chose that moment to burst in on them. "It's after three. I have to get you home before your parents kill me."

Julie stood upright. "You always had the most awful timing." Kevin groaned.

"Give her a kiss and say good night," Jake dictated.

"You're not off the hook yet, sweetie," Kevin whispered as she kissed his lips lightly. "Good night, Julie."

"Good night, Romeo." Jake snickered as he led Julie to the door. "We'll see you tomorrow."

As they stepped into the corridor Julie blinked against the bright fluorescent lights. So many things had happened in the last few hours, things that had changed her whole train of thought. She almost felt as if she had suddenly become a different person. Maybe she had. Because it seemed that she had finally grown up. Maybe she had come to see what life was all about. Maybe it was time to start living for tomorrow instead of getting lost in the memories of yesterday. Maybe it was time to let Scott's memory rest in peace.

Never before had Julie experienced so many feelings and all coursing through her at the very same time. And all because she had finally come to realize what the word love meant. It was the greatest feeling in the world. Suddenly Julie looked up at Jake. "What?"

"I'll meet you by the stairs," she said simply.

"Now what?" he groaned.

"I have some unfinished business to settle," she said and then went back into Kevin's room closing the door behind her. If she hadn't known better she would have thought that he had been waiting for her. At least, that was how it had seemed.

"Forget something?"

Immediately Julie went to his side. "I couldn't leave, Kevin." She bent down close to his ear. "Not until I told you how much I love you."

He kissed her lips gently. "I love you too," he whispered placing a hand to her cheek. "Now go home and let me get some sleep."

When she walked out of the door this time there was a spring in her step. This time it seemed that this was only the beginning. And this time there would be no regrets. This was the beginning of a new book. Now all she had to do was close the old one.

Epilogue

Five months had soon passed and Kevin was well on his way to a complete and successful recovery. His arm, although just slightly scarred, was the only evidence that he had been in any kind of accident at all. There had been no scarring to his face either. It was truly amazing! Just as it was truly a miracle, a miracle that Julie thanked God for daily. The surgery that Kevin had undergone had been required only to remove his spleen, which had been the cause of his internal bleeding. Once that objective had been achieved, his recovery had progressed from that point forward.

Although Julie hadn't originally planned on attending college she had enrolled for the next upcoming session. She had gotten a job at the local supermarket but that hadn't been good enough. She wanted a career. She wanted to become something, someone who would make a difference. It was very important that she achieve a goal. So she signed up for the general courses that she knew that she would need but did not choose a major. She knew in what direction she wanted to go but her parents had said that she had plenty of time before she made that decision.

On her one day off, usually in the middle of the week, she did some volunteer work at the local hospital. She loved being with the children. She found great joy, especially in working with the child cancer patients. A few weeks ago she had found an old box in the back of her closet packed with stuffed animals and without a second though she pulled it out and brought it down to the hospital. You would have thought it was Christmas that day. But the joys that it brought to all of those children made Julie believe that not only was she making a difference but that she was doing something for Scott as well. That it was somehow all connected. That she was making a positive influence in someone's life. These children meant the world to Julie and she would do anything she could to make their lives just a little bit better. She felt a true connection to them and to their families. It wasn't an easy job but it had its many rewards.

Everything in her life was slowly falling into place. She had to admit that lately life had been rather kind to her. Not only had she survived a horrible car accident but she had also lost her first love but she had somehow survived it. And she and Kevin were in love. They had surely come a long way since Camp Wiskle. As Tracey had stated from the beginning it had certainly turned out to be a summer to remember. In fact, Julie couldn't remember a time when she had been happier.

Then there were those times when memories of Scott would creep into her thoughts. The pain would sometimes hit her from out of a clear blue sky. She would be reading a book and it would strike or she'd be washing the dinner dishes while gazing out of the window and bang, it would hit her like a ton of bricks. And the pain could be staggering at those times. It could actually steal her breath. Then there were other times when the pain was a constant ache. Those were only some of the times she missed him. But wasn't that normal? Wasn't that only a part of the natural grieving process? Hadn't Scott been the one to teach her all about love? He had been the first young man that she had ever really loved. It should not have come as any surprise at all as to why he had truly left his mark upon her heart.

After leaving Camp Wiskle Julie had overcome many obstacles. She had definitely grown as a person. She had even gone so far as to have given her heart to Kevin. Sure, they were taking it slow. They had to, for both of their sakes. He understood when she needed time to herself. Especially if one of her kids, as she fondly referred to them, wasn't taking well to their treatments, and she was upset, Kevin always made sure that she had her space. There was always something going on at the hospital. There were good days and there were bad days. There were days when they were floating on a cloud when one of her kids went into remission and there were days when things did not go smoothly. Kevin helped her through it all. There were also plenty of times when he had cried right along with her. The work she did at the hospital sometimes took a lot out of her but it made her feel complete. It was something that she felt compelled to do. It was something that she wanted to do. And she especially needed for her family, as well as for Kevin, to understand and support her. Thank goodness they did.

Janet was steadily closing in on her due date and Matt was practically beside himself with worry. They had only discovered recently and quite accidentally that they were having a little boy. They were ecstatic as was the entire family. All Janet had to do was call Matt's name and he was off and running. It seemed that he was more nervous than his wife was about giving birth to their child. Jackson and Marie were tickled pink about becoming grandparents. They had even gone so far as to convert Matt's old bedroom into a nursery for the newest member of the Finch family.

Steadily life seemed to be moving on and it was right after the holidays when Julie asked Matt to take her to the cemetery for the first time. There was something pulling her there and although she wasn't sure exactly what it was she did know that it was definitely the right time. In her heart she felt led to close the last page in that book. Maybe that would close off the many memories that surrounded her from day to day that she had of Scott. Then again, Julie knew better than that. Scott was a part of her life and he always would be. He owned a large piece of her heart. Somehow closing that chapter in her life was not going to be easy. A part of Scott would always be with her. Time might heal some of her wounds but her heart would never be completely free from Scott. In the past few months she had come to accept that.

The cemetery was a half hour drive from home. Matt had been quiet for most of their small journey. She knew that this was just as hard on him as if was for her. Maybe even more so, considering he had at least been aware of Scott's illness. "Did he talk about it at all?" she asked softly.

"Talk about what?" Matt gave her a quick glance as she had broken the silence that had surrounded them for the longest time.

"His illness." Her brown eyes were wide.

"Not really. He tried to get around it. I think he tried to forget about it."

"You never talked about it, Matt. You never said a word…"

"I promised Scott that I wouldn't. It was the only promise I could make to him and not break." He sighed wearily. "I never realized that you and he… I always thought he was too old for you. He *was* too old for you," he reiterated. "I really can't say what I was thinking. When I first found out about the both of you I hit the roof. I never thought in a million years. I still don't know how you both pulled it off. I was mad as…" He made a small face before continuing. "But something changed that day, for the both of us. There was no way that I was ever going to understand what he was going through. No way on this earth but I did know that

Scott may have hidden a lot of things but his feelings for you were genuine."

Julie stared out of the window, her eyes burning with unshed tears. "And believe me he didn't have to tell me that."

"I just wished he would have told me," she whispered.

"It wouldn't change anything."

"But I could have told him..."

"He knew, Julie."

She could not imagine how she would have felt had she known that Scott was going to die. It may have actually been better for the both of them that she hadn't known. After all, it had been the way that Scott had wanted it. She had to respect him for that. It must have been really hard on Scott's parents. Although she hadn't known the specifics surrounding Scott's illness she was well aware of the constant pain that losing him had entailed. The pain was a daily reminder of how fragile life was and that she had to go on. And going on meant taking chances.

As they passed on through the large iron gates leading into Pine Lawn's Cemetery Julie's heart rate nearly doubled. "He's buried at the top of the hill and under a big oak tree," Matt said softly. "His parents chose one of the prettiest cemetery's in the state," he said softly as though there were people around and he was trying not to be overheard. "Are you all right?" He glanced in her direction as they drove up the long winding hill.

She was far from okay. That was a fact they both knew. "I think so." She breathed as her fingers closed around a single small budding purple iris which had been resting on her lap. She would have opted for a single red rose but the purple flower had some significance for the both of them. It meant much more than she cared to think about at the moment.

"If you're not up to this..."

"I have to do this, Matt," she said before he could protest any further. "It's the only thing that I haven't done. In my heart it's the one thing I have left…" Her voice caught but she hurried on. "I shouldn't have to tell you that."

"You know how he felt about you." Matt parked the car on the side of the small road. "What more is there left to know."

Julie bit her bottom lip thoughtfully. There was a lot more that she wanted to know. Sometimes the thoughts were so overwhelming that they could almost make her head spin with their intensity. "Sometimes it doesn't feel like it's enough." Her voice broke and she got out of the car quickly. She had come this far and she was going to see this through to the end. The very end. She owed Scott a lot more than just a simple goodbye.

The great oak tree wasn't far from the street. It was a very large cemetery with winding roads and all different kinds of trees. There were oak, maple and gigantic pine trees just to name a few. There was only the faintest of a whistle as the wind blew through the trees on that day. They were surrounded by the most beautiful granite and marble stones all around. There was the scent of fresh flowers which filled the crisp winter air. "They only have a marker." Matt said softly from just behind her. "Maybe we should have waited until there was a stone…"

"No." As she bent down she placed a trembling hand to the cool metal grave marker. All it read was Scott's name. There were no dates. There were no flowers. It was bare, for now anyway.

"I know his parents have already ordered the stone. But I think that they have to wait until the ground settles before it can actually be placed on the grave." Matt was babbling and they both knew it. "There's still another box in the basement that I haven't gone through."

"It's okay." She touched his arm as she knew he was trying to make her feel more comfortable. "I'm okay, Matt." She had tears in her eyes as she placed the small purple iris beside the metal marker.

"I'll give you a few minutes alone." He then turned and walked back to the car truly leaving her alone.

Julie ran her hand lovingly across the cool metal marker lightly. There was so much that she felt she needed to say. There were so many words that she'd never been given the chance to say and never would have the chance to say. All the maybes that she could never articulate were almost as though quickly moving water running down the drain. The moment had come and the moment had gone. There were so many things that Scott had taught her. And although they had run out of time at least they had been granted the time to love at all. She always thought of that when she was feeling sad or angry. There was always a reason when a special person touched someone's life. Scott had touched her life as no one else ever had and probably never would. And she would always love him for that. And there were people that understood that and there were people who would never in a million years understand half of that. Those were the people she really felt sorry for.

The tears that she had been holding back for so long had now only began to fall. But it was okay. It was something she would get through. It would take time to heal. "Goodbye, Scott," she whispered. "I love you." Her voice quaked as her bottom lip trembled. "I will always love you." Then she gained her feet and walked back to where her brother stood waiting for her. "Let's go home, Matt."

At that moment Matt turned back for one last look at the gravesite but Julie did not. In fact, there would be no more looking back for Julie. Coming here had somehow made her a stronger person and finally she felt almost free from the past at that moment.

The last words had been spoken. The last page had been turned. The last chapter was finished. Finally the book could now be closed. But all of Julie's past reflections of Scott would never be forgotten.

Meet

Sandra Bonaldi...

To Sandra Bonaldi writing is as natural as breathing and there are times when her characters demand their stories to be told. Sandra finds that she works best while multi-tasking and welcomes the inevitable challenge that writing sassy romance offers always opting for that happily ever after.

Life is about keeping it real. While her children are now adults she and her husband, Tom, are now able to pursue their passion for creativity on a broader scale. Writing has been one of Sandra's passions but raising a family came first and now her two Rat Terriers Chase and Chelsea have no problem collecting on all the leftover hugs and kisses.

Sometimes we need to be reminded of the simple things – A feel good love story that has you believing that yes, you can come through a horrible ordeal and still believe that happily ever after does exist...